VERTICAL
EXPOSURE

A Dan Courtwright Mystery

VERTICAL EXPOSURE

PAUL WAGNER

A Dan Courtwright Mystery

Published by Albicaulis Books

Dan Courtwright, VI: Vertical Exposure
© Paul Wagner 2023

ISBN#: 979-8-9856058-8-4

This is a work of fiction. Names, characters, businesses, places, events, locales, and incidents are either the products of the author's imagination or used in a fictitious manner. Any resemblance to actual persons, living or dead, or actual events is purely coincidental.

Published by Albicaulis Books

Napa, California

albicaulis.com

First Edition

chapter 1

Ranger Dan Courtwright was not excited about the way he was going to spend the next two days. Maybe worried was a better way to describe it. Or anxious. Something to explain the tightness in his stomach as he drove the highway into Stanislaus National Forest. He was signed up to take a rock climbing class that was supposed to add to his skills on the Search and Rescue Team. The only problem was, Dan hadn't climbed seriously in about ten years.

Ah, hell. Let's face it. He'd never climbed seriously. But in college at least he had done some climbing with the club at Humboldt State, and he could point to a few walls in Northern California where he'd somehow found his way to the top. Some of the others in the club were a lot better than he was, and on at least one climb they had pretty much dragged his sorry ass up to the top.

But that was years ago. He wanted to say more than ten years ago, but it was getting closer to twenty now. And he wasn't sure he was going to be able to keep up with the rest of the people in the class. He knew he couldn't keep up with the woman sitting next to him in the passenger seat of his car, Katie Pederson.

He was probably going to be the oldest one in the class. As the saying goes, "There are old climbers and bold climbers, but no old, bold climbers." At least that part fit. He was old, and definitely not bold. The only question was whether he was a climber at all.

That morning he'd stopped off to pick up Katie, a young woman who also worked for the Stanislaus National Forest. He'd watched Katie climb a couple of years ago while they were retrieving some human remains in the middle of the Emigrant Wilderness. He knew that she was a lot better climber than he was—steady, solid, and confident. And if the rest of the class was like her, it was going to be a challenging two days.

"I'm really looking forward to this," Katie told him as they drove along. "Should be lots of fun."

Dan tried to make his smile look authentic. "Let's hope so," he offered.

Katie noted his reticence, and chuckled. "You'll do fine, Dan," she said. "You don't always have to be the best." She looked at him. "This will be good for your personal growth."

Dan wondered when, exactly, young people like Katie—she was a good ten years younger than he was—concluded that it was perfectly acceptable to talk that way to their elders. He realized, with a start, that it was probably during the time that he was about her age.

"Do you know anyone else in the class?" Katie asked him.

Dan shrugged and shook his head.

"I know Blake is going to be here," she said. Blake Vanden was another colleague, about Katie's age. "But he stayed with friends up here somewhere around Long Barn," she added, as a way of explaining why Blake hadn't accepted Dan's offer of a ride.

Dan nodded to show he understood. Blake was nearly as tall as Dan's six foot four, but his muscles hadn't caught up with his bones. When he walked, he jangled along like a marionette, all elbows and knees. Unfortunately for Dan, on a rock wall Blake looked and climbed like a giant spider, effortless and agile.

Next to him, Katie sipped an orange juice and looked out the window, apparently enjoying the view.

"Oh!" She suddenly turned to him. "You know who else is going to be here? At least, I think she is?"

Dan glanced at her, then shrugged again and shook his head.

"I saw on my feed that Suzi Muller was taking this class."

Dan gave her a quizzical look. "I'm not sure I know her…"

"Suzi Muller, Dan. She's a total legend." Despite Dan's general mood, Katie's enthusiasm made him smile.

"Tell me," he suggested.

"She was, like, one of the first women to do SAR work in the Rockies," Katie explained. "Now she's down in SEKI."

Dan took this in. SAR was search and rescue. SEKI was Sequoia/Kings Canyon. That would explain why he hadn't heard of her. Dan had always worked well north of the national parks in the southern Sierra Nevada.

"She started, like, a long time ago," Katie continued. "Boy, the crap that she must have had to put up with. You know?"

Dan murmured his agreement.

"Anyway, she's out of Fresno or Visalia or somewhere," Katie said. "And she totally rocks. She's mentored a whole bunch of younger women into this stuff. I love her."

Dan smiled. He was proud of the fact that he had mentored a few young people as well. "Sounds like someone I would like to meet," he said.

"Oh, you will absolutely love her, Dan," Katie said. "She's this tiny little woman, short blond hair, kinda perky, but she doesn't back down from anyone."

Dan grinned. "Okay, that sounds great."

"Oh, and she is just an animal as a climber," Katie added. "I mean, off the charts great. She might even be one of the instructors.

She probably is."

Dan's smile faded just a bit. "Cool," he said quietly, still forcing a smile. "But I thought Rod Arquette was teaching this one," he said.

Katie shook her head dismissively. "That's his name on the climbing school, but I bet he's way too full of himself to show up to teach a lousy SAR class. Unless it's pretty advanced. Then he might do it."

Dan thought this over. The day wasn't getting any better.

He gave a salute to Doris and the Summit Ranger Station as he drove by and soon found himself following a dark blue Prius.

"That car looks familiar," Katie said. "The "Save Mono Lake" bumper sticker next to the electric vehicle badge. I think that's Suzi Muller. That's her!" Katie looked to Dan as if she wanted him to try to flag the car down from behind.

Dan took a deep breath and let it out slowly. Maybe the class would break up into teams and he could climb with Katie. That would be good. They could take things at their own pace. But she would probably jump at the chance to climb with this Suzi Muller.

Blake? Dan didn't think that would work very well. Blake was an independent kind of guy. He'd clamber up the wall and then wait impatiently while Dan would probably struggle along.

He took another slow, deep breath. If his boss Steve Matson hadn't more or less pressured him into taking this class, he could be back at the Summit Ranger Station filling out wilderness permits and giving advice about campfires.

He drove past the horse stables and continued on to take the road out toward Gianelli trailhead. At least the class was going to be in one of the most beautiful spots on the planet. As he followed the little Prius along the road, the sunlight through the trees on the old road seemed warmer now.

He heard Katie take another sip of her juice. "I love this road," she said contentedly. "How great is it that we get to do this today?"

Dan tried to give her a big smile. "Pretty great," he agreed.

"And rock climbing on top of it!" she enthused.

Dan nodded and smiled again, this time not quite so broadly.

chapter 2

It was a group of eight. Dan and Katie were among the last to arrive. They parked right next to Suzi Muller, who waved to them and then climbed out of her car.

Dan watched as Katie gave Suzi a big hug and then turned to introduce her to Dan.

"Oh, I've heard all about you," Suzi said. "It's great to be able to put a face to some of those stories."

Dan gave an embarrassed grin and shook his head. "That's all they are," he said. "Stories. Katie has told me a few about you, too."

Suzi just laughed. "If you hang around long enough in this business, the stories come with the territory," she said. "At least none of the ones about you weren't too bad…"

Dan grinned. "Well, that's a relief."

Suzi gave a nod of her head towards the other climbers who were assembled over by the trailhead sign. "At least not like some of those guys." Her face contorted into a grimace.

Dan and Katie exchanged a quick glance.

"What do you mean?" Katie asked.

"Oh, they're just guys being guys," Suzi said. "See the tall guy over there with the hat?"

Katie followed her gaze. The man was wearing a hipster-style fedora and sported a short trim beard and dark-framed glasses.

"Jim McDougal," Suzi told them. "He's harmless, if you don't mind somebody who talks too much and laughs too loud at his own jokes. A bit of a space invader, too."

Dan gave her a quizzical look.

"He always stands just a bit too close to you," Suzi explained. She pushed her hands out in front her herself, as if to shove him away. "I like a bit of space, you know? Keep your distance, sailor."

Dan grinned. He could see why Katie liked this woman.

"But the other two, in the camo gear?" Suzi asked. "From the Mariposa Sheriff's department. They don't really get it. I think they'd be happy if the only women they ever met were either cooking for them or sleeping with them."

Katie gave a grunt of disgust. "God, I hope I don't have to climb with them," she said.

"Oh, you will," Suzi said. "And you'll do it with a smile." She paused, looking at Katie. "And if they give you any crap you'll give it right back to them, always with a smile—one that makes them feel just a little bit worried that you might be laughing at them."

Dan chuckled and shook his head. "This is sounding like less fun every minute."

Suzi glanced at him. "Who's the tall skinny guy?"

"Oh, that's Blake," Katie offered. "He's sweet. Good climber, too."

Someone over in the larger group gave a sharp whistle and waved at them, urging the three to hurry up.

Suzi hoisted her daypack on her shoulder and turned to Katie. "Let's go show 'em," she said. Then, turning to Katie, she said. "And don't worry, I've got your back."

Dan tagged along behind the two women, hoping that Suzi might have his back, too.

As they walked over to the trailhead, Katie asked quietly, "Did either of you get a text message this morning? Something about Rod's second wife…"

Dan was about to answer that he had, indeed, seen a message, when Suzi waved it off. "God, I get tired of people sticking their noses where they don't belong," she said.

And they left it at that.

Just as the group was slowly gathering, one more truck zipped into the parking lot. The driver hopped out and started jogging quickly toward the group.

Dan heard Suzi's muttered comment next to him. "Ooh, better hurry, Hideo. It's not like you to be late."

In front of the group, Rod Arquette waited as Hideo Saito joined the group and gave a quick but sincere apology for being late, accompanied by a small bow, his hands folded in front of himself, his head nodding.

Suzi gave him a discreet wave and smile, and Hideo returned the favor, then quickly turned his attention to Rod Arquette.

Rod Arquette clapped his hands together and asked everyone to pull up a log around an old fire ring at the trailhead. Dan made a mental note to remove the ring. Camping was not allowed at the trailhead itself, and that fire ring sent the wrong message. The group slowly came together and sat down, some on logs, some on rocks.

Once everyone was seated, Arquette made it obvious he was going to wait as long as it took for the conversations around the ring to stop. It took a while, and gave Dan a chance to study the man.

Arquette was wearing a stretched out blue tank top and a pair of black nylon running shorts, and both were faded and dirty. His arms, bronzed and roped with muscles, glistened in the light as he put his hands on his hips. While his hair was graying around the edges, he still wore it long enough to look slightly wild.

He looked around at the group as if he were an eagle seeking the easiest prey, or perhaps a bull elk waiting for his next challenger. As the group quieted down, conversations breaking off one by one, Arquette put one foot up on a log in front of him, about to ascend the steps of the stage.

His head was held high, his chin jutted out, and his eyes peered at them from underneath deep brows. Dan noticed the bent leg was showing just the tiniest of trembles, a wiggling in the muscles that gave him away. Certainly not from physical strain? Nope. Dan decided that Rod Arquette was just showing the slightest sign of stress. Or fear.

"I'll wait," he said once, pointedly, and then even Jim McDougal finally stopped talking and looked at him.

He waited three, four seconds more--and then began to talk. "You may think of today as an exercise, or training," Arquette said dramatically. "But it's not. It's life and death."

He looked around at the group, letting this sink in. "Anybody who thinks otherwise can leave right now."

The nearer of the two deputies shifted his seat, and Arquette immediately glared at him. The deputy froze, staring back like a deer caught in the headlights.

When all was still again, Arquette continued. "What you learn today will save someone's life if you learn it well. And if you don't, there's a good chance they die. Think about that for a minute." He let the statement hang in the air.

Dan resisted the impulse to glance at Katie, maybe even to roll his eyes. This kind of ultra-macho approach had never worked well with him. Arquette gave him a few minutes to think about whether he could stand it for two full days. It wasn't long enough for Dan to come to a decision.

Dan took one more deep breath and let it out slowly and quietly.

Rod Arquette glanced at his assistant, a quiet young man over by their pile of gear, and nodded to him. The young man hurried over with a coil of climbing rope and handed it to him.

"What's this?" Arquette asked, holding it up.

Of course it was an awkward moment. Everyone knew that Arquette was setting someone up to fail here. They kept silent. Finally, Blake answered, "Ten-millimeter climbing rope."

Arquette stared at the rest of the group, forcing them to agree or disagree. Dan found these methods childish.

"It's what keeps you from ending up in a shapeless pile of blood and guts at the bottom of the cliff," McDougal offered.

Arquette waited again, to see if anyone else would offer a suggestion. When they didn't, he started talking again. "It's a tool," Arquette explained, holding the coil of rope high. "It's exactly as useful as the person holding it."

Dan wondered how much longer this would go on. His eyes slowly drifted up to catch a Steller's jay that had heard the commotion and come to see if it meant there would be crumbs on the ground. Dan settled in and watched the jay, quietly making a bet with himself that the jay would get bored and leave before Arquette stopped talking. Dan bet it would.

The bird hopped from branch to branch, getting closer each time to the group, tilting its head from side to side to inspect. But the ground was empty. There was no food here today.

Dan won the bet, but only by a minute or two.

At first, Dan's concern about the climbing seemed misplaced. For more than two hours the workshop consisted of Rod Arquette and his assistant Andrew MacRostie "Yeah, go ahead, call me Andy Mac," the young man said with a sheepish smile, going over the key safety precautions they needed to observe in a climbing situation, and particularly a rescue. They were drilled on knots and procedures, asked to repeat acronyms and mnemonics, and challenged with a series of potential disasters for which they were required to come up with the appropriate action steps in response.

At every step they were asked to demonstrate exactly what had been covered, including tying and re-tying the knots several times, and checking the work of others in the group.

Sitting next to Suzi, Dan often heard her mutter a quick answer under her breath, which helped both him and Katie look just a bit more prepared than they might have been.

By the time that Rod Arquette called for a short break, Dan was impressed. "Suzi, I think you could probably teach this course," he suggested.

She shook her head. "Frankly, I don't have the patience for it," she answered over her shoulder as she turned and headed for the outhouse, Katie quickly following her.

Which left Dan in the company of Jim McDougal.

"So," Jim said loudly, and walking over to stand close to Dan. Too close, Dan noted. "You're the big ranger guy that solves murders, huh? Jim McDougal." He stuck out a hand and gave Dan's a firm shake, pulling him closer. And then with an almost conspiratorial tone, he leaned in and asked, "Does that murder stuff keep you pretty busy?"

Dan pried his hand away from McDougal's grip and noted that the two sheriff's deputies were now eyeing him with distrust.

"Right now, I'm busy enough just remembering all this information, and worrying about the rest of today," Dan told him with a smile. "I don't need any more excitement…"

"Ah, hell, this is easy," McDougal assured him. "You've

probably done this stuff a thousand times already. Isn't that part of your job description? This should be a piece of cake for a ranger like you."

Dan gave him a small smile. "Let's hope so," he said. He could see that the two deputies were looking at him and quietly discussing something. And chuckling.

Blake came over to say hello and shake Dan's hand. It was a relief to see him turn to McDougal and introduce himself as well.

"So you work with Sherlock here, eh?" McDougal said to Blake, pointing at Dan. "Does he ever do any work, or does he just sit around playing the violin between cases?" McDougal laughed loudly at his own joke.

Blake muttered something about Dan doing more than his share of the work, but his comment was overshadowed by Rod Arquette calling everyone back to class.

As they reassembled, Rod's assistant Andy asked if they had any questions from the morning session. There was lots of murmuring and shaking of heads. Andy turned to Rod and suggested it was time to move to the rock.

"Yeah, I have a question," McDougal said. "Anybody else getting messages on their phone about this guy's marriages?" he asked, pointing to Rod Arquette. "I mean, it's weird, right?" He looked around expectantly at the group, as if seeking approval, smiling all the while.

To his right, Dan heard Suzi give a small groan. "Oh, for god's sake…"

In the awkward silence that followed, McDougal defended himself. "What? I was just asking." He was still glancing around the group. "I think it's weird. What's the deal?"

Up in front, Andy MacRostie was looking at Rod Arquette. The old climber stared at McDougal and then looked at the rest of the group. His mouth was slightly open, and his tongue slowly worked its way along the top of his lower lip, his eyes narrowing into a frown. He shook his head with disgust.

"The first ingredient of any climb is trust," Arquette said. "Without trust, you have nothing." He stopped to stare at the group. His voice was quiet, but angry. "Right now, I don't have any trust in any of you."

He stopped again and allowed his eyes to roam over the whole group. Dan swallowed.

"And I'm not going to climb with any of you," Arquette said. He turned to Andy. "You do the rest of the class." And he turned his back on them and walked over to the pile of gear they had assembled.

Andy cleared his throat and gave a sigh. It seemed to Dan as if Andy was not completely surprised. Maybe this was not the first time he had been left in this kind of situation. "Okay," MacRostie began. "Let's review just a bit from this morning, and then we'll make a couple of teams and practice what we've been talking about."

Rod Arquette had picked up a small day pack and was heading up the trail, his back to the group.

As the group watched Rod Arquette, Andy MacRostie now waved his arms at the class. "If I could get your attention here?" he asked.

chapter 3

After dividing up all the gear, they hit the trail. Dan noticed that Suzi somehow volunteered to take on more gear than anyone else, and she also managed to pass the two deputies while they took a short break to catch their breath on a steep part of the trail. Katie was right behind her.

Dan noted that the camo clothes the deputies were wearing were at least a half size too small, as if they had gained weight over the years but didn't want to admit that they couldn't still fit in the clothes they'd worn in their twenties. He gave the two men a nod and a smile as he passed them. They nodded back but didn't return the smile.

It didn't take more than twenty minutes for them to reach their destination, a massive granite rock face, and Dan was surprised to see they were at the top of the cliffs, not the bottom. He didn't want to appear too concerned, but he did take a look over the edge. It was a long way down. Andy asked Suzi to help him set up some anchors so that they could run some top belays to the cliffs. Apparently, they were going to rappel down first.

They wedged their feet into their climbing shoes—Dan had always hated the crush these shoes put on his oversized feet—and one by one they indicated that they were ready to tackle the rock.

But before they could start, Andy brought them over to show how they had rigged the anchors—balancing the load, making sure the stress didn't overstrain any part of the rig, and checking the redundancy of the anchors.

Dan liked that they would rappel first. Rappelling may look scary to those who haven't climbed, but it's a whole lot easier than climbing up a steep face. And quicker.

Just when Dan thought he knew what was coming, Andy asked for volunteers.

"For what?" Jim McDougal asked loudly, looking around with a grin. "I want to know what I'm getting myself in for."

Andy smiled. "We need a couple of victims."

Dan took a quick glance around. Neither of the two deputies was going to step forward. And Suzi and Katie weren't either. Blake always wanted to be hands-on for everything. That left Hideo, McDougal, and Dan.

Dan raised his hand. "I'm in."

"Good," Andy acknowledged him. "And how about you?" he asked, looking at Jim McDougal.

Slightly embarrassed, McDougal agreed. "Sure, I'll play nice on this one."

"The rescue scenario is this," Andy explained. "We've got a climber on the face of a cliff, and we have to lower him down to rescue. You've climbed up to him, and now you have to lower him down. Remember, whatever is simplest and safest."

Dan took a glance over the edge of the cliff. It was an impressive amount of vertical exposure.

"So we need two teams here," MacRostie continued. "Three people for each rescue, and the victim."

Dan was still standing close to Suzi and Katie, and they quickly volunteered to help him. Andy pointed to Hideo Saito and asked him to be the third person on the team.

Jim McDougal turned to Dan and said, "Race you to the bottom. Last one there is a rotten egg." And then laughed just a little too loudly.

MacRostie held up his hand. "Hold it, folks. This is no joke. This is absolutely real life, and if you are not a hundred percent focused on the task at hand, this exercise can go wrong in a big hurry. And when I say go wrong, I mean…fatally wrong." And then looking directly at Jim McDougal, he said, "No more jokes."

McDougal's face twisted into a silent apology and tried to look appropriately cowed. He waited for MacRostie to turn his back and then looked at the rest of the group and shrugged.

MacRostie gathered the group over at the edge of the cliff and talked them through all the steps they would need to follow. He talked them through the diagnosis process and coached Dan through his answers, leading them to believe that he had a broken arm, and possible internal injuries, but he was lucid, and his helmet seemed to have protected his head from injury.

Dan tried to remember all they had learned that morning and was relieved when Suzi immediately took charge of their group. Within minutes she had them rigged up properly and she, Katie, and Hideo all began to work together to lower Dan and Hideo down the cliff.

Dan was facing Hideo Saito with his legs wrapped around him "like a lover," MacRostie reminded them, and his unbroken arm around Saito's neck. Both were tied into climbing harnesses for safety. Then Hideo was slowly lowered down the cliff by Suzi and Katie, his feet walking backwards down the face of the rock.

Other than the mildly uncomfortable fact that his face was only inches from that of Hideo Saito, it was a walk in the park. Within a minute or two he felt Hideo's feet swing down, and both Dan and his rescuer were now standing on a ledge, some fifty feet below the two women.

Hideo carefully set some protection in the rock and tied Dan into it before disengaging and waving to Katie and Suzi up above. "We're good," he called up to them.

Dan looked around. The ledge was large—at least six feet deep and thirty feet wide on the top of a huge granite mass. Beyond the edges, it dropped off down into the canyon, some hundred and fifty feet below.

"Not a good place to go for a stroll," Andy MacRostie cautioned from above. "There's a lot of exposure."

He then explained that the next stage of the drill was to execute the same kind of rescue, but it would be up to Suzi to rescue Katie, or vice versa.

"He's going to stick us all on this ledge and make us climb up for our lunch," Dan heard McDougal say from his spot just a few feet away on the ledge.

Dan looked up the sheer wall and wondered if he could climb it. But before he could make up his mind, he saw Katie stepping off the top of the cliff with Suzi wrapped around her.

This was a more complicated maneuver, because Katie had to control their descent by managing the rope, while Suzi sat in her lap. From above, Dan could hear Suzi talking quietly, giving tips and encouragement to Katie as they came down the rock. Hideo was managing a safety top-line belay from below.

Dan and Hideo helped them unrope once they made it to the ledge, and Dan couldn't help but notice the smile and flush of accomplishment that washed over Katie's face. She was loving this.

Over on the other team, one of the deputies was a bit hung up halfway down the cliff, with Blake on his lap. His feet had slipped off the wall, and the two were now hanging from the rope. With some huffing and puffing, and a bit of help from Blake, the deputy managed to get back into position and make it down to the ledge.

"How hungry are you?" they heard Andy MacRostie call from above.

Hideo's stomach suddenly gave a loud growl and Suzi laughed at the embarrassed look on his face. "Some of us are pretty hungry," she called back.

"The ropes are all set," MacRostie explained. "So you can climb and belay each other from there, or, if you want, we can practice a hoist rescue from there. But that will take longer. If you want to eat now, we can do the hoist rescue after lunch."

Hideo's stomach gave another groan, and he quickly apologized to the group. "We can do the rescue. Really," he said.

Suzi took a quick glance around and called up to MacRostie. "Let's have lunch," she said. "I'm hungry."

Turning to the rest of her team, she asked, "Who wants to go first?"

Katie immediately stepped forward and volunteered. "I'm still in the harness, so I'll go."

Suzi set up to belay her, and Katie smoothly started up the rock. Dan had seen her climb once before, and he was reminded of how confident and easily she moved over the granite. Below her, Suzi was smiling and nodding as she tended the belaying rope.

Over on the other team, Blake was stepping into a harness, and would soon follow Katie. Dan looked at Hideo. "Do you want to go next?" he asked.

Hideo waved his hands in front of himself as if he were making a tortilla by hand. "Either way. If you like, you can go first," he said.

Dan shook his head. "After you."

When Katie made the top she sent the rope back down, and Hideo tied himself in. He took a deep breath, then another. Dan could see that his eyes were closed as he faced the wall. One more deep breath. Then, eyes open, he began to climb, not quite as smoothly as Katie, but he had clearly learned from Katie's approach. Where Katie had felt around for the next handhold, Hideo already knew where it was.

Dan continued to study the wall. He could see the first couple of holds for the climb, but beyond that it looked very tough, almost slick. He glanced at Suzi, who met his gaze.

With a wink, she pointed to a spot behind him, where a crack led up the side of the cliff. "You don't have to climb this," she said, pointing to where the rope fell down from above. She stuck her chin out toward the crack. "Just go up that. I can still belay you from here, or they can from above." She shrugged, as if to say, why make life hard on yourself?

Dan looked at her. "You think?" he asked.

She gave a snort of derision. "Give me a break," she said. "Do you think anybody cares about how you get to lunch?"

Dan chuckled and turned to look at the crack. He could easily see a route there. He looked back at Suzi.

She grinned. "You'll still be up there way ahead of these guys," gesturing to the other group behind her. The first deputy was just starting up the wall and was already huffing and puffing, his sweating face was just inches from the wall of granite.

Hideo topped out and sent the rope back down. Dan climbed into the harness and, with a quick call to Suzi to let her know he was climbing, he began working his way up the crack. As Suzi had suggested, it was dead easy. Maybe a 5.5 or 5.6. He kept his weight on his feet, and kept his ass in, but still worked up a sweat as he struggled up it. There was one spot where he needed every bit of his six foot three inches to reach a good handhold, but he made it to the top without a hitch.

As he climbed over the top, Katie greeted him, "Nice work, Dan." She then moved past him to call down to Suzi. "I'll get the belay on you, Suzi."

And then, turning back to Dan, she grinned, "This won't take long."

chapter 4

Dan wandered over to pull his lunch out of his day pack. The group began to settle in, some sitting on rocks, Katie and Suzi on a fallen log, and Blake just plopped on the ground.

Dan was always amused by what people brought along to eat on the trail. It looked like Blake had mainly handfuls of nuts and berries. No wonder the kid never put on a pound. The two cops from Mariposa each pulled out a big deli sandwich, complete with chips, an apple, a cookie, and a soda. Dan suspected that they had stopped by to buy something pre-packaged on the way this morning.

Of course, Hideo had a kind of bento box, which fascinated Suzi. "What do you have in there?" she asked, barely containing her glee. "I love it."

While Hideo quietly talked her through all the items in his lunch, Dan looked at Katie. To his surprise she wasn't eating much.

"You not hungry?" he asked.

She patted her stomach and made a grimace. "I've been nibbling on stuff all day," she said. "Maybe I'll eat something later."

Dan offered her what he had: a bit of cheese, some crackers, dried fruit, a few energy bars.

Katie shook her head. "I'm okay," she reassured him.

Andy MacRostie stood up and walked away from the group, staring at his cell phone.

When Suzi noticed MacRostie had left, she turned on Jim

McDougal. "What the hell were you thinking?" she asked. "Don't bring that stuff up here."

McDougal gave her an exaggerated look of innocence. "What? I can't ask a simple question? I mean, it was the elephant in the room. Somebody had to ask."

"No, they didn't." Suzi corrected him. "How would you feel if you were the target of that kind of thing?"

McDougal shrugged. "Happens all the time. If it's important, I respond. If not, I ignore it."

Suzi gave him a withering glare and turned to Katie. She took a moment to compose herself and then said, "You sure looked good on that rock today."

The deputy whose name tag read "Bianchi" agreed. "Yeah, you did."

Suzi glanced over at him. "Fast and clean, too," she said. "I think you get the top grade today."

Katie gave a small sarcastic laugh. "Yeah, right. Not like you."

Officer Bianchi stood up and came over to Dan and offered his hand. "Del Bianchi" he said. "Mariposa County. I've been doing SAR for about twenty years now."

Dan shook his hand and said it was nice to meet him.

The other deputy joined them. "Jack Meadows," he said. "Same as Del here. Same place, same time. We started within a year of each other."

"Suzi, how long have you been doing this?" Katie asked loudly.

Suzi rolled her eyes. "I started in Fresno four or five years ago," she said. And then, while the deputies both exchanged a quick glance, she added, "But before that, I did damn near twenty-five years out of Boulder."

Blake asked her about Colorado, and Suzi became enthusiastic about the Rockies. That changed the subject once and for all, and the group was soon deep in conversations about which mountains were the most fun and which were the hardest to climb.

Dan followed the conversation, but didn't join in. He was happy to listen to the stories and chuckle at the jokes.

After a few minutes, he felt a tap on his shoulder. Andy MacRostie was there and asked if he could have a quick word.

Dan agreed and stood up, following Andy off along the top of the cliff until they were out of earshot and sight of the rest of the group. Andy gave a look in their direction and then leaned in to Dan. "I'm sorry to bother you, but I was wondering if you have a minute to talk about something…"

Given that he'd already followed Andy this far, Dan gave a nod and prepared himself to listen.

"You heard about that text this morning? The one about Rod's second wife?"

Dan grunted to show that he had.

"Did you get it, too?"

Dan nodded. "And I know Katie Pederson did. But we didn't think it was important."

Andy exhaled loudly and thought for a minute. "Yeah, well, maybe it isn't. But it also isn't the first one. Did anybody else get it?"

Dan shook his head. "I don't know. Jim McDougal obviously did, and I got the impression that Suzi Muller did. I don't know about the rest."

Andy took another deep breath and turned to look over the canyon that spread out below them. "This has been going on for a while," he said. "Rod's become a target, somehow. Seems like every class we teach, everything we do gets hacked by somebody."

Dan opened his hands up in front of himself and said: "I'm not really up to speed on all this social media stuff, but have you reported it to anyone?"

"Three weeks ago Inyo County said they'd look into it," Andy replied. "But I think I know more about this stuff now than they do. And last week over in Mono County they really didn't even want to take a statement. They think it's a waste of time. And sometimes I think it's more than just social media. A few weeks ago, somebody slashed Rod's tires. I don't know if that was connected, but if it was…"

Dan thought about his friend Cal Healey in the sheriff's office in Tuolumne County. He doubted Cal would have much expertise in this area either. Cal's daughter Lisa probably knew more about it than he did. Still, he offered: "You could try the Tuolumne Sheriff. At least I can vouch for the fact that they won't ignore you completely…"

Andy thought this over while he stared out over the canyon. Then he turned and looked at Dan. "Would you be able to look into this at all? I mean, you are pretty good at this stuff." There was just a hint of begging in his voice.

Dan shook his head slowly. "I am not the guy to know what to do about something like that," he said. "I'm okay with a shovel or a McLeod, but with social media I wouldn't even know where to start."

Andy gave a derisive snort. "Yeah, well neither does anyone else. At least you're willing to listen."

Now Dan turned to look out over the canyon. Even in the harsh light of midday, he could see the patches of trees and shade far below, down by the upper fork of the Stanislaus. Just a sliver of the rushing water was visible between the trees. "How long has this been going on?" he asked.

"Months. Maybe a year," Andy answered. "Just a steady stream of nasty emails, texts and stuff."

"Have you tried tracing it?"

Andy responded with a sad sigh. "I've been learning. Everybody I talk to says that the texts all seem to come from burner phones. No way to trace them. Email accounts that pop up and then get deleted. It's like playing whack-a-mole in the dark…with your eyes closed."

"If they all get sent to people here, then it has to be somebody who has access to your media accounts, right?" Dan asked.

Andy gave a cynical laugh. "Yeah, except that we've been hacked so many times," he said. "I guess it's all part of their… attack."

Dan sighed. "I wish I could help you," he said. "But I really don't know the first thing about this, and I couldn't do anything even if I did find something. I think your best bet is law enforcement, and just keep trying until you find someone who can do something. I can connect you to the Tuolumne County Sheriff. If I do that, they'll at least listen to what you have to say."

Andy turned to look at him. "Do you think there's anybody in Tuolumne County who knows about this stuff?"

Dan shook his head. "I really don't know," he answered. "But I know who to ask."

chapter 5

The afternoon was spent hoisting the victims back up the cliff face. This was much slower, harder work, and as the heat from the sun warmed up the granite, it turned the whole exercise into Bikram yoga, as well.

Meadows and Bianchi, the two deputies from Mono County, had soaked their camo gear right through. Dan was aware of how often he had to stop and wipe the sweat off his face. Suzi had taken to looking after Katie, making sure she didn't get dehydrated, and giving her the shadiest spot on the ledge to rest. That spot got smaller with each passing hour. Only Blake and Hideo seemed impervious to the heat.

By three o'clock, they had all managed to get back up to the top of the wall, victims included, and Andy MacRostie called another break. "Make sure you are drinking enough water," he warned them. "If you are suffering, you can't help anyone else. And pretty soon, we'll have to pull your sorry ass out of here. Not what you want when you're working SAR."

Dan flopped down in the shade of a huge Ponderosa pine and looked up. High above him, he could see the green needles were gently swaying in a breeze. He wished that he could feel it down where he sat.

Hideo saw him looking up. "It would be nice to have some of the air down here, wouldn't it?" he said to Dan.

Dan smiled and nodded. "Or we could climb up there and enjoy it."

Hideo laughed quietly. "I think I've had enough climbing for now," he answered.

Jim McDougal came over to sit with them, a huge bottle of blue sports drink in his hand. "Gotta love this stuff," he said. "Tastes like camel urine, but it does the job." Then he offered his bottle to Dan and Hideo. They both demurred.

Suzi and Katie sat down nearby, and McDougal got their attention. "You guys hear about this big new resort they're putting in over by Dodge Ridge?" he asked. "It's supposed to be massive, like a thousand rooms?"

Dan knew that the project was far from approved. "A long way to go before that gets final approvals," he said. "They still haven't done their environmental impact studies."

"Ha!" McDougal exploded. "Those guys have so much money, they'll just make up an EIR and print it on nice green hundred-dollar bills. The county won't say no to that."

This was too much for Suzi Muller. "What the hell are you talking about?" she said. "They have to get it past Fish and Game, Forest Service, and a bunch of local groups that are really concerned. And if that doesn't get the supervisors to listen, they'll take them to court."

"Except that most people around here would be damn happy to give up three hundred acres of forest to get the jobs and money that thing would bring into the county," McDougal replied. "Money talks."

"Until they see the traffic impact report," Suzi answered. "Everybody loves jobs, but they never want to live with the traffic and more expensive housing that come along with them. It always seems like a good idea until you have to live with it."

"You think that people won't be happy to see the value of their homes go up?" McDougal challenged Suzi.

"Sure, people who own homes," she agreed. "But renters? All they'll see is their rent go up. And by then it will be too late for them to do anything about it. They'll just have to drive farther to commute."

"This county could do with some investment," Jack Meadows suggested. "It would be nice to see some of the roads get fixed."

"Yeah," Suzi answered. "But first you'll have a lot more cars on those roads. You won't see the taxes for years, but the traffic will come right away. And wait until your favorite fishing spots get discovered."

Dan smiled. He had heard these conversations for years, both around the community and in public meetings. He knew there was no easy answer. And he wasn't about to suggest one.

"Does the Forest Service have anything to say about this?" McDougal asked him.

Dan shook his head. "Not from me. Not here. We'll participate in the EIR process and weigh in where we see any issues."

"Right," McDougal said sarcastically. "I bet…"

Just as the discussion looked as if it might get more heated, Andy MacRostie appeared from behind the tree and cleared his throat.

The group looked up at him expectantly.

"I want to go over everything that we did today, and make sure that we're all comfortable with what we've learned and what we've done."

The review lasted another hour or so. While it seemed to be more than was necessary, Dan remembered his classes on how to do a training. "Tell them what you are going to tell them. Then tell them. Then tell them what you told them." He had to admit that MacRostie had the playbook down.

With a promise of more fun in the morning, he asked them to help get the gear back down the trail and loaded in his truck before they left.

This time Dan made sure that he carried more than his fair share and gave Suzi a break.

When they got near the trailhead Suzi, who was in the lead, turned her head and said, "It looks like we have a greeting committee."

Dan looked ahead to see two women looking up at the group. They had set up a folding table with what looked like drinks and snacks.

Suzi stopped and waited for Jim McDougal to catch up to her. "That's Rod's wife and step-daughter," she said to him pointedly. "Cheryl and …I think her daughter is Sam. See if you can mind your manners."

"We have cookies and drinks for everyone," Cheryl called out to them. "Help yourselves. Don't be shy. We have lots!"

She was somewhere between thirty-five and fifty-five, Dan guessed. Her hair color was soft brown, with a bit of gray that could almost be mistaken for blond. Only the small wrinkles around her mouth and eyes, and the fact that she had a teenage daughter, gave away enough to make him think of forty-ish or more. Her figure was enough like her daughter's to prove a family resemblance, slim but not skinny, and athletic.

The snacks included brownies, and Dan was quick to sample them.

Within minutes the rest of the group had arrived and stowed the gear in Andy's truck. The snack table had been heavily attacked, and the cold drinks were gone. "We have more, but they're not on ice," Cheryl explained.

When Dan walked over to thank her, Cheryl Arquette pointed to him. "You're Dan Courtwright?" she asked.

Dan nodded. "Guilty as charged," he said with a smile.

"We need to talk," Cheryl said.

Dan gave a glance to the rest of the group and followed Cheryl to the other side of her car.

"Rod absolutely hates getting other people involved in this," Cheryl said. "But we've got a problem."

She went on to describe not only the messages, but a series of problems in their camps and workshops. "Stolen gear, stolen food, vandalism. It's a mess. And no matter where we go, this stuff seems to follow us."

Dan asked her, as he had asked Andy MacRostie, if they'd reported anything to law enforcement.

"Sometimes, but Rod can't stand that." Cheryl said. "He thinks it's just something between a practical joke and harassment. And he thinks he can take care of it himself."

"And you don't?" Dan asked.

Cheryl leveled her gaze at him. "Well, it hasn't stopped yet," she said.

Dan promised to keep an eye open during the workshop but stressed that it was really best to get someone from the Sheriff's Office involved. "They handle most of the criminal stuff here," he said.

Cheryl sighed. "Yeah. I know. But it's hard to get their attention about this kind of thing."

Dan told her about Cal Healey, and then noticed Katie was

trying to catch his eye.

He broke off the conversation with Cheryl and walked over to her.

"This climbing really tired me out," Katie said. "I'm ready to go whenever you are."

Dan quickly agreed, and they were soon off down the road, the breeze that Dan had wished for now blowing in through the open windows of his vehicle.

For the first few minutes of the drive, they were silent, both tired from the day's work, and from the amount they had been asked to absorb. But soon the cooling air brought them back to life.

"Those brownies were good," Katie offered.

Dan chuckled. "I bet you were ready for them," he said. "Did you eat anything earlier in the day?"

Katie shook her head.

After a short silence, she explained. "I guess I should tell you. I'm not very hungry in the morning these days." And before he could fully react, she added, "I'm pregnant…"

"Wow!" Dan enthused. "That's great! I didn't know…" And then he stopped. She might not be married, so there was nothing to be gained by diving into that pool. "That you were. Pregnant. But that explains a few things."

Katie laughed. "Yeah, I didn't want you to spend tomorrow worrying about me."

"Well, I will," Dan assured her. "But now for a completely different reason."

Katie smiled. "Yeah, okay."

"So when are you due?" Dan asked. "Is it okay to ask that?"

Katie gave him a sweet smile. "I'm just over four months," she said. And then, patting her stomach, "It will be a while before I really start to show."

Dan chuckled. "Man, for someone who was carrying an extra passenger, you sure did great today."

Before Katie could reply, Dan's phone pinged to let him know he had a message. And a strange beep from Katie's side of the truck indicated she had as well.

As Dan drove he saw Katie check her phone and then groan. "Jesus…"

Dan glanced at her. "What's wrong?"

She held out her phone to Dan, who shook his head to show her he couldn't read the message while he drove.

Katie said, "It's a poem, I guess:

Rod can't run,
Arquette can't hide,
from Janice Scott's
suicide.
Burma Shave.

They shared a startled look with each other.

Dan took a deep breath and told her about his conversation with Andy MacRostie. He didn't go into great detail but let her know that text was something of a pattern.

"Ugh," Katie answered. "Cyber-stalkers are the worst."

Dan told Katie that he would follow up with Andy, and also let Cal Healey, his friend in the Tuolumne County Sheriff's office, know about it.

"I bet they can't do anything," Katie said. And then, pointing with her phone, she directed Dan to note the turn-off to her house in the tiny community of Confidence.

As they arrived in front of the house, she asked Dan if he wanted to take a look inside. "We just bought it like a few weeks ago," she said. "And now we have to get it ready."

Dan glanced at his watch, then looked at the old farmhouse, clearly a remnant from a prior era. He knew that Kristen would be working late this evening, and staying at her place.

"Sure, I'd love to see it," he said.

"Oh, good," Katie said. "And you can meet my wife."

And for the second time during the car ride, Dan found himself wondering just exactly what Emily Post would have suggested he say in this situation.

He smiled and said, "Cool."

chapter 6

By the time Dan got home that night, he was starving. Katie and Shauna had invited him to stay for dinner, but that seemed too much like imposing on them. He begged to take a rain check and return when he could bring Kristen, and maybe they could offer to add something to the party.

He checked the fridge to see what he might be able to forage. There was some cooked asparagus and some cold salmon that Kristen had brought home from her job as a caterer. Dan checked carefully to make sure there was enough of her delicious dill sauce. Maybe there was enough for both the salmon and the asparagus. Some French bread, better than half of a bottle of white wine, and some of Kristen's pickled veggies filled out the menu.

He had just set it all up on the table—he'd nibbled a couple of asparagus spears with his fingers as an appetizer—when his phone beeped again. He leaned over to see a message from Andy MacRostie, asking him if he had received the nasty Burma Shave poem.

Dan wiped his fingers off on his napkin and sent back a quick affirmative. And when MacRostie asked him for Dan's contact at the Sheriff's office, Dan knew it was time to give Cal Healey a call.

"What's up, Dan?" Cal answered his phone on the second ring.

Dan started to tell Cal about the SAR training, and about Rod Arquette.

But Cal interrupted him. "How do you like working with Tweedledee and Tweedledum?" he asked.

When Dan didn't immediately answer, Cal laughed. "The two guys from Mariposa County. Have they flexed their muscles and told you how tough they are?"

Dan chuckled and told Cal about Suzi Muller. "I think they're just a little bit afraid of her," he explained.

Cal laughed. "God, I'd like to see that in live action. They must be squirming."

"They don't have room to squirm," Dan said. "Not in the tight shirts they're wearing."

Only then did Cal ask him about Arquette. "So he's getting some emails or something?"

Dan explained what he knew and told Cal to be expecting a phone call from Andy MacRostie. "I've been telling him how smart you are, so I figured I'd better warn you that he might be expecting you to live up to the billing."

Cal met this with a short silence. "I think I'm safe," he said. "As long as it's you that thinks I'm smart, I think I can cover that."

Dan grinned. "Don't have to run faster than the bear, right?"

"Just have to run faster than you, Dan," Cal agreed.

"I'll give MacRostie your contact info," Dan said.

"Sure," Cal answered. "We can add him to the list of people we probably can't help…"

"Isn't the cyber-crime division of the Tuolumne County Sheriff's Office up to speed?" Dan asked.

"We're as fast as that dial-up modem can take us," Cal answered with a chuckle. "But if we can't do anything, maybe we can turn it over to someone else, if it's serious."

"Andy MacRostie thinks it's serious."

"Are they getting any specific threats?" Cal asked. "That would make a difference."

"I don't know, but I'll let MacRostie explain it all to you."

"Okay," Cal agreed. "Say hi to my buddies up there."

"Will do," Dan said. "Which one is Tweedledum?"

"The dumb one," Cal replied.

Dan laughed. "Thanks. That narrows it down…"

Dan had just finished tidying up the kitchen when Kristen knocked on the door. He rushed over to open it.

"Want some company?" she asked. Dan grinned. "Always. And you don't have to knock first, either." Dan noticed a couple of food containers in her arms, and asked her if she needed help bringing in anything from the car.

"No, thanks," she said. "But I have had an interesting day…"

She plopped herself down to lie on Dan's sofa and let out a long sigh.

Dan loved to see her on the sofa like that, relaxed and apparently happy.

"Wow," she said. "What a day. I almost don't know where to start."

"You know what they always say…" Dan encouraged her.

"Start at the beginning," she answered. "Okay…" And she began her tale. She had been hired to cater a dinner for twenty-four people down at one of the big houses right down by the lake. The house was huge, with big picture windows facing the lake, and its own boat dock. The kitchen was larger and better equipped than the kitchen she used for her catering company.

"A true McMansion," Dan offered.

Kristen agreed. "It was. Giant houses for giant egos. And it was for only two people! The other people were all guests."

"So what was the occasion?" Dan asked.

Kristen shook her head. "No, it was some kind of meeting, really, a bunch of people talking about that new resort they're talking of building. I guess one of the people there was the developer, and he was talking to the rest of them about how wonderful it was all going to be."

"Man, that thing is getting all kinds of attention," Dan said. "We were talking about it today at the SAR training."

"Well, according to this man, it's the greatest thing to ever happen to Tuolumne County," Kristen said.

"Was he trying to get people to invest?"

Kristen shook her head. "I don't think so. I think he just wanted people to know about it and support it."

"And did they?" Dan asked.

"They seemed pretty enthusiastic," Kristen answered. "The guy even talked to me about it."

Dan smiled. "Somehow, I don't see you as the ideal investment partner for something like that," he said.

"Actually, he was more interested in my cooking," Kristen continued. "He kind of offered me a job."

"Doing what?" Dan couldn't hide his surprise.

"They're going to have a 'world-class' restaurant," Kristen said, making finger quotation marks around the term world class. "He said I would be perfect as the executive chef."

"You would be," Dan laughed. "But don't take the job until you find out how much it pays."

"That's what was wild," Kristen said. "He offered me more than twice what I'm making in a good year right now. And he promised that I'd work a forty-hour week and a normal schedule."

Dan looked at her carefully. Normally he would have thought

she'd laugh this off. But she didn't seem to be smiling. And he readily understood the attraction of more regular hours.

"Are you serious?" Dan asked. "Was he serious?"

Kristen shrugged. "Who knows? He seemed to be serious. He brought me out of the kitchen so that they could all give me a round of applause. That's always nice. And he paid his bill. Not only that, he gave me about a thirty percent tip on top of it."

Dan eyebrows shot up. "Wow. That makes for a profitable night."

Kristen agreed. She still wasn't smiling.

"But?" Dan asked her.

She shook her head. "I don't know. I mean, my first reaction was that it was a ridiculous idea." She paused.

"Which means you had a second reaction, which was…?"

"I don't know," she repeated. "And the good news is that I don't have to decide any time soon. They won't be open for at least eighteen months." She looked carefully at him. "So how was your day?"

"Interesting," Dan replied. He gave her a quick summary of the climbing workshop and the cast of characters.

Kristen smiled at his descriptions of Bianchi and Meadows, and immediately wanted to know more about Suzi Muller. But when Dan mentioned that Katie was pregnant, Kristen came alive.

"Wow! That's so exciting!" Kristen's eyes lit up. "When is she due?"

Dan was slightly pleased with himself that he could remember this. "She's about four months along," he said.

Kristen quickly counted off the months on her fingers. "So, October, more or less."

Dan told her about Shauna and the house, and Kristen sat back, smiling. "They must be so happy. Their own house, a baby on the way. Big adventures ahead," she said.

chapter 7

At breakfast the next morning, Kristen was all smiles. "Are you ready to get rescued again?" she asked as she stood by the toaster.

Dan sighed. "One more day, that's what I'm telling myself."

"You'll have to tell me how Katie does," Kristen asked.

"Don't worry, she'll do fine, just what you would expect," Dan said.

"Well, make sure she takes care of herself," Kristen suggested.

"I will," Dan promised. "But I think Suzi's there ahead of me. Did you do any more thinking about that job they offered?"

"Oh, I thought about it," Kristen said off-handedly. "I'm not going to worry about it. If they're serious, they'll contact me again in about a year, and then I'll have to make a decision."

Dan took a big spoonful of granola and started chewing. That seemed the safest course of action right then.

"They certainly are trying to drum up support," Kristen said. "Not that I'm complaining, but that dinner last night cost them a bundle, and it was only for a small group of people."

"Important people," Dan mumbled through his granola. "You can bet on that."

"Oh sure," Kristen agreed. "Judge Marley was there, and the family that owns that big ranch over by Jamestown…and a couple of the supervisors."

Dan grunted. "They'd better be careful, or they'll be in violation of the Brown Act. You're not supposed to meet or gather to discuss any business unless it's in public. No private meetings. Were there only two supervisors?"

Kristen raised her eyebrows at him. "Yeah, they even talked about that. And apparently this guy Lenhardt, the developer, has hired the daughter of one of the supes to be his PR person for the project."

Dan shook his head in disbelief. "Jesus, these guys just think the rules are for everyone else…"

"Oh, they're really working it," Kristen answered. "What's the name of that guy who's teaching your workshop?"

"Rod Arquette?" Dan suggested.

"That's him. He's going to be the director of activities, or sports, or something. At least that's what Woolford said."

Dan sighed. "They are working it," he agreed.

Kristen smiled. "Next thing, they're going to offer you a job."

Dan gave a short laugh. "Not likely," he said. "I don't think I'm their kind of guy."

And with that, and a nice long kiss from Kristen, he got his gear together and walked out to his truck.

It was the same group again at the trailhead, but this time everyone was on a less formal basis. They chatted and joked among themselves while Andy MacRostie unloaded the gear for them to carry up to Burst Rock. Jim McDougal was as loud as ever, and this morning he seemed to think it was a good idea to poke fun at Hideo, who had been the first to arrive.

"No chance of you being late two days in a row, eh, Hideo?" McDougal pronounced the name as if it were "hideous" without the last letter.

"It's Hi-DAY-oh, asshat." Suzi corrected him. And then to

Hideo. "Did you sleep well last night?"

At that point MacRostie called them all together, and they began the hike up to the granite cliffs where they would hold their workshop.

Dan grabbed three ropes and a sling of hardware and noted that MacRostie had asked the two deputies to carry the rescue litter that they were going to use. "You guys should be able to do this; work as a team," MacRostie suggested.

As they started up the trail, Dan noticed that MacRostie made an effort to hike next to him.

After a hundred yards, he heard MacRostie ask quietly, "Did you get that poem last night?"

Dan grunted an assent. He sensed that MacRostie didn't want to draw attention to the conversation.

"Just more of the same," MacRostie said.

Dan gave him time to continue but didn't hear any more. "I did mention this to my friend in the Sheriff's Office," Dan offered. "So if you want to give him a call, he'll know what it's about."

Out of the corner of his eye, Dan saw MacRostie give a small nod. "Thanks. I'll try to do that in the next couple of days. Not that it will do any good."

The training for the day focused on how to use a litter to carry a victim to help. And while it started with the basics of carrying the litter and making sure the victim didn't end up on the ground, or worse, by the middle of the morning it became clear that they were going to spend the rest of the day working on the cliff face.

"You going to volunteer to be the victim again today?" McDougal asked Dan. "If you thought yesterday was exciting, try going for a ride in a metal bed on the side of a cliff."

But Andy MacRostie explained that they would not be asking

anyone to ride in the litter. "We'll start with it empty," he said. "And at the end, if we think we're ready for it, we'll load it up with some weight. But no people. That's a risk we don't need. And that underscores a key element about this technique. Hoisting someone off a cliff on a litter is inherently dangerous. We don't expose ourselves or the people we're rescuing to unnecessary risks. Ever. What's our mantra? Simplest and safest."

Once again they reviewed how to diagnose injuries, and which patients would be appropriate for a litter rescue. And they practiced with the litter, first on level ground, and then on the steepest sections of the trail. Just before lunch, MacRostie directed them to take the litter off into an overgrown grove of Jeffrey pines. He loaded up the litter with as many day packs as he could find, and they spent the next hour negotiating over logs, through brush, and around boulders carrying the litter without dumping the packs.

It was the kind of joint effort that required real teamwork, and Dan was happy to be working with Suzi Muller again. The older woman seemed to be able to take charge without giving orders, and their team always seemed to be on the same page. It was a skill Dan knew he needed to learn.

During their lunch break, Dan was surprised to see Rod Arquette reappear. The older man quietly pulled out his lunch and sat down on the edge of the group, not really making any comment, other than to nod at Andy MacRostie.

The conversation at lunch started with some comments about the training, but quickly circled back around to the new development project. Dan noted that Rod Arquette followed the conversation carefully, but made no mention of any contact he might have had with the developers.

But during a brief lull in the conversation, Jim McDougal

wasn't satisfied with that. "So what do you think of all of this?" he asked Arquette. "Wanna see a huge development go in right outside the front door of Yosemite?"

Arquette stared at McDougal as if he could will the man to disappear.

He couldn't.

With a very measured voice, Arquette said, "You know, it's really frustrating. All I've tried to do is give classes and workshops, and I've been hassled out of just about every county and forest and park in the Sierra." He looked directly at the two deputies. "Mono County, Inyo, Kern, John Muir Wilderness, Ansel Adams, El Dorado, Toyabe," Arquette paused to let this sink in.

Dan remembered all too well confronting Arquette about an unlicensed climbing camp a few years ago in the Stanislaus National Forest. He wondered if Arquette remembered. He hadn't mentioned it in his list.

"Makes you wonder how those developer guys are managing to pull something like that off." Arquette continued. "And if maybe they aren't playing by the same rules." Again he looked directly at the deputies.

McDougal snorted. "Developers have money," he said. "And they're waving the money and jobs in front of people like it's the vision of the promised land. Who's gonna say 'no' to that?"

Rod Arquette didn't respond to this. He just continued to stare at the deputies.

As they wrapped up lunch, Cheryl Arquette joined them.

"Did you bring us goodies again?" Jim McDougal called out to her.

She gave a tiny smile and shook her head. "Not today," she said. "Sorry."

"Oh man, I was looking forward to brownies," McDougal continued. And then, in a lower voice, "And that cute daughter, too,"

He grunted when Suzi Muller elbowed him hard in the ribs. "Don't be an asshole," she said.

McDougal shrugged and joined the rest of the group for the final afternoon of the training.

For the next three hours they practiced managing the litter on the face of the cliff. They raised it and lowered it. They practiced moving from above and tracking it along the face of the cliff as it moved. And they managed to add the daypacks for weight, and do it all over again.

By a little before four o'clock, they were all at the top of the cliff, the litter was safely stowed, and there were smiles and handshakes all around.

Andy MacRostie congratulated them on a job well done, and they thanked him for his instruction.

"Yeah," McDougal cheered. "We didn't need that asshat Arquette for any of this. You did a great job!"

Which was exactly when they noticed Rod Arquette walking up the trail toward them.

chapter 8

If he had heard McDougal's comments, Rod Arquette didn't allow that to show.

He quickly called them together and asked them to participate in one more exercise.

Watching Arquette, Dan realized that the man didn't trust Andy to do this part. And as MacRostie stepped back, Dan realized that MacRostie knew it, too.

Once again, Rod Arquette waited until he had their full attention. "I want you to take some time to think about what you've learned today," he said. "Not just about ropes and gear, but about people and about yourself." Arquette paused to let this sink in. "It's too easy to pack up and head out of here full of smiles and endorphins, and leave everything you've learned behind."

There were some murmurs in agreement with this.

"So here's what I ask you to do," Arquette said. "We have an hour. You have an hour. Use that hour carefully. Mindfully. I want you to find a space up here—a place where you can focus your mind. Find that place and sit there. Sit there for an hour, and think about what we've done today—how we've done it, how you are going to do it again if and when you need to."

Arquette paused and looked around. "Go. Find a spot in the forest, or on the granite, and think calmly about it. About the world. About your role in the world. Take off your shoes, if you want.

You'll feel the ground better. Take off your clothes if you want..."

From somewhere behind him, Dan heard Suzi mutter under her breath: "I'm not stripping for you, ya dirty bastard."

But Arquette ignored her. "Go," he said. "I'll ring a chime when we're done. We'll let you know. Go."

Dan was delighted with the assignment. He watched, briefly, to see which directions the others chose. Bianchi and Meadows (Dee and Dum?) headed back down the trail. Dan knew that wouldn't lead to anywhere peaceful.

Katie, Blake and Suzi all started out walking together along the use-trail on the top of the cliff to the right, heading further out into the sunlight and glaring granite. McDougal looked at Hideo Saito and said, "Looks like we go this way, Hideeeo," and pointed to the left along the cliff, where another faint trail led. Hideo waved Jim forward and invited him to lead the way.

Dan smiled. The one direction nobody had chosen was the one that led up over the top of the ridge, away from the cliff and away from the trail. There was not even the hint of a use trail to follow. Dan headed in that direction. A granite ledge and a few downed trees created an immediate obstacle, and he picked his way over and around them, but soon broke out into more open forest.

There were large slabs of granite here, and clusters of bent, stunted junipers that had struggled every winter against the storms, and every summer against the sun. In between, patches of white sand, rough decomposed granite, made small flat areas like lakes and puddles, sometimes connected with each other, sometimes not. And from the top of the ridge he could see mountains off in the distance—the Emigrant Wilderness.

Dan kept walking. He loved this landscape. The sky was an intense blue you only see at high elevation. A fox had left a small pile of scat on one rock, a marker to let others know of his existence. In one patch of sand Dan crossed the tracks of a few deer, a doe and two fawns, he noted, moving up into the high country for the summer. Most of the sand was untouched, not another footprint to be seen. And it was silent except for an occasional sigh from the wind or a bird calling for friends.

He loved the feeling of breathing this clear thin air as he walked, the gentle breeze drying the sweat on his skin before he could even feel it. He kept walking. Up ahead, he could see the ridge drop away. He checked his watch. It had now been a quarter of an hour since he left the group. He was supposed to be sitting still, thinking about the class. But the ridge ahead called to him. He'd never hiked here before. Who knew when he would come back again? And he had at least another forty-five minutes. That meant at least another fifteen until he needed to turn around. He checked his watch one more time to make sure. He stood with his hands on his hips and looked around for the best route forward through the trees and white granite.

That was when he heard the gun shots.

Three shots, carefully spaced out. They were quite a distance away, back toward civilization, of course. With a groan he turned towards them, back towards the trail. He couldn't ignore them. Most likely, there would soon be more. Even if he was supposed to be at the workshop, he was still on duty. He knew he needed to make sure that whoever was shooting was doing it safely. He turned and started walking back towards the shots. The ridge would have to wait for another day.

As he walked back, Dan listened carefully. The last thing he wanted to do was walk into the range of someone firing off their gun. It could be the last thing he did. He called out, asking them to hold their fire, listening for an answer.

Which was why it took him longer to walk back than it had taken him to walk out on the ridge. By the time he was close to the workshop group, he decided that the deputies would have reacted as well. He might as well check with them.

But when he arrived at the workshop's old fire ring, Dan was surprised to find it empty. Confused, he stopped to listen. Somewhere off along the cliff he thought he heard voices and began to walk towards them.

There, beyond those trees, was a group of people. He could see McDougal's hat, and that short one looked like Suzi Muller. He checked his watch again. Had he misunderstood? It was only forty minutes after Arquette had told them to break for an hour. Maybe the others had decided thirty minutes was long enough. Typical.

Dan walked towards the group. As he stepped out from behind the last group of trees, he saw Deputy Bianchi turn around and suddenly drop to one knee and point a gun at him.

"Freeze!" he yelled. "Stop right there!"

Dan halted and raised hands slowly. What the hell was going on here?

"No, wait, that's Dan," he heard Suzi say.

Deputy motioned him forward, still covering him with his gun. "Where have you been, Courtwright?" he asked suspiciously.

Dan pointed over his shoulder carefully. "Where I was supposed to be. Over on the ridge, you know. Thinking about the class, like Arquette said." It was a lie, but a sweet little white lie.

"Are you armed?" the deputy asked.

Dan gave a little snort and shook his head. His hands were still up.

Deputy Meadows walked over to Dan and gave him a very cursory pat down, then met the eyes of his colleague and shook his head.

Bianchi lowered his weapon. "We have a situation here," he said.

"Suzi Muller interrupted him. "Rod Arquette's been shot, Dan," she said. And then added, "Dead."

Dan looked quickly at Meadows, standing next to him, who stared back silently.

"What the hell?" Dan asked. "Did you see who did it?" But even as he asked the question, he'd already sensed the answer.

"Did you call it in?" he asked.

Both deputies answered. "To Mariposa dispatch," Bianchi said. "They'll pass it on..."

Dan walked over to his pack and pulled out his radio. They might as well hear it directly from him, too.

chapter 9

Jim McDougal was getting impatient. "We've been sitting here for more than an hour," he said. "You'd think they could let us get out of here."

Deputy Bianchi wasn't having any of it. "Not until the Sheriff gets here and releases you," he said. "They'll want to take a statement from everyone."

McDougal looked at Dan as if asking him to confirm this. Dan shrugged. "Until they get here, we all sit tight," he said.

"Ah, hell," McDougal said. "They know where we live. They can track us down. It's not as if any of us is a suspect."

Deputy Meadows stood up and walked over to him. "Until the Sheriff gets here, we're all suspects, you included," he said.

McDougal gave him an ironic salute, "Yes, sir."

Katie and Suzi Muller were sitting apart from the group, talking quietly as they looked out over the canyon. On the other side of the group, Cheryl Arquette was sitting with Andy MacRostie. He had his arm around her shoulders, which continued to shake.

It was MacRostie who had found the body, Dan had learned. And not long after, Cheryl had started screaming, then sobbing. An hour later, and she was still obviously terribly shaken.

Hideo Saito suddenly looked up at Dan, and then pointed into the air, opening his eyes wide.

As Dan listened, he could make out the steady thump of a

chopper. He looked at Hideo. "That could be them," he said.

One by one, the people in the group began to strain their necks, searching the sky for the incoming chopper, which was still hidden in the trees.

Just as Suzi Muller called out "I see it!" and pointed to a spot over Dan's shoulder, Dan noticed someone limping up the trail toward them.

He looked carefully, then smiled. He would recognize that limp anywhere.

"Sheriff's here," he said, and stood up to walk over and shake Cal Healey's hand.

Cal was breathing hard from the climb up the hill.

"Damn," he said. "Couldn't you guys do this on flat ground?"

Dan gestured over to Bianchi and Meadows. "I think you've met these guys?"

Cal reached out and the three men shook hands.

Bianchi immediately started giving Cal a report on the incident, with Meadows standing by to add commentary.

Dan could see that Cal was taking it all in as he surveyed the group. When his eyes met Dan's, he gave a quick nod.

"Okay. I've got a couple more people on the way," he said. "First I want to take a look at the victim, and then we'll start taking statements." He said this loud enough for the rest of the group to hear.

McDougal gave a sigh, looked at his watch, and sat back down, shaking his head.

Bianchi and Meadows began to walk Cal over to the cluster of trees that held Rod Arquette's body. Cal stopped for a moment. He asked Meadows to stay with the rest of the group and gestured for Dan to join him.

The scene wasn't pretty. Arquette's body was folded up next to a large log. His clothes were soaked in blood from his chest to his knees. His head was turned away, but there was a black stain in the dirt below it as well.

"Three shots," Bianchi said. "We heard them. Not all at once. More like Bang, count to five, Bang, count three more, then the last Bang."

Cal looked at Dan, and Dan gave a quick gesture to show that he agreed.

"I was way the hell over on the other side of the ridge," Dan said. "But that's what I heard, too. At least, from what I could tell. There were some echoes off the granite."

Cal knelt down next to the body and delicately reached out to move Arquette's head. His eyes traveled down the body, his hands carefully pulling cloth out of the way at times.

Still crouching down, Cal leaned back and gave a deep sigh. "All three shots hit him," Cal said. With his fingers pointing like a gun, he pretended to shoot. "Bang, bang, and bang." The last one Cal pointed at Arquette's head.

"That's got to be the last one," he said. "No need to keep shooting after that one."

Bianchi agreed. "Each shot gets a little more accurate," he said.

Cal sat thoughtfully. "Maybe, yeah. Close range. Don't need a rifle to do this."

Behind them, they could hear the chopper looking for a place to land.

Cal turned to Dan. "Who are these people?" he asked. "Any problems over the weekend?"

Dan shook his head. "Nothing worth killing him for," he said. "He left most of the teaching to his assistant, that guy MacRostie."

Dan pointed to Arquette's body. "He only showed up a couple of times to say hello."

Cal looked at Bianchi. "Where were you?"

Bianchi pointed back down the trail. "Deputy Meadows and I were a couple hundred yards down there."

"Did you see anybody hiking up or down the trail?" Cal asked.

Bianchi shook his head. "Nobody, either direction."

Dan wondered if they would have noticed, given their assignment from MacRostie.

"If somebody had walked up or down that trail, would you have noticed?" Cal asked.

Bianchi nodded soberly. "I think so," he said. "We weren't just staring off into space,"

Cal looked around and took a deep breath. "Okay. I'd like you to go over and collect everyone. Make sure nobody leaves. We're gonna need to talk to them all, and it's going to take some time."

Bianchi nodded and walked back to the group.

Cal turned to Dan. "Did you see anything that might indicate that somebody wanted to kill this guy?" he asked.

Dan shook his head. "But remember, this is the guy that's been getting all those texts and stuff," he said. "So somebody doesn't like him."

"Yeah," Cal sounded dubious. "But enough to kill him?"

Dan turned and joined Cal in staring at the group.

"Talk me through the characters here," Cal asked him.

Dan identified each of the members of the training, including Andy MacRostie and Cheryl Arquette.

When he was finished, Cal waited for a minute. When Dan said nothing more, Cal took over. "So everybody is up here, supposed to be off on a spirit animal search, or something. And Tweedledee

Bianchi says nobody came up or down the trail."

He looked at Dan. "Where does this trail go from here?"

Dan pointed over the ridge. "Powell Lake, the whole Emigrant Wilderness."

"Is there another way to get here?" Cal asked.

Dan shook his head. "Not a convenient one," he said. "It would be a long hike. And you'd have to get in and then get back out again."

Cal shook his head slowly. "Yeah, not likely…"

Dan heard the chopper land on the granite over on the top part of the ridge.

Cal looked at him. "We're going to have to spend some time up here," he said. "Maybe once we get done with the crime scene, you can help the guys chopper this body out." He pointed with his head.

Dan agreed. "Are you going to need some help with them?" he asked, looking at the group of people gathered around Deputy Bianchi.

"Yeah," Cal said with a sigh. "But I've got a couple more LEOs on their way that can help with that."

Dan nodded. "Okay. Let me know what you need from me."

Cal looked at his friend. "Got an alibi?"

Dan smiled sadly and shook his head. "Not unless you'll take the sworn testimony of a couple of squirrels and noisy blue jay."

Cal snorted a short laugh. "Great."

"I can provide a character witness, if you want," Dan offered. "But it's only the local Sheriff. I don't imagine that will carry much weight with you."

Cal shook his head. "Not where I come from," he said. "If that's all you've got, you're in some serious shit,"

"I figured as much," Dan said.

He watched as Cal walked over to the group and start the

investigation. He sent a text to Kristen to let her know he would be late back to his place.

chapter 10

It was dark by the time Dan got back home that night, despite the long days of early June.

He was surprised to see his neighbors Walt and Ruth in the living room, seated on the sofa and deep in conversation with Kristen.

There was an awkward pause while Ruth apologized for being there so late. "You must be exhausted," she said to Dan.

He smiled and shrugged. "It was a long day."

"What took you so long, Dan?" Kristen asked, a note of worry in her voice.

Dan shook his head. "There was a bit of a situation up there," he explained. He didn't want to go into detail about it in front of Walt and Ruth.

Ruth's wrinkled face took on another furrow of worry. "I hope it wasn't anything serious," she said.

Dan just shrugged. "Yeah, it was," he said. "But it's not my problem now."

Kristen continued to look at Dan with concern.

Ruth began to gather her things and looked at Walt. "We should go," she said.

But Kristen held out her arm to ask her to wait. "No, that's okay," she said. "At least tell Dan why you came over."

Ruth considered this for a moment, looking at Walt for permission. Finally, she said, "Well, I don't know if you know much about it, but we're worried about that big new development they are planning up by Yosemite."

Dan gave a sad smile. "Yeah, you and everybody else," he said. "We had quite a conversation about it at the training session this weekend."

"And what did people say?" Ruth asked. "Were they worried about it, too?"

Dan shrugged. "Some were. Some seemed to think it was a good idea. Lots of different views."

Walt nodded silently.

"And what do you think?" Ruth asked.

"I've got some concerns," Dan said. "I'm not sure they've thought the whole thing through. But that's why we have EIRs and public hearings."

Ruth's head bobbed up and down vigorously. "You know, we moved up here years ago from Walnut Creek," she said. "We loved that it was rural and wild. But every year there's more traffic. They keep building bigger roads. And it seems like Walnut Creek is just moving up here to find us again."

Walt gave a sad smile. "Well, we came up from Walnut Creek," he said. "Maybe we started it."

"Oh, don't be ridiculous, Walt," Ruth turned on him. "You know that's not true."

Walt shrugged. Nearly as tall as Dan, he towered over his tiny wife, but he wasn't in the habit of contradicting her.

Ruth turned back to Dan. "So what are you hearing about it, Dan?" she asked. "I mean in the office…"

Dan shook his head. "I think the forest service is waiting to see the final plan before they take a position," Dan said. "That's what they usually do."

Ruth harrumphed. "I hope they don't wait until it is too late," she said. "Those developers are certainly shaking the trees and bushes for friends."

Dan saw that she was holding a flyer about the project in her hand and looked at Kristen.

"We got one of those, too," Kristen said. Then, after a pause, she added. "And they've even offered me a job."

"What?" Ruth exclaimed. "Oh, you can't be serious! You're not going to take it, are you?"

Kristen shook her head. "I don't know. I'm not sure it's really right for me."

"It certainly isn't!" Ruth continued. Then realizing that she might have overstepped, she apologized. "I don't mean you wouldn't be good at it. I just mean...well, never mind."

Kristen smiled at her. "It's a long way off right now," she said.

Walt cleared his throat. "You know that they've hired the daughter of one of the supervisors to be their flak," he said. "I would think that violates some kind of conflict of interest law."

"Oh, they'll try anything," Ruth said. "They're so greedy for money. And people here are so shortsighted. They only see the money and the jobs. They don't see the traffic, and housing costs, and the crime."

Walt patted Ruth on the arm. "Dan looks like he's beat," he said. "We should let them get on with things."

Ruth glared at him, and Dan thought she was going to argue, but then she looked at Dan, and then Kristen. "I'm sorry," she said. "I just get so worked up about this. It makes me so mad."

Kristen smiled at her. "That's a good thing, Ruth. It means you care," she said. "We need more people to do that around here."

Ruth took a deep breath and then gave a quick nod. She patted her thighs with her hands twice, as if to call the meeting adjourned, and stood up. Walt joined her quickly.

And with that they quickly said their goodbyes and left to walk back to their house next door.

Dan smiled and looked at Kristen. "Welcome to the neighborhood," he said.

"They're sweet," Kristen said. "She even brought over some cookies, then apologized for how bad they are."

Dan laughed. "Are they bad?" he asked.

Kristen shook her head. "They're delicious. But she said she felt embarrassed to bring food to a chef."

Dan licked his lips. "I think I better try one to make sure," he said.

As he walked over to the kitchen counter, he heard Kristen, "What took you so long up there?" she asked. "I thought you'd be back hours ago."

Dan told her about the shooting, without going into too many details.

"Oh, my god," Kristen said. "His poor wife. How awful."

Dan agreed. "Yeah, and Cal and his team showed up and wanted to interview everyone and get as much information as possible."

"Did you tell him about that guy who was complaining about the hate mail and everything?" Kristen asked.

"Yeah, I'd actually told Cal about that yesterday," he said.

"Do they know who did it?" Kristen asked.

Dan shook his head. "No idea, at least not yet. There were ten people up there, and none of them has an alibi," he said. "And from what we can tell, nobody has a motive. It's not an easy situation."

"I guess Cal is going to be busy," Kristen said.

"Yeah, and he had most of the department up there helping

him with the questioning," Dan said. "He saved me for last. I think he kind of wanted to get my take on it all after he'd heard from everyone else."

"And what did you tell him?" Kristen asked.

"That I had no idea," Dan said, with a dry chuckle. "That wasn't much help. But ten people. All of them had the opportunity. None of them have alibis, and I don't think any of them had a motive, at least not from what I saw over the course of the weekend."

"Couldn't it have been someone else, someone not at the training?" Kristen asked.

"Maybe," Dan said. "But there were people from our group along the trail in both directions, so it would have been hard for them to get in and out."

Kristen considered this. "Sounds complicated," she said.

"Oh, and no gun," Dan added. "He was shot, but we didn't find the gun."

"Didn't Cal search everybody?" Kristen asked. "Could he do that? I mean, legally?"

Dan sighed. "Yeah, well, he asked for permission, and everyone agreed. But he didn't find anything."

"That's weird," Kristen said.

Dan shook his head. "It's the middle of the wilderness. The gun could be anywhere down a ravine, off a cliff, under a rock or up in tree…"

Kristen put her arms around Dan's neck and looked up at him. "At least you're back here, where I can keep an eye on you," she said.

Dan smiled. "You can be my alibi tonight," he said.

She kissed him. "I hope I won't have to go into too much detail," she said.

Dan laughed and kissed her back.

"Oh," Kristen said, breaking off the embrace. "You got a phone call this evening, before Ruth and Walt came over. I took a message."

She handed him the slip of paper.

Dan didn't recognize the name or the number. "Did he say what it was about?" he asked.

Kristen shook her head. "No, but that's the same guy that tipped me thirty per cent the other night."

"The developer?" Dan asked.

Kristen nodded.

Dan held the paper in his hand. "I guess it's a good thing you didn't mention this when Ruth and Walt were here."

Kristen smiled. "He didn't say what he wanted. Maybe he wants to offer you a job, too."

Dan laughed. "Because I am such an influential leader of the community?"

"Exactly," she said. "Not to mention a suspect in a murder investigation, apparently."

"Yeah," Dan said. He looked at her. She was radiant in the soft light of the table lamp. "I think I'll wait to call this guy back."

chapter 11

The next day, Dan was surprised to see Andy MacRostie walk into the Summit Ranger Station.

Out of the corner of his eye, Dan could see Doris slowly begin to drop back into the back office. He knew she wanted to listen to this conversation, but she also knew it didn't concern her. Dan turned and asked her if she could please check the women's restroom to make sure it was fully supplied.

Doris murmured her assent and walked past MacRostie and out the door. Dan knew he would have to give her some explanation later.

"How are you doing?" he asked MacRostie.

MacRostie shook his head. "Still coming to grips with it all," he said. His eyes glanced up at Dan's then quickly looked off toward the bookshelves on Dan's left. "I certainly didn't expect that," MacRostie said. He gave out a huge sigh.

Dan let MacRostie's sentence hang for a while. Then he said, "I'm not sure anyone expected it. How is Cheryl?"

MacRostie shrugged. "Okay, I guess. I mean, how do you expect her to be? She's a wreck."

Dan asked if her daughter was with her.

MacRostie shook his head. "No, she left yesterday morning for her dad's place," MacRostie said. "I guess that's good." He gave another sigh. It was clear that MacRostie was struggling for some kind of control.

"What about the climbing camp?" Dan asked. Rod Arquette and MacRostie had been running a camp for young climbers out of Pinecrest Lake.

"We've given everybody a couple of days off," MacRostie said. "It's kind of a mess."

"I can imagine," Dan said.

"They're mostly young kids," MacRostie said, "The camp is a big adventure for them—young kids living life large. But this is something else completely. I mean, they worry about a missing 'biner, or wanting to be first on a climb."

"Not exactly life and death stuff," Dan agreed.

"I mean, to them it is," MacRostie said. "You lose your girlfriend, you lose a credit card. You don't want to climb with somebody because they were mean to you…It's all important to them. But nothing like this."

"Sounds like you're a family counselor as much as a climbing instructor," Dan said.

MacRostie agreed. "But it pays the bills, man. Well, barely. At least we can keep the doors open. And now, I don't know what's going to happen."

Dan asked if MacRostie had told Cal Healey about all the hate mail messages and social media posts.

"Yeah, for what good it will do," MacRostie answered. "He said they'd look into it, but I doubt they have what it takes to figure that stuff out."

Dan came to Cal's defense. "They may not have it in-house, but the shooting took place on federal lands. That means they can call in the FBI," he said. "My guess is that Cal will do that."

The words seemed to have a powerful effect on MacRostie.

"The FBI? Really?"

Dan let that sink in.

"That would be…well, maybe they can figure things out better," MacRostie said.

Dan looked up to see Doris walking back in the door. He smiled at her. "Everything good?" he asked.

She nodded and came back around behind the counter.

Dan introduced her to Andy MacRostie, and she offered her condolences.

MacRostie thanked her, but he was still obviously shaken. "I guess now I don't know if I should be worried. I mean, whoever did this might…Well, I'm worried about Cheryl."

"Oh, poor woman," Doris said.

Andy MacRostie agreed. "It seems to me that she could be in danger," he said. "But she won't do anything. She's a wreck."

Dan and Doris murmured words of sympathy.

"Maybe you could talk to her," MacRostie said to Dan. "Just hear her out. I think it would be good for her to talk it all out, and maybe have you give her some advice."

Dan shook his head. "If you seriously have some concerns about her safety, she should contact the Sheriff's Office," he said. "They can also provide security if she is in danger."

MacRostie shook his head. "She won't do that,' he said. "She doesn't take it seriously. And they see her as a suspect. That's not quite an ideal situation to ask for help."

Doris looked at Dan. He knew what she was thinking, but he was going to hold firm here.

"If you really think there is a danger, you need to tell that to the Sheriff's Office," he insisted.

He saw Doris fidget to his left. "It's not my job, and there is nothing I can do that would help."

MacRostie and Doris both looked at Dan. It was clear they both disagreed with him.

"Sorry," he said. He shrugged and shook his head. "I just don't think I can help her."

After a long pause, Andy MacRostie finally accepted Dan's answer. He said goodbye to both Dan and Doris and walked out the door.

Dan turned and held up his hand to Doris. "You know there's nothing I can do there," he said.

Doris nodded. "I know. But I feel sorry for the poor woman. Somebody should talk to her."

Dan gave a pointed look at Doris and raised his eyebrows. "And?"

She shook her head and turned away. "Somebody who knows and cares about her," she said. And quickly turned to fuss with the maps behind her.

It was just after lunchtime when Doris took a phone call and turned to Dan. She put her hand over the mouthpiece of the phone and said, "someone named Eric Lenhardt? I didn't get the company…"

Dan shrugged and reached out to take the phone from Doris.

"Is this Dan Courtwright?" the man on the phone asked.

"Yes, it is."

"Mr. Courtwright, my name is Eric Lenhardt, and I'm with Willoughby Partners. Have you heard of us?"

Dan gave a sigh. "I think so," he said. "You're the group behind the new resort?"

"Exactly," Lenhardt agreed. "Good for you."

Dan wasn't sure congratulations were in order. "What can I do for you?" he asked.

"Well, I'd like to get a chance to meet you and let you know a little more about our project, from the horse's mouth, as it were. Would you have time to do that?"

Dan thought this over. "I'm not sure," Dan stalled. "I think the Forest Service probably has its own team looking at all of that."

"Oh, I'm sure that they do," Lenhardt agreed. "I was thinking that we'd like to talk to you more on a personal basis, rather than an official one."

That did not seem like fun to Dan. "I try to keep a pretty low profile on most of these kinds of projects," he said. "There's an obvious concern about conflict of interest and all."

"I understand completely," Lenhardt replied. "And I really respect that. But there may be some other reasons for us to meet."

Dan was getting suspicious. "And what would those be?" he asked.

"Well, we're doing our best to meet with many of the top leaders in the community," Lenhardt explained. "From bankers to environmentalists. Business owners to outdoors people. Just letting them know what's going on. We think they deserve that, given their roles in the community."

Dan thought about Ruth and Walt. He wondered if they had made the list. He doubted it. "Yeah," Dan answered. "I'm not sure I fit the bill."

"I appreciate your candor," Lenhardt continued. "And your modesty. But I think you fit the bill pretty nicely. You've been recommended by a number of people."

Dan chuckled. He could only imagine who might have done that. "Really?" he asked. "Like who?"

"Well, a number of people," Lenhardt said. "Rod Arquette, the famous rock climber, for one."

The man obviously hadn't heard the news. "Was he working with you?" Dan asked.

"Well, he was," Lenhardt admitted. "An amazing guy. Really impressive."

"But?' Dan prompted him.

"Rod has a lot of irons in the fire," Lenhardt said. "In the end, I think this was just one iron too many for him. He simply didn't have the time. That's when he suggested we talk to you."

Dan considered this. "Sounds like you had some big plans for him," he said.

"Well, we were hoping he would join us as our outdoor specialist, giving our guests the chance to learn about the area and explore the kinds of activities that make it so special," Lenhardt explained.

"So kind of a camp counselor, huh?" Dan asked. He couldn't keep the skepticism out of his voice.

"Well, we'd like to think of it as so much more than that," Lenhardt said. "It would be an opportunity to create a whole community of people, really engaged people, who love this area, and would be dedicated to protecting it for the future."

Dan smiled. "Sounds attractive," he said. "Protecting it from what?"

Lenhardt didn't miss a beat. "You know the dangers that our mountains face every day, Dan," he said. "You know the budget cuts, the lack of focus, the lack of purpose. We're creating a community that would fight to fix all of that."

Dan shook his head. "I don't think I'm your guy, Mr. Lenhardt," he said.

"Don't be too quick to decide," Lenhardt said. "You haven't

really given me a chance to explain this—how we work, and how we would work with you. It's an amazing opportunity."

"Thanks," Dan said. "But I don't think it's right for me."

"I understand your concerns," Lenhardt continued. "I would have the same concerns, if I were you. But I think you owe it to yourself to sit down with us, if only for half an hour, and really get a sense of what we're talking about."

"Sorry," Dan said. "I'll leave this to the Forest Service…"

"You haven't even heard how much we are willing to pay," Lenhardt stressed. "Believe me, we are making a real investment in our team."

Dan remembered what Kristen had said. "I can imagine," he said.

"And you're still not interested?" Lenhardt asked.

"Not really," Dan admitted. "It's not what I see myself doing."

"Well, I appreciate that, Dan." Lenhardt said. "And I respect it. I won't push any harder. But I do want you to know that the offer to meet with us still stands. We'd love to sit down with you and tell you about us, and about the project."

"I'll keep that in mind," Dan said.

"And we would still be interested in talking to you about our community advisory panel," Lenhardt said. "We're looking for people to give us honest insight into how we can best proceed. You would be an ideal candidate."

Dan shook his head. "No, thanks." His patience was wearing thin.

"Well, let me ask you then, Dan. Do you know anyone else you think we should talk to? Anyone in the community who would give us the kind of input we're looking for?"

Dan looked at Doris, who was helping a family find the right hike for the day. He thought of Ruth and Walt, and how angry they had been.

"You know, I don't really think so," he said.

chapter 12

It was late that afternoon when Dan got a call from Cal Healey on his cell phone.

"Got a couple minutes?" Cal asked.

Dan assured Cal that he did.

"We're tracking down all kinds of things with this Arquette case," Cal said. "I'm wondering if you've heard anything about some of this stuff."

"Shoot," Dan encouraged him.

"Maybe not the best choice of words, Dan," Cal said. "But yeah, okay. Number one. Have you heard anything about problems up at Arquette's climbing camp? Anything at all?"

Dan thought back to his conversation with Andy MacRostie. "I had Andy MacRostie in here this morning," he told Cal. "He said there were the usual issues—something like stolen boyfriends, missing credit cards, that kind of stuff. Andy didn't seem to think it was very important."

"No, I don't think we worry much about that," Cal agreed. "Anything else?"

"We had some issues with them a couple of years ago, when they were running a school up here without a license," Dan said. "But they've been completely above board this year, got all their paperwork and everything."

"Good for them." Cal didn't sound convinced.

"Andy did say that they'd run into problems in some of the other jurisdictions," Dan added. "You might check with Mono County, or some of the other National Forests. But with us, they've been clean."

"Okay, thanks," Cal said. "Could I ask you to reach out to a couple Forest Service people in those areas to see if they might know anything?"

Dan looked at the clock. "Is an email good enough to start?" he asked. "I can follow up on the phone with anyone who might have something."

"Sure. Thanks, Dan." "It's just that we're buried here. We know about all the text messages and everything. We've got some people working on that. Did MacRostie say anything about drugs? Illegal drugs? Ever hear anything about that?"

"No," Dan answered. "Not a peep. But I'm not sure he would have mentioned that. I mean, he's trying to run a business there, and that kind of stuff would probably kill it. Especially if it got exposure in the press."

"Well, we'd sure as hell have something to say about that," Cal agreed.

"He did say that they were struggling to make ends meet, or something like that," Dan added. "Maybe that's a way of adding a bit to the bottom line?"

Cal considered this. "Yeah, maybe." He sounded skeptical. "I'm thinking more about some of the climbers."

"Andy made it sound as if most of them were pretty young," Dan said. "More like a summer camp than anything else. I know kids do drugs, but…"

"No, it doesn't seem like they'd have the connections to deal with the kind of stuff we're tracking," Cal admitted. "And they are kind of off in their own world up there. I don't think they even get down to Sonora that often."

"It's not that far," Dan said. "But it seems like they wouldn't be able to go down there without the rest of the kids knowing about it, at least not more than once or twice."

"Yeah," Cal agreed. "I guess I'll go talk to them and see if I can find one or two who might be doing that. Did MacRostie say anything else to you?"

Dan thought back to the conversation. "I told him that if he had concerns, he should talk to you about them, not me," Dan said. "He was concerned about Cheryl Arquette, said that she should be worried about her own safety."

"Okay," Cal replied. "I'll have someone go up and talk to her. Did he mention anything specific?"

"No, not really," Dan said. "He said she seemed really upset. He was afraid whoever did this might go after her next." He didn't mention her concerns about being a suspect.

"Not likely," Cal said. "I don't think this was an attempt to wipe out the family. If it were, why didn't they shoot her right then and there?"

"Yeah, good point," Dan agreed. "Unless they got scared off by someone."

"Possible," Cal answered. "Possible, but not probable."

Dan heard Cal sigh.

"Are you making any progress on this?" he asked Cal.

Cal gave a dry chuckle. "Progress? As in figuring out who did it? No. But it's early days. We haven't found the gun yet. Cheryl tells us that Arquette owned a 32-caliber pistol. Coroner says that's consistent with the wounds. But we don't know where that gun is. It could be just about anywhere now."

"Are you still searching the area?" Dan asked.

"Yeah," Cal answered. "Can you guys keep it closed off a bit longer?"

"Whatever you need," Dan said. "Just confirm with Steve Matson and we'll do it."

Cal answered this with a long silence. A long silence. When it continued, Dan asked, "Are you still there?"

"Yeah, I'm here," Cal said. "And I'm thinking about Mrs. Arquette. Why would she worry about her own safety, unless maybe she knows something that makes her worried?"

"Well, it was MacRostie who said that, not her," Dan said. "But if she knows something about that, why hasn't she told you about it?"

"I think I'm going to ask her that myself," Cal said.

"She might be worried about talking to you," Dan said. "MacRostie said she was concerned that she would be considered a suspect."

"She is a suspect," Cal said. "You always look at those closest to the victim first."

"But?" Dan asked. There was something in Cal's tone that made Dan think he wasn't convinced.

"But there are none of the obvious reasons," Cal said. "There was no insurance policy. No insurance company would touch that guy, given how he makes a living. And she owned the house before they were married. She kept it in her name. The climbing school isn't worth much without him."

"What about affairs, or another girlfriend?" Dan asked.

Cal snorted. "He had at least five of them in the last few years. She didn't care. Says that she knew he'd always come home to her. She was his home."

"She is what, his third wife?" Dan asked. "Any chance one of the other two might be angry?"

"Oh, that's an idea. We never would have thought of that, what with all that hate mail and everything," Cal said appreciatively. "You're a smart guy, Courtwright, I don't care what other people say about you."

Dan chuckled. "Happy to help, Cal. Anything for our boys in blue. Or, in your case, some kind of sickly tan."

chapter 13

Dan had the next two days off, and he planned to spend them taking care of a few things around his cabin. They were already well past the fire safety season, so the leaves and pine needles had all been raked, and the branches and other detritus from the trees had been piled up and burned months ago.

But there was always more to do. And now that Kristen was here, he found himself wanting to do even more.

Rod Arquette's murder wasn't his problem, and he knew it. But he couldn't help thinking about it. Somebody up at the training knew who did it. Dan was sure of that. The question was who?

But he also knew that he thought best when he kept busy, working on something and letting his mind wander.

He had built a small fountain in the backyard for the birds, and it was a never-ending source of entertainment for the birds, and maintenance for Dan. This time the pump had stopped working entirely. He cleaned out the intake of the pump, checked the tubing up to the top of the fountain, and was just about to conclude that he needed a new pump when he checked the reset button on the outlet. After forty-five minutes of work, he fixed the damn thing with a single push of a finger.

At least Kristen would be happy about that. She liked the fountain and loved the animals it attracted. And later in the season the forest was even drier, which meant that the animals needed the fountain even more. By the end of the summer, she was sure they were going to have an entire ecosystem around the little pool of water.

The animals would cluster around, just like the people at the SAR training. Dan hoped they wouldn't murder each other, but he knew from experience that a blue jay or squirrel was a likely victim, usually thanks to a fox or local feral cat.

And then there was the woodshed.

They had used up most of the wood over the course of the winter, and there was only about half a cord left. He would need to get at least another cord and a half before the next winter, but before then he needed to re-stack what was there already. As they had burned up the wood, they always seemed to pick out the best pieces with each trip, and that meant that the last half cord was a sorry pile of odds and ends, some old lumber, quite a few pieces that were just a bit too big to burn in their stove, and the odd pine cone or rotten log thrown in as well.

That took the rest of the morning, and by the time he was done, he was covered in dirt, dust, and spider webs. He hadn't seen any black widows, but he knew they were there, and gave himself a quick check before coming back into the house.

It had started out cool, but by now the forest was plenty warm, and Dan had worked up enough sweat to get the back of his shirt wet. What he really needed was another shower. And maybe a nap. Having a day off was turning out to be hard work.

When he came in for lunch, he realized how much cooler it was inside, and decided that he would have to check his email sometime this afternoon—probably right around three or four, when it would be hottest outside.

He made himself a turkey sandwich, tossed a few of Kristen's homemade pickles on the plate, added the tag end of a bag of potato chips, and grabbed a jug of lemonade. But when he opened the door to take all that outside to eat on the picnic table by the fountain, the heat hit him again, and he turned right around and sat down at the kitchen table.

By the time he was done with lunch, he'd polished off the entire half gallon of lemonade, and had decided that any outside work could wait until tomorrow morning.

He flicked on his computer and sat back, waiting for it to boot up.

A string of emails cascaded with a series of chimes into his mailbox, most of them in response to his queries about Rod Arquette at the various neighboring National Forests. Carol down in Prather called Arquette an arrogant sonofabitch and said that if it hadn't been for his assistant, Andy, they would have banned him from the whole National Forest. But Andy had begged, pleaded, and filled out every form in triplicate, including liability insurance. And he had lived up to his word. They'd had no other problems. But if Arquette ever showed up without Andy, Carol would be happy to tell him to go to hell.

Dan smiled as he read that one. He'd seen Carol in action once, and he had no doubt that she was absolutely capable of fulfilling that promise.

Over in Inyo the email had been forwarded to someone Dan didn't know. And the response was considerably more circumspect. But reading between the lines, Dan could see that Arquette had not made any friends down there, either.

There were three other responses, all of them more or less the same. And the guy in Humboldt-Toyabe, who knew Dan well, actually called Arquette an "entitled son-of-a-bitch," and told a story about him ignoring a direct command from one of their rangers that nearly ended with Arquette getting arrested. Again, it was Andy MacRostie who stepped in and smoothed things over.

Dan picked up the phone and dialed Cal Healey's number. Cal didn't answer, so Dan left a message to say that he had heard back from his colleagues and would be happy to share the information.

His work on the computer done, Dan looked outside. The thermometer on the porch read eighty-nine degrees. That was way too hot to work out there, even in the shade. And it wouldn't get any cooler in the next few hours.

There was a slight sense of relief when Dan remembered that he had promised Kristen to clean up the area underneath the downhill section of the house. It was always cool in there, even on the hottest days. With the lemonade gone, all he had to drink was ice water. He took a jug of that under the house, turned on the bare fluorescent lights to illuminate the scene, and considered exactly what he needed to do.

There was lumber to stack, a bunch of cardboard moving boxes to break down and recycle, paint cans to either save or throw out, and he wanted to organize his tools, which now lay about on shelves and the floor. Oh, and he would need to sweep the floor in there, too. It was covered with what would turn out to be a cardboard box full of dust, dirt, sawdust, and trash.

He sat down on a sawhorse and thought about where to begin. It certainly was cool in there. If he worked slowly and deliberately, it just might take him the rest of the afternoon.

Which it did.

When he heard Kristen's car he checked his watch, and saw that it was nearly six p.m. The ice water was long gone. He took a look around the basement. It looked great.

Well, maybe it didn't look great, but it looked a lot better than it had at noon. And that was good enough for Dan. He hoped it would be good enough for Kristen, too.

He heard her talking to someone on the phone and left his cool cavern to join her up in the house.

But when he walked in the door, she took one look at him and held up her hands. "Stop! Stop right there! Oh my god you are filthy!"

Dan chuckled. "I've been working," he said.

She fixed him with a stare. "I can see that," she said. "But how can you bring all that stuff into your house? How about you come around to the back door, and strip off those clothes before you come inside?"

Before Kristen had started staying over at his place, Dan would have simply walked into the bathroom and cleaned up in there. He looked at her. She met his gaze.

"Really, Dan," she said. She was not joking.

He gave a sigh and nodded. He walked around to the back porch and stripped to his underwear, then stepped into the house.

"Like this?" he said, holding his arms out to his sides so she could appreciate the look.

Kristen gave him a quick smile. "Leave those clothes right there outside, and I'll throw them directly into the washing machine," she said. "And you may want to take two showers."

Dan smiled. "Want to join me?"

Kristen laughed. "Only for the second one," she said. "And Cal called. He got your message and wants you to call him back."

Dan leaned forward and Kristen allowed him to give her a brief kiss on the lips while she held her hands back to avoid touching him.

He grinned and walked off to take a long shower.

When he got out of the shower, Dan checked with Kristen about dinner. "Do I have time to call Cal?" he asked. "Or should I wait until after?"

Kristen waved her hand around at the kitchen. "It's all leftovers tonight," she said. "So we can eat whenever you want. All I have to do is heat a few things up."

Her eyes scanned him from head to toe and she smiled appreciatively. "Very nice," she said. "Much better than before."

Dan laughed. "I'll call him now. It shouldn't take too long. And then we'll have the rest of the evening free."

chapter 14

Cal picked up on the first ring. "What have you got for me?" he asked Dan.

Dan told him about the response from his contacts in the various forests, and summarized each of the emails, one by one.

"He seems like a really popular guy." Cal said sarcastically.

"No question," Dan answered. "But I'm not sure any of this helps you much. I think it's pretty unlikely that anyone from the Forest Service should be on your list of suspects."

"Except for you," Cal corrected him.

Dan laughed. "Yeah, but it's hard to tie all this stuff to someone who wanted to murder him."

"Did any of your friends mention any issues with his clients, or these kids at his camps?" Cal asked. "No drug deals, no violence, nothing like that? Any consumer complaints to anybody?"

"Most of what they mentioned had to do with him not following their rules," Cal said. "I didn't get anything back about any other problems. I can't guarantee that they would know about that kind of stuff, but they didn't mention it at all. And if it had been serious, they would have told me. Seems like MacRostie was the key to the whole thing. Without him, I think Arquette would have been in deep shit a few times. MacRostie always stepped in to save him, at least for a few days."

"That's what I'm getting, too," Cal said. "Seems like a lot of people didn't like him, but nobody seems to have a real motive to kill the sucker."

"So you've got no suspects?" Dan asked.

"Oh, hell, I've got suspects," Cal said. "I have the ten people who were there when it happened, or at least close enough to have had the opportunity. And the guy had a 32-caliber handgun that we can't find. The coroner says that matches the murder weapon. So assuming that gun was up there and used to shoot him, I have ten suspects with means and opportunity." He left the sentence hanging.

"And you don't have anyone with a motive?" Dan suggested.

"Not right now I don't," Cal agreed. "I've got people sending hate mail to the guy, but I don't know who they are. So far, it's all from burner phones and fake email addresses."

"Did you talk to his wife?" Dan asked. "You know what they say..."

"Yeah, I did," Cal said. "She is still in bad shape. You know, there are times that this job is really unpleasant, and questioning a woman whose husband has just been shot is one of those times."

"Hmm. Yeah, I bet," Dan said. "Is there any reason to believe that she shot him?"

"Not that I can see," Cal said. "She clearly loved him. She's absolutely destroyed right now—shaking, sobbing. Sometimes incoherent. She's asked us to leave her alone. Says it's too painful. She'll answer any questions, but only in writing through her attorney."

"Does that seem suspicious to you?" Dan asked.

Cal shook his head. "Not really. Not given the circumstances."

"She did seem pretty happy, I mean when I saw her the day before, on Saturday," Dan asked. "What about Andy MacRostie??

"Same problem," Cal said. "He's not upset like the wife, but he came right out and told me point blank that he didn't do it, and I have to say that I think I believe him. His career is tied to Arquette, and now he's out of a job."

"So if Cheryl didn't do it, and MacRostie didn't do it…" Dan said.

"We looked at his step-daughter," Cal said. "But she left the night before to go with her dad. She is now in Patagonia."

"Wow," Dan said. "That must be nice."

"That leaves eight other people," Cal said, refusing to get sidetracked.

"Including me," Dan said.

"Including you," Cal agreed. "You're a pretty sorry excuse for a suspect, Courtwright, but right now I've got to hang on to every suspect I can."

"Happy to help, Cal," Dan said.

"Thanks for following up with the Forest Service folks," Cal said. His voice sounded tired.

"Happy to do it, seriously," Dan said. "Hey, did you learn anything about Arquette's previous marriages? That was what the hate mail was about."

Cal sighed loudly enough for Dan to hear it clearly over the phone. "Yes. And no. Two marriages. First one right out of college, two kids. She lives somewhere in the East Bay, Berkeley or El Cerrito. Happily remarried. Doesn't really fit the profile of a jilted lover. And her husband was in Tucson on business."

"What about the kids?" Dan asked.

"We're checking," Cal said. "But the older one is in college in Colorado, and the younger one is in high school down there. No reason to believe they were up here at all. But we'll check. We're checking everything."

"And the second one?" Dan asked. "Second marriage," he clarified.

Another long pause.

"Janice Scott," Cal said. He waited for Dan to respond.

"Uh huh. Yeah." Dan said. "Did she commit suicide?" he remembered the poem on his phone.

"Apparently she did," Cal said. "She married him when she was just out of high school."

"Ugh. That would make her a very unlikely suspect," Dan said dryly.

"Very unlikely," Cal agreed.

Dan thought this over. "But someone cared enough about that to send a bunch of us a poem about it," he said. "Someone who knew her? Her family? That's got to be it."

"Yeah, we're on it," Cal said, still sounding exhausted. "Just like we're on everything else."

"Well, somebody was sending those texts," Dan said.

"Yeah," Cal agreed. "If you get any more, let me know."

"Find the texter, find the murderer?" Dan suggested.

But Cal wasn't in the mood. "Just let me know if you get any more, okay?"

Dan promised he would.

chapter 15

The next morning, just as Dan was getting ready to make a list of things to do around the house, he got a call from Katie Pederson. She asked him if he had a few minutes to talk, or if she should call back another time.

"I know it's your day off, Dan, and I don't want to intrude on that."

At first, Dan was worried that she would want to talk about the murder, and that wasn't something he wanted to do with her. Not that he suspected Katie of being involved in any way, but he didn't think it was a good idea for them to talk too much. Stories get changed that way, and memories get altered. It doesn't help things, later.

But she barely mentioned the murder. Instead, she started telling Dan the story of how she bought her house. And she explained that it might take a few minutes to tell the whole thing.

Dan opened the back door of the cabin and walked out onto the deck. He settled into one of the big Adirondack chairs, put his feet up on the deck railing, and told Katie to take her time. It was still cool enough to be pleasant, the sun was streaming through the trees in big, golden bands, and Dan happily considered that he had nowhere to go.

"Did you ever wonder how we could afford a big house like this?" Katie began.

Dan told her that he assumed that Katie and her wife made enough money to afford it.

"Well, that's true," Katie admitted. "But only because we got a screaming deal on it."

She went on to explain the whole situation. The house sat on almost five acres of land, and should have cost a lot more, but it also came with a condition.

"There's an old lady living here, and there's a condition on the deed says that she can stay here as long as she likes." Katie explained. "So, basically she can stay here until she dies."

That seemed like a complication to Dan, but he didn't say anything.

Katie went on to explain that the condition had been placed on the property about six years before, as part of the will and living trust of the owners at that time. "It's written right into the deed and the title report, and it cannot be changed," Katie added. "The old lady here, her name is Lucilla, was the sister of the owner. That's why they set it up that way."

"Why didn't they just leave her the house in the will?" Dan asked.

Katie let out an exasperated sigh. "Good question. But they didn't. They had a reverse mortgage on it, so maybe that was the reason. Anyway, Lucilla lives here in the back of the house. She has her own set-up there, kitchen and everything. So it works."

"But,…" Dan suggested that there was more to the story.

"Well, not really any 'buts,'" Katie said. "It works. We're paying off the bank for the house, and Lucilla's a sweetheart. We get along great. She does amazing things out in the garden."

Dan gave a chuckle. "Yeah?"

"Okay," Katie admitted. "Why did I call you? Because Lucilla seems to think that there are some strange things going on in the house. In the attic. She keeps hearing noises up there, and she's worried."

"An old house?" Dan asked. "Could be squirrels. Or birds, or bats. Up here, there are lots of possibilities."

"Yeah, we know that," Katie replied. "We've had a pest guy come out and look at it, and he said there was no evidence of anything like that. Not that he seemed very interested. I think he maybe was just too busy right then."

Dan suddenly felt a slight twinge in his gut. "Katie," he began, "What do you think is going on?"

"I don't think anything is going on," Katie assured him. "But I don't seem to be able to convince Lucilla of that."

Dan could hear the frustration in her voice. "And you think I can convince her?" he asked.

Katie let out a sigh. "I don't know, Dan. But could you come up sometime and just take a look around? I've told her a little bit about you, and I think it might help to have you reassure her."

Dan let his head fall back until it rested on the back of the chair. He was now staring at the pines and cedars that towered over his house, with a few patches of blue sky between them. He must have done that for a few seconds, because soon he heard Katie again.

"Dan? Are you there?" she said. "Did I lose you?"

"No," Dan jerked himself upright. "No, I'm here. I can come up sometime. I'm not sure it will do any good or anything, but sure, I can come up and have a look."

Another big sigh came from Katie, this one of relief. "That would be wonderful, Dan. I am so grateful." She would have gone on longer, but Dan cut her off.

"Not a problem," he said. "When were you thinking?"

"Well," Katie's voice suddenly became about ten years younger. "I know you're off today, and I am off today…" She let the sentence hang.

Now it was Dan's turn to take a deep breath. He thought about the work that needed doing around the yard. And how hot it would be today. And how much cooler it would be up higher, where Katie's house was.

"Well, sure," he said. "What about this afternoon?"

"Oh, God! You are a saint!" Katie gushed. "That would be so great. I'll never be able to thank you enough."

Dan smiled. He never minded when people owed him a favor or two. He rarely collected on the debts, but it was nice to know he had them in his pocket.

chapter 16

When Dan arrived at Katie's house, she came out to greet him. "I think Lucilla's feeling a bit under the weather today," she said quietly. "But let me see if she'll come out to say hello."

She walked around the back of the house, and Dan could hear her voice making an effort to be bright and cheerful as she talked to someone back there. He stayed out front, not wanting to make his presence an issue to the old woman.

After a few moments, he heard Katie saying "He's just right here, out front. Come say hello."

And Katie came around the corner of the house, gently leading a much smaller old woman by one arm. The old woman wore a long dark cotton skirt that reached the ground, with an almost tribal pattern of brown, tan, black, and a tiny bit of bright red. Around her shoulders she wore a shawl, although it was already well into the eighties this morning, and underneath the shawl was a pale lavender sweater. Her hair, pulled back into a tight bun, was almost completely gray with a few strands of black.

But the thing that struck Dan most was her eyes. They were deeply set in her narrow face, tucked in underneath a ridge of bone and dark eyebrows. It was as if she were peering at you from underneath the roots of a tree.

Dan smiled and gently said hello.

Lucilla stared back at him, her eyes searching his face. He

thought maybe she was looking for a clue, something that would remind her of who he was. What she didn't do was smile.

Her mouth twisted into a kind of grimace, but she didn't say anything.

"Do you want to tell him about the noises you've been hearing?" Katie asked her, helpfully.

Lucilla gave a quick shake of her head.

"He's really good at solving mysteries," Katie offered. "I thought he could help us figure out what was going on. What was making the noises you hear."

Dan liked the way Katie included herself in the problem. That was smart people management.

But Lucilla wasn't having any of it. She still hadn't spoken, but she turned around and started to walk away, back towards the porch and the entrance to her part of the house. As Katie tried to follow her, Lucilla looked back over her shoulder.

With her head she motioned towards the house. "They make lotta noise," she said. "Upstairs. Too much noise." Her accent was heavy and gave the words a darker tone. And then she turned and walked back around to the side of the house into the garden.

Dan could see rows of vegetables there, and up above, a beautiful section of roses.

Katie gave Dan an apologetic shrug. "I'm sorry, Dan," she said. "She's a little out of sorts today."

Dan shook his head and smiled. "No worries. Let's take a look upstairs and see what's going on."

Katie led him through the house back to the laundry room. Once there, she pointed to a section of the wall and a trap door in the ceiling. "That's how you get in," she said. "I hope you can fit."

Dan inspected the wall. Artfully crafted into the woodwork of the house was a ladder that he would not have noticed, delicately carved, and perfectly fit together. He gingerly tested the first step, and grabbed onto the side rails and gave them a shake. The ladder was strong, too. "This should work," he said.

"When you get to the top, you have to push the little door out of the way," Katie explained.

Dan reached up with one hand and tested the hatch. After an initial resistance, it popped free on one side, and he was able to push it open and clear the way into the attic.

"I think I'll wait here," Katie said.

Dan remembered that she was expecting, and agreed it was a good idea. "I'll let you know what I see."

He eased his head up over the edge of the hatch and looked around. It was dark in the attic, and it took his eyes a few minutes to adjust from the bright sunlight of the laundry room below.

"There's a lot of boxes, I guess," Katie offered. "We just moved in, and haven't really unpacked everything."

"I can see that," he said with a grin. "Let me get up here and see…"

He climbed up the rest of the steps of the ladder, and now stood under the ridge of the roof. There, he could stand, but he would have to crouch down to explore around the edges. He could see flares of daylight coming in from around a few of the eaves. That might mean there was room for a squirrel or other animal to get in.

He eased his way around one stack of boxes. The floor was plywood. He was grateful for that. At one end he could see a small window that let in some light through the gable. The boxes had been stacked in towers, all close to the hatch, as if someone had decided to put them all up there as quickly as possible.

"There's a lot of stuff up here," he called down to Katie.

"Yeah, I'm sorry," she said. "Some of it is, like, Christmas stuff. And some is stuff we won't need for a few months, until the baby comes."

Dan crouched over and edged his way into a more open area in the attic.

"And there's some stuff we really don't need, but didn't want to throw out," Katie continued. "Plus some stuff from the previous owners."

Dan squeezed between a nice old rocking chair and the last stack of boxes. Over by the little window he could see some furniture: a chair, a dressing table with a lamp on it. It almost looked like someone had set it up as a little corner retreat.

"What's this furniture?" he asked Katie.

"Just stuff that was left here from before we moved in," Katie said. "We might bring the rocker down once the baby is here."

Dan walked over to the dressing table. There was a dusty hand-held mirror on top, and he noticed a broken comb and a hairbrush beside it. They didn't look nearly as old as the furniture—maybe from the 1970's he guessed.

Dan crouched down next to the dressing table and looked out the window. From there he could see some of the garden, and part of the barn.

As he looked out, he suddenly had the strong sensation that there was someone else in the attic with him. Someone or something was behind him. He froze for a moment.

He put his hand on the dressing able and slowly craned his neck to look around. From what he could see, the attic was empty. But the sensation was so strong that he stood up, too quickly, and cracked his head on one of the rafters.

Katie must have heard the thud. "Are you all right?" she called out from below.

Dan rubbed his head and looked around the attic. "I'm fine," he said.

And that was when he noticed the rocking chair. It was slowly rocking back and forth, ever so slightly, as if something or someone had bumped it.

Dan was sure that he hadn't touched it on the way in.

He stared at it for a few seconds. For some reason, he was covered in gooseflesh—something that hadn't happened to him in years. The chair slowly came to a stop. Dan took a step, testing the floorboards to see if they moved, if that had been what set the chair in motion.

Nope.

He took another step and cast his eyes around the attic. Maybe a rat on one of the chair's runners? Wouldn't he have heard that?

Slowly, Dan walked back towards the hatch, looking behind boxes, easing around towers of boxes, the light from the window behind him turning his shadow into that of a giant.

There was still a series of chills running up and down Dan's spine, even in the warm air of the attic.

"Do you see anything?" Katie called up to him.

"No," Dan answered, hoping the tremor in his voice didn't give him away. He looked at the rocker again and did some quick calculations. It was now over the part of the house that Lucilla inhabited. He carefully slid it over the floor, placing it firmly over Katie's part of the house, and wedged it in place against the roof and rafters. At least that way it wouldn't move.

Dan went back and stood over the hatch. From here he could see very little past the boxes. He still felt that shiver in his spine and was grateful that the hatch backed up against the wall. At least this way, no animal could jump on him from behind. Or anything else.

He carefully climbed down the ladder, every nerve in his body alert to a noise. As he ducked his head out into the laundry room, he saw Katie below him.

"Well?" she said.

He shook his head. "I didn't see anything," he told her, shaking his head.

chapter 17

That evening Dan told Kristen about his visit to Katie's house. He didn't go into great detail about his experience in the attic, but he told her about meeting Lucilla and the noises upstairs.

"I hear she's quite the character," Kristen said. "I've never met her, but I've heard all about the house."

Dan looked at her in surprise. "Really?" he asked. "What do you know about it?"

"Well, I don't know the whole background," Kristen admitted. "But one of my waitstaff knew the young couple that bought it before Katie. And yeah, they lived in one part of the house, and the old lady lived in the other."

"And?" Dan prompted her.

"And they spent a lot of time and money fixing up the place," Kristen said. "Did you notice the kitchen?"

Dan grunted to let her know he had.

"That's one thing they did. They even asked me to suggest a good layout, and I got them a couple of discounts on the stove and fridge."

Dan smiled. "Did you get a designer's fee?" He knew she wouldn't have asked for one.

Kristen laughed. "You know me better than that. I was happy to help. And they did a ton of work in the garden, too," she said. "There was even a team from their church—it was one of these small, home churches. They went up there and spent a couple of days doing major projects for them."

"Well, it still looks good," Dan said. "I guess Lucilla does a bunch of the work there now."

Kristen thought about this. "That's what I've heard," she said. "They get all sorts of great veggies, and the rose garden is a showpiece. What ever happened to all that furniture? I heard the attic and barn were just full of old stuff."

Dan told her about the dressing table and rocker in the attic.

"Yeah, I heard that they had kind of a little memorial up there for her sister Lydia, like a little shrine, but I heard there was a lot more than that," Kristen continued. "Did you look in the barn?"

Dan laughed. "It wasn't an inspection tour," he said. "Well, it was, but only in the attic. I didn't get in the barn. Next time I'll have to let them know that my girlfriend wants me to inspect the barn."

Kristen shot him a glance. "Good," she said evenly. "And make sure you do a good job. I wouldn't want you to miss anything."

Dan laughed again. "Got it."

He told her that Katie would be placing a few rat traps around the attic, just to make sure.

Kristen seemed to be lost in thought. "You know," she said. "That couple broke up. I guess that's why they sold the place. She just took off and left him. He was at some conference in Idaho, and when he got back, she was gone. Not a word or a note. I think he took it pretty hard."

She reached out and took Dan's hand.

Dan squeezed her hand. "If you're going to leave me, please make sure you leave a note," he said.

"If I leave you," Kristen said firmly, "you'll damn well know why."

That night after dinner, Dan decided to tell Kristen about his experience in the attic.

"It reminded me of when I was a little kid," he said. "We lived in a house on a dark street with lots of trees. And my job was always to take out the garbage."

"Doesn't sound too scary," Kristen suggested.

"You wouldn't think so," Dan agreed. "But the garbage cans were around on the side of the house, on the far side of the garage. And every night I dreaded that trip. I knew what was coming. Going out the front door, there was a light, and so that was no problem. But going across the front of the garage, I could always feel the fear starting to rise in me."

"What were you afraid of?" Kristen asked.

"I knew what was out there, waiting for me," Dan said. "It was huge—taller than I am now. And for a little kid, that was gigantic. And it had no face. At least, I couldn't see its face. It was covered in a tattered old black shroud, that was filthy. And it just towered over me."

He looked at Kristen, who seemed appropriately serious.

"I mean, I never actually saw it," he said. "But I knew it was there. And it knew I was coming. You couldn't see the face, it was just a black hole there in the hood, but sometimes I thought it might have a veil over its face, or maybe that was just white bone showing through. And it was icy."

Even now, Dan began to feel the chills in his spine.

"With a long arm, and a single, bony finger at the end. I knew it would never get me if I saw it coming," Dan said. "Somehow, it wouldn't attack me then. But when I turned my back on it, when I got around to the dark side of the garage and had to open the garbage can—that's when it started to creep up on me."

Kristen was silent, watching him. Their eyes met briefly, and Dan glanced away before he continued.

"And so my back was to the trees and the darkness," Dan said. "And I knew that it was there. It was reaching out with that bony finger to get me, with the black shroud making very quiet, kind of whispering sounds."

"I knew I couldn't turn around," Dan said. "For some reason, I knew that if I confronted it, it would all be over. So I always threw the bag of garbage into the can, and slammed the lid down, and raced back across the front of the garage. I could feel it right behind me, just inches away with that bony finger reaching out."

Kristen smiled sadly and shook her head. "It sounds terrifying for a little kid."

"It was," Dan agreed. And after a moment, he added. "And I felt a little bit of that up in that attic in Katie's house."

Kristen stared at him. "Did you turn around to see?" she asked.

Dan nodded slowly. "There was nothing to see. But the rocking chair was moving a bit, back and forth."

She continued to search his face. "But did you see anything else?"

Dan shook his head. "No," he admitted. "And I knew it was silly. But even though I knew it was silly, I still had that feeling that something was weird up there. Something was wrong."

Kristen squeezed his hand and stood up. "Next time, I'm going with you," she said. "I want to see this."

Dan laughed. "There wasn't anything to see," he explained.

"There wasn't anything for you to see," she corrected him.

"Oh, and you have ESP?" Dan questioned her.

"I have a woman's intuition," she replied. "And I am really curious."

"Curious and brave," Dan said. "Are you sure you want to confront my childhood demons?"

She smiled. "They're your demons, not mine, Dan."

Dan stood up and she gave him a hug. "Thanks for listening," he said. "Probably sounds pretty crazy, huh?"

She squeezed him hard and gave him a deep kiss, then leaned back to look at him. "It is really crazy," she said. "Like you. Crazy. And wonderful. And you were probably a very sweet little kid."

Dan laughed. "I'm not sure my sixth-grade teacher would agree with that," he said.

She kissed him quickly and turned to tackle the dishes.

"You know," he said, "there is a whole theory about people who imagine things like monsters and boogeymen."

Kristen handed him a dish towel and pointed to the dishes drying in the rack.

"It has to do with evolution," he continued. "It goes back to when we were far from the top of the food chain, back when we were competing with Neanderthals. If a group of people were walking along the trail, and one of them heard something, most of them might just say that it was the wind in the grass. But one of them would be sure it was a lion or some other terrible monster, coming to eat them."

He dried the wine glasses and put them in the cupboard. Kristen handed him a plate.

"Of course, most of the time, it was only the wind in the grass," he said. "But every once in a while, it really was a lion. And sensing that, even if you were wrong a lot of the time, was a survival skill. Because it helped the rest of the tribe become more aware, more careful."

Kristen handed him the other plate and pointed to the silverware still on the table. Dan collected it and brought it to her.

"So do you think that you are more sensitive to that kind of thing than most people?" Kristen asked.

Dan shook his head. "Not really. Those were just childhood fears. I think most people have them," he said. "But who knows? Maybe they really do play a role in the fight or flight reflex."

"Would that also work with tall monsters who attack small children?" she asked with a smile.

"Of course!" he laughed. "You never know when one of those is around."

Kristen wiped her hands on a dish towel and smiled at him. "Well, it's also a survival skill to share stories about your childhood with me," she said. "It greatly improves the chances you will... continue your genetic line."

Dan burst out laughing. "Do you want to do that now, or later?" he asked.

"After we finish the pots and pans," she said.

chapter 18

Dan was back at work the next morning at the Summit Ranger Station. It was an odd day. A rare summer storm had filled the skies with low clouds, and it was threatening to rain. In June, that was rare indeed. But Dan hoped that even a few small showers would help reduce the fire risk for a few days. The woods were already far too dry for safety, and they had restricted campfires to fire rings and gas stoves since Memorial Day.

It was Doris who took the phone call. Dan overheard her trying to talk the caller into forgetting whatever it was he was complaining about, but she clearly failed. Two or three minutes into the call, he heard the tone of her voice change, from discouraging to helpful, and she began to take a few notes.

When she hung up she looked at Dan with a sour expression. She waved the note at him. "There is a car up on the Pinecrest Peak trail, and it's been there for a long time," she said. "This guy thinks it's been abandoned, and that we ought to do something about it."

Dan walked over to take the note from her. "Silver Honda Accord. That's it? The guy didn't get a license plate?" he asked.

Doris shook her head. "No plates on the car," she said. "Whoever left it there probably took them off."

Dan gave a disgusted sigh. "Great. Now we not only get to protect the forest and maintain the trails, we also get to tow away abandoned vehicles."

"At least this one seems easy to get to," Doris suggested.

Dan agreed. "Yep. I'll go take a look after lunch."

If the weather had been better, it was a drive that Dan would have enjoyed more. But after the first bridge over the creek, he began to think about the steeper sections he'd have to face later. If it really did start to pour, those roads could quickly become more problematic.

The road twisted through the mountains, going past the trail to The Gargoyles, and sometimes opening up onto small meadows that were already drying out in the summer sun. Other times it wound through the forest, clouds of dust rising up behind Dan's truck as he powered up a rise, or negotiated a hairpin turn.

He knew it would take a while to get all the way to the end of the road, but he also doubted that anyone could get a passenger car all the way to the end. It was possible, with very careful driving, but they had probably decided to stop before they left their oil pan on a rock.

Then again, maybe they had hit a big rock, and that's why the car had been left. Dan knew from experience that getting a car towed out of this area was not a cheap proposition.

He drove past the campground and over the bridge, then turned onto the spur road that led up to the trailhead parking for Waterhouse Lake and Pinecrest Peak. It occurred to him that it would have been more enjoyable to hike up to the Peak from Strawberry. It was only a few miles. But then again, he might need some of the tools in the truck.

The car wasn't hard to spot. It was parked at the trailhead and underneath the weeks of accumulated dust he could see that it had some kind of graphics or paint on the side. He couldn't read them through the dust.

He pulled up and parked near the edge of the lot. Dan usually took a certain amount of pride in finding a parking spot that would be well-shaded, but today there was no need. The gloomy clouds took care of that.

He slipped the gearshift into park and climbed out of the truck, leaving the door open. Even from here he could tell that the windows on the car had been smashed. At first he thought that had been done by someone trying to steal what was inside, but then he realized that they had all been smashed.

He walked a quick circuit around the car. Overhead, the tall pines were sighing with the wind, which seemed to be picking up. He gave a quick glance at the sky and noted that it seemed to be a bit darker now. Rain would probably follow soon.

The caller had been correct. There were no plates on the car, and the only identification was a small, square sticker on the rear bumper. Dan wiped the dust off to read that it was a parking permit for Diablo Valley College from twenty-two years ago. He wondered if the college would still have records going back that far.

He tried the door handles on the passenger side, and they were both locked. He hoped he wouldn't have to climb in through the back window, which was totally smashed. He gave it a careful inspection as he walked around to the other side of the car. It would be a tight squeeze, but he could probably do it, headfirst. That would not be fun. And the dust on the car would coat his shirt and pants.

The rear driver's side door was locked as well, but Dan gave a quick sigh of relief when the driver's door opened easily. He peered inside, taking stock of the interior. With the back window shattered, it wouldn't have surprised him to find an animal living inside—a squirrel, or even a raccoon or a skunk.

He proceeded cautiously.

Inside the driver's door, Dan quickly spotted the VIN and took a photo. At least that was still here and would help trace the car. The stereo was gone. There was no telling if it had been worth anything. Dan couldn't imagine a twenty-year old stereo would sell for much on the black market, but maybe it had been upgraded more recently.

The back seat had been torn to shreds. Judging by the strands of fur, Dan guessed it had been a raccoon. He carefully looked under the seats, and in the pockets on the back of the front seats. They were empty. He slowly eased into the driver's seat and checked the glove box, the windshield shade, and the center console for any identification or documents, but came up empty. The car had been cleaned out. Even the trunk was empty—the spare tire was there, but it was flat.

Dan heard the sharp pang of a drop of rain on the roof of the car. He looked at the windshield to see that the clouds were lower, and the ridge across the canyon was now indistinct, blurred by falling rain. He checked again around the interior of the car but found nothing to help. The rain was now splattering on the roof.

He got out of the car and took one more circle around it. He considered wiping the dust off to read the graphics and decided that it wasn't worth the trouble. The VIN was all he would need to trace the car.

A gust of wind buffeted him, and the rain now changed from a few fat drops to a steady downpour. Dan raced back to his truck and slammed the door behind himself. The rain was now beating on the roof like a carwash.

Dan pulled out his radio and called dispatch. He gave them the location of the car, plus the VIN, and asked them to run a trace on the car. And he watched the rain pour down.

There was no reason to wait. He started the truck and put it into gear. The wipers scraped noisily across the windshield, and Dan turned the truck around.

As he peered through the windshield, he could see that the rain was washing off the dust of the old Honda. He stopped, facing the car, and wiped off the inside of his windshield, which was fogged up from his damp clothes. He had to do it twice, and then turn on the defroster. Slowly, he began to see through the foggy glass.

The color of the graphics had begun to wash into visibility from the dust. Dan made out a letter here and there. And he realized what the words said, and he sat back in his seat. He watched as the rain cleared more and more of the dust off the car. But he already knew what it said.

He grabbed his radio again and called the Sheriff's office. They would certainly want to know about this.

There on the side of the car were two words: "Arquette. Murderer."

The Sheriff's Office patched him through to a deputy who asked him to wait for them to arrive, and to make sure nobody else touched the car.

Dan hung up the radio and turned off his engine. The windshield wipers froze, half-way through their cycle, leaving the wipers pointing somewhere up in the sky.

Out the rain-splattered side window, Dan could make out the steep road, now running with rivulets of water in the two tire tracks down the mountain.

chapter 19

It didn't surprise Dan that Cal Healey was the officer to arrive. When he'd heard the deputy on the radio tell him to wait at the car, he'd known it was going to be a priority.

Cal's vehicle pulled up around Dan's, and then parked next to it. By now the rainfall was steady, and Dan had given up using his windshield wipers. He sat in the truck, windows fogged up and splattered with rain, and waited for Cal to get out of his vehicle.

He waited for quite a few minutes. Just as he was about to get out of his own truck, he saw Cal's door open. The Sheriff knocked once on his passenger side window, and then opened the door and climbed in.

"What the hell's going on?" Cal asked, not really of Dan, but just as a general observation.

He was holding a clipboard and staring at the abandoned car.

Dan turned on his engine, and with it the wipers and the defroster.

"Don't bother," Cal said. "I saw the thing just fine."

Dan shrugged and turned the engine back off. "Did you get the VIN number?" he asked.

Cal looked at Dan and shook his head in displeasure. "Oh yeah," he said. "We got it. Did they tell you?"

Dan shook his head. "Not me. I haven't heard anything since I called this in."

"And you just happened to find this?" Cal asked. There was clear suspicion in his voice.

"Nope," Dan explained. "Somebody called in to Summit to tell us about an abandoned car up here. I came up to check it out."

"And you found this…" Cal led him on.

"And I found this," Dan agreed. "I wouldn't have even called you, but the rain washed enough of the dust off for me to read the letters on the side." He paused here. "I figured you'd want to know about it once I saw that."

Cal nodded, and the two men sat in Dan's truck for a few moments without further comment.

Cal broke the silence. "This sucks," he said.

Dan looked at his old friend. Cal looked tired, older than Dan remembered. "Have you got any further on this thing?" he asked Cal.

"Not really," Cal said. "Although, technically, I shouldn't talk to you about it, because technically you're still a viable suspect."

Dan smiled. "And my motive?"

"Fuck that," Cal said. "I have ten people with the means and opportunity. It's like a fucking Agatha Christie movie. I have no people for whom I can find a motive."

"I have always suspected Colonel Mustard in the library with the candlestick," Dan said.

Cal gave him an ugly stare. "He doesn't have a fucking motive, either."

Dan considered this. He pointed to the truck. "Seems like the motive has to be tied to Arquette's second wife," he offered. "That's what all the texts and things were about."

"You think?" Cal was angry. "If we could find anyone who had a connection to her, that would be right. But we can't. Her father died in a car crash about ten years ago. Her mother has alcohol-caused dementia and is in some kind of a care home in Redding. I've got suspects all over the place with no motive, and a clear motive with no fucking suspects."

"Were there other kids in the family?" Dan asked. "Or a previous boyfriend?"

"A brother," Cal admitted. "James, or Jimmy. Last seen living rough on the streets down by Venice Beach, years ago. Our contacts down there seem to think he probably isn't with us anymore. They're checking."

"Boyfriend?" Dan reminded him.

Cal shook his head. "Not in high school, anyway. She was kind of mature for her age, in more ways than one. She didn't hang out much with the other kids in high school."

"So nobody with a connection to Janice Scott at all..." Dan summarized.

"Well," Cal corrected. "That's not completely true. Do you see that car over there? The one with the letters painted all over it?" He paused to let Dan react.

Dan just waited.

"That car was last registered to someone named Janice Scott," Cal said.

"When was that?" Dan asked.

"About fifteen years ago," Cal said. "It was her car. No record of what happened to it after she died. But there it is."

Dan looked back at the car. "So somebody has kept it all these years?"

"You would think so," Cal said. "I did manage to ask Cheryl Arquette about it. I mean, you'd think that if it belonged to Janice, and she was married to Rod, that Rod would end up with it. But

Cheryl says she's never seen it, never heard him talk about it."

"What about someone at her school?" Dan asked.

"Working on that," Cal said. "It was a long time ago. Teachers have moved on, students are hard to track down."

"It doesn't sound like you're having a lot of fun," Dan said.

"I hate this shit," Cal said. "I'm used to breaking up fights down at the Boogie Bar, or arresting some son of a bitch for beating his wife, or the wife for shooting her drunk husband," he said. "Somebody is fucking with us on this one. And I don't need that."

"It's got to be like every other case," Dan said. "You just keep tracking down leads and eventually they get you to where you need to be. You just have a ways to go on this one."

Cal blew out his cheeks. "We haven't even started on this one." Then he looked sharply at Dan. "Unless you want to confess? That would solve a lot of problems for me."

Dan laughed. "Nah, you can't pin this one on me, copper," he said. "Do you want to get out and check out the car?"

"No," Cal said. "But I guess we have to."

Dan shook his head. "I don't have to. I already did it once, got wet, and called in the proper authorities."

Cal gave him a disgusted look. "Put on your raingear and give me a hand," he said. "I can use all the help I can get right now."

chapter 20

As they looked over the car, Dan gave Cal a quick outline of what he had found. Cal followed him around, both of them bent over in the rain as if that would somehow keep them dry. It didn't. By the end of the inspection, their pants and shoes were completely soaked, and Dan had a steady drip of water down the back of his neck.

"This car's been stripped clean," Cal said when they were done. "Except for that fur in the back. Is that a raccoon, or did you get a haircut back there?"

"Wrong color," Dan said. "Mine is a much richer brown."

They stood in the rain. Drips formed on the front brim of Dan's hat, hanging on for a moment before falling down, sometimes hitting his face, sometimes not. He reached up and tried to wipe the water off, which sent a cascade of water down his wrist and soaked his arm. He looked at Cal, wondering how long the Sheriff would keep him standing out in the rain.

"I need you to keep this quiet," Cal said to Dan.

"Well, Doris already knows about it," Dan said. "She took the call this morning."

"No, I don't mean about the car, per se," Cal said. "I mean the graffiti. If anybody asks, you just found an old car, and the Sheriff's Office towed it away."

"Got it," Dan said. "I think I can manage that. Anything else?"

Cal took a deep breath and let it out. "No, not really. Let's get out of the rain. How are things with you and Kristen?"

"Good," Dan assured him. He knew that Cal's wife Maggie would want to know. "Really good."

Cal grinned appreciatively. "Great. Maggie will be happy to hear it."

Dan pointed to the car. "This case keeping you busy?"

"Oh man, you have no idea," Cal said. "That guy Arquette was kind of famous, apparently. We've got reporters from all over calling about it. Mainly climbing and outdoors magazines, but newspapers, too."

Cal slipped in behind the wheel of his SUV and Dan joined him in the cab. Cal turned on the engine. He knew it would take more than a few minutes to clear the windshield with both of them inside.

"Sounds like fun," Dan said. He knew how much Cal hated talking to the media.

"Yeah," Cal said sarcastically. "Tons of fun." He reached up with a rag and tried to wipe off some of the condensation on the windshield.

Dan thought it was time to change the subject and told Cal about his visit to Katie Pederson's house. "You're trying to solve a simple little thing like a murder, and I'm tackling the really tough problems—ghosts in the attic."

"I should tell some of those reporters about that," Cal suggested. "I bet they'd love the story. Let's get the hell out of this rain and you can tell me all about it."

"Thanks," Dan said, laughing. "But I don't think Katie would appreciate getting her house on the national news." Cal passed him the rag and Dan tried to wipe down his side.

Dan explained his visit to Katie's house, but he left out the sense of dread that he'd felt.

"Did you meet her wife?" Cal asked.

"Only briefly," Dan said. "She seemed nice enough." He wondered why Cal had asked.

"They get a lot of grief from some of the good Christian locals," Cal said. "I sure hope it doesn't wear them down."

"They seem pretty happy in the house," Dan said. "Except for the ghosts."

Cal looked at him. "Let me know if you think any of that stuff could be…neighbor-related," Cal said. "We've got some small-town people here with small minds. It wouldn't surprise me to find out they're trying to make life difficult for those two."

Dan hadn't considered that possibility. "I'll let you know," he said. "I didn't see anything like that when I was there, but I'll check again."

Cal didn't react. The two men sat in silence for a moment, listening to the rain.

"That house has quite a history," Cal said. "Did Katie tell you about it?"

"Yeah, about the old couple who made sure that, what's her name, Lucilla, always has a place to live…" Dan said.

"No, I mean before that," Cal explained. "It was the old Clementi family homestead. I think they moved here sometime in 1850s. I don't know when, but a hell of a long time ago."

"The house looks like it," Dan said.

"They had quite a place there for a while," Cal continued. "Apples. That was big. And they made wine, too, at least until Prohibition. Did a little mining, and had a store over in Tuolumne for a while. They even called that little valley down there "Dago Valley" since the whole Italian family lived there for a couple of generations.

"That's one they've probably changed by now," Dan said.

Cal laughed. "Maybe. I think it might have been Cesare who named it that himself."

The SUV was beginning to warm up, and Dan could see a small section of clear windshield, down at the bottom where the defrost vent was.

"Anyway, I guess old Cesare was the last one," Cal continued. "He grew up here but didn't hang around. Everybody else was gone, and the place was falling apart. But back in the 1980s he came back and started living here again. And he fixed it up some. They'd already sold off most of the land in bits and pieces over the years, but the house was still standing."

"I noticed there was some creative carpentry along the way," Dan said.

"Oh, hell, Cesare wasn't the kind of guy to let a building code get in his way," Cal chuckled. "Or get a permit, for that matter. But he was a pretty good cabinetmaker. And he was out there in the country. He pretty much did what he wanted. Nobody ever checked on any of that. And nobody complained."

Dan wondered if talking about this was helping Cal sort through the murder investigation. At least he seemed to have calmed down. Dan decided to play along. "Did they have any kids?" he asked.

"No, no," Cal corrected him. "Cesare was on his own. Lydia came later, about five years later. She was related to him somehow, second cousins or something. Anyway, even then they were old, and nobody here gave a damn. Just two old Italians making things work in their old age." He was lost in thought for a few minutes.

Dan noticed that his side window was now clearing up as well, from the front vent.

"She was a sweet old lady," Cal said. He looked at Dan. "Lydia.

She used to give out homemade cookies on Halloween, and if you were walking by and said hello, she'd always pull out a carrot or something from her garden and tell you to give it to your mom."

Dan smiled. "And did you?"

Cal laughed. "Half the time, I just ate it on the way home. But that was just to get back at the old man. He'd yell at us and tell us to stay the hell away from his apples."

Dan grinned. "And did you?"

Cal snorted. "Of course not. At least, not until Lucilla arrived. That was about the time that old man Clementi, Cesare, fell off a ladder in the barn and died. And damned if Lucilla wasn't even meaner than he was. With him, it was all kind of a game. He'd give you holy hell for stealing a couple of apples, but that's all. We knew the worst that would happen was that he would chew us out. With her, it was warfare."

Dan gave Cal a questioning look.

"Shit, she took to carrying a shotgun around," he said. "And she wasn't afraid to use it."

Dan's eyes grew wide. "Did she ever hit anyone?" he asked.

Cal shrugged. "Nobody ever told us about it if she did. My kids swore it was true, for what that's worth. She's a tough old bird."

"And she's Lydia's sister?" Dan asked.

"Older sister," Cal said. "When the family left Sicily, Lydia was just a baby. And I guess that they left Lucilla behind or something. Anyway, I guess you heard she has quite an accent."

Dan smiled. "Yeah, I did notice that."

"So she got left behind with relatives or something," Cal said. "And then came and tracked down Lydia here later. Lydia didn't remember very much about it, because she was just a baby when it happened."

"Wow," Dan said. "Can you imagine leaving your daughter behind?"

Cal was shaking his head slowly, back and forth. "Different times back then, I guess. This was right after World War II. Lots of crazy stuff in the world, that's for sure."

"What happened to Lydia?" Dan asked.

"She died a few years ago," Cal said. "It caused a bit of a stir, because nobody could figure out what to do with the house and all. But Lydia had made out a will. She gave the whole thing to the local school. I think she wanted them to have like a farm or something to teach the kids about agriculture. But she didn't want to throw Lucilla out, so she could live there as long as she wants, or as long as she's alive. And then it went to the school."

"Wait a minute," Dan said. "So how did Katie and Shauna buy it?"

Cal grinned. "Never underestimate a lawyer," Cal said. "The school figured out a way to sell it now, and get the money now, and still abide by the terms of the agreement. That's what they did. They got a new computer lab out of it."

"And Katie got a house out of it," Dan added.

"Not at first," Cal corrected him. "A young couple bought it first, but they had some problem, and the wife took off and left him. He filed a missing persons report, so we looked into it."

Cal paused here, and Dan shot him a questioning look.

"Nasty guy," Cal said. "Very verbally abusive. She finally had enough. We found out she was in a shelter, and then moved out of the area."

"Ugh," Dan grunted. "Is he still around?"

"Yeah, over in Soulsbyville," Cal said. "But she left for good. So the husband had to sell the house. Of course, he blames the whole thing on his wife. Anyway, that's how Katie and her friend bought it."

"Wife," Dan corrected him.

"Wife," Cal agreed. He turned to stare at the car again.

The windows were now completely clear, and Cal said that he ought to get going. He had work to do. Dan looked at the abandoned car and gave him a nod. "Good luck," he said.

Dan opened the door. The rain was still splattering on the roof, but he thought it might have eased up some. He climbed out of Cal's SUV, slapped his hand on the roof to say goodbye, and ran for his own vehicle. As he inserted his key and started the engine, he checked in his mirrors to make sure he wasn't going to back into Cal's SUV, but the Sheriff had already put his car in gear and was starting to drive back down the mountain.

Dan waited for a couple of minutes for the windshield to clear, and then followed him.

chapter 21

Dan was in no hurry to get back to the Summit Ranger Station. He was still thinking over all of what Cal had told him, and so he decided to take the longer, loop road around Herring Creek Reservoir and the watershed that surrounded it. The road was solid, rock more than dirt. Rough gravel in places, and plenty of washboard, but it was still stable in the rain. He told himself that he could always explain that he was late because he was inspecting it.

Which was true.

But he was also giving himself time to think. He hadn't had enough of that lately, and this was as good a chance as any. He took the road slowly, happy that he didn't have to push it hard through the washboard surface. That always rattled his teeth. Even as the rain lightened up, the trees were glistening silver, dripping with water. Occasionally a puff of wind would send a shower down from the trees above him, drops rattling on the metal roof. The mountains above him were hidden by the thick gauze of the clouds.

He stopped once to check out a camper parked near Bloomer Lake. He saw somebody moving around inside when he stopped his truck there. They waved at him through the window and he waved back. Nothing to see there, so he drove on by. And he stopped again where an overeager plow operator had carved out enough material to block the gutter on the side of the road. It only took him a minute or two to clear that out with a shovel, and then he watched as the pool of water slowly disappeared down the hill.

By the time he got back out to pavement, it felt good to have the smooth surface of the road under his tires, despite the numerous potholes. Minutes later, he pulled into the parking lot at the Ranger Station and parked as close as he could get to the front door. There weren't many cars in the lot, and he didn't think anyone would mind if he tried to keep dry.

Once inside, he took off his jacket and tried to dry off. Doris gave him a few minutes to set himself straight before she brought him up to date on the day's activities. The main issue was a noise problem in one of the campgrounds, but Larry had offered to handle that. Larry always volunteered for the duties that most closely approximated law enforcement.

Thanks to the rain, most of the campers were staying close to their campsites, which kept the traffic down in the Ranger Station. Doris had even had time to tidy up a bit and organize their map drawer, which was always getting re-shuffled.

"Katie Pederson called you," Doris said. "I think she might come by later today."

Dan gave her a questioning look.

Doris held up her hands in front of herself. "I don't know," she said. "I'm just passing on the message. That's all she said. If you want to know more, you'll have to call her."

Dan grinned and shook his head. "Nah, that's fine. Looks like it will be a quiet afternoon here, anyway."

"It has been so far," Doris agreed. "I'm just waiting for…"

She stopped as Dan held up his hand. "Don't say it, Doris," he said. "You'll jinx it. Just let the experience wash over you like a gentle breeze…"

"Until some camper has an emergency," Doris said dryly.

Dan sighed with exasperation and shook his head. "You couldn't leave it alone, could you?"

It was at least another hour before Katie walked in the door. She greeted them both and chatted away with Doris about the weather and then moved on to Doris' grandson Travis—a topic Doris never tired of discussing.

Dan glanced at the clock. They would close up in twenty minutes, he wondered just how long Katie was going to talk to Doris. He hoped she wouldn't ask him to stay late.

Doris must have noticed, because she quickly summed up Travis' latest accomplishments and discreetly walked to the far end of the counter, leaving Katie and Dan with a bit of space.

She asked Dan how his day was going, and he told her about the car—not the graffiti, but the car—and about his drive back through the back roads in the rain.

"Sounds like a perfect way to settle your mind," she said.

Dan nodded. "Or at least, zone out for a bit. It sure was nice."

Dan asked about how things were going with the house and Lucilla. "Heard any good noises recently?" he joked.

That remark apparently hit a nerve. Katie's face took on a pained expression, and she lowered her voice. "Yeah, not good, really." She glanced over at Doris, who quickly became very interested in a stack of memos in front of her. "I was hoping to talk to you about that."

Dan gave an encouraging nod. He was having a hard time matching the intensity and anxiety that Katie was bringing to the conversation.

"Well, Lucilla is still claiming to hear all sorts of noises from the attic," Katie said, her voice tinged with frustration. "I really don't know what to do about it." As she spoke, Dan noticed that Katie had started to fidget with her hands.

"Have you talked to Shauna about it?" Dan asked. "What does she think?"

"She thinks the old girl is completely bats," Katie said. "She thinks we should just ignore the whole thing."

"And you don't?" Dan suggested. He was hoping to calm her down. Letting her talk it out might do that.

"We have to live with her," Katie said. "Not forever, but for a while at least. We have to live in the same house. I don't want her to hate us." Her eyes were suddenly and intensely focused on Dan.

Dan backed up and thought this over. "Okay. And you haven't heard anything, or Shauna?"

Katie shook her head vigorously. "Nothing. It's got to be all in her imagination."

"Well," Dan said. "Seems to me you have a few options. One, you can tell her she's crazy, and ignore her." As Katie began to protest, Dan held up his hand. "And you've already told me that's not going to happen. So let's eliminate that one. Two: you can continue to try to find these noises that she's hearing." That was a close escape.

Katie looked at Dan. "Yeah, that's what I was thinking."

"What does Shauna say about that?" Dan asked.

"She's away for a few days on business," Katie said. Dan could see she was a little uncomfortable with this.

"So maybe you can take care of it while she's gone?" he asked. And without her knowing, he thought.

Katie agreed that this might be possible.

"Maybe you could set up a wildlife camera up there?" Dan suggested. "At least that would show if anything is moving around."

"Oh, good idea," Katie agreed. "That would really help." She seemed to be relaxing a bit now.

"Of course, any disembodied spirits in there won't show up on the camera," Dan said, trying to lighten the mood. He gave a short chuckle, then stopped when he saw Katie's reaction.

Again, Katie had fixed him with a glare.

"Just kidding. But if the camera doesn't show anything, you still have one more option," Dan said.

"What's that?" Katie asked.

"You can just pretend that you hear the noises too, and tell her that you hope they stop soon," Dan said.

Katie shook her head and stared at him in disbelief. "Don't be a jerk, Dan," she said. "That's crazy."

Dan backpedaled and gave her his most innocent look. "Not crazy at all. You'd just be making an attempt to live a little bit in her world."

"Dan!" Katie said. "I'm not going to lie to her." She was clearly appalled.

Dan shrugged and gave up. He gave her an apologetic grin. "I'm just suggesting options, Katie. Sounds like the best one right now is the wildlife cam." He glanced over at Doris. Somehow, even though Doris was pretending not to listen, she was communicating her disapproval very clearly.

He softened his voice. "Do you have a wildlife cam you can use?" he asked gently.

Katie looked down at her feet and shook her head. "I guess I could get one in town…"

Dan smiled. "I've got one you can use. I'll bring it by tonight and help you set it up."

Now Katie was nodding a bit more vigorously than she needed to.

"Hey," Dan said to her. "This isn't a big deal. Five years from now you're going to look back on this whole thing and think it is funny as hell."

Katie looked up again, and Dan saw the frustration in her face. Doris met his look with a scowl.

"Or not," he said.

chapter 22

Dan did not know what to expect when he told Kristen about the conversation with Katie. But that didn't keep him from being surprised by her reaction.

She had been working on something in the kitchen while they talked, but now she stopped. Dan wondered what can of worms he might have opened here.

"Okay," Kristen said. "When should we go up there?"

"Well," Dan said, stalling for time. "I was thinking of going up there right away, before dinner."

Kristen continued to look at him. "Sure," she said, wiping her hands on a dishtowel. "I can be ready in a couple of minutes."

Dan walked out into the backyard to collect the camera. It only took seconds, but by the time he came back inside, Kristen was ready.

"I thought we could bring a few of these cookies," she said, holding up a pink bakery box. "At least that way we won't have to eat them all."

Dan laughed. He loved Kristen's desserts, but they had decided that sweets were a luxury that was adding too many pounds to their body weight. "Good idea," he said. It was nice to think of Kristen as an ally in his awkward conversations with Katie.

On the drive up to Katie's house, Kristen asked him about Lucilla.

"I've heard people talk about her like she's some kind of force of nature," she said.

Dan tried to describe the old woman. "She's very dramatic. That's the word I'd use. Doesn't seem to care. Uses a hammer when a gentle tap would do," he said. "I think it's just the way she is. She comes from a different time and place." He didn't want to color Kristen's first impressions too strongly.

As they pulled up in front of the house, they could see Lucilla out in the garden, working with a hoe. Dan waved to her, but the old woman turned away and went back to her hoeing without any response.

Katie came hopping out onto the front porch, a big smile on her face. "Hey! I wasn't really prepared for company," she said, looking at Kristen. "But I'm so glad you're here."

She quickly ushered them inside, as if she wanted to get out of sight of Lucilla, and then began fussing over Kristen's cookies and apologizing for not having anything to offer them.

Kristen waved her apologies off. "We're just here for a few minutes," she said. "And you'd be doing us a favor to help us eat these up."

"Did you see Lucilla?" Katie asked them.

"She's working out in the garden," Kristen said. "I'd love to meet her. Do you think she'd like one of these cookies? I mean, if you want to share?"

"Oh, absolutely," Katie agreed. "I've always wondered if she has a sweet tooth."

Katie went to her cupboard and handed a plate to Kristen, who selected a couple of cookies and put them on the plate. "The way to an old woman's heart," she said, giving Dan a wink.

Katie led the way as the three of them went out the door. Lucilla was still in the garden, her dark clothes giving her the air of a woman in mourning. This evening she was up in the middle of the roses. The hoe kept up its work, whacking at the weeds with metronomic regularity. Dan wondered how long she could keep that up.

"She really loves those roses," Katie said to them quietly. As they walked closer, Katie called out, and the three of them joined Lucilla up in the rose garden. The old woman's eyes fixed on Dan. "The ranger," she said darkly. "I don't forget."

Katie introduced Kristen, and Dan watched as Kristen offered the plate of cookies to Lucilla.

But what followed shocked them all. Lucilla took one look at the plate and shook her head violently, as she took a step backward.

"I made them myself," Kristen said. "They're yummy."

Lucilla looked at the plate suspiciously. Hesitantly, she reached out her hand and picked up the plate, lifting it up to her nose to smell it. Then she picked up a cookie and took a tiny bite. Her face crinkled into a grimace and she spit the cookie out into her hand. She shook her head again and handed the plate and the remains of the cookie back to Kristen.

"No good!" Lucilla uttered the words like an oath.

She shook her head violently and handed the plate back to Kristen. "You take them," the old woman said, pointing back to the house.

Dan froze. So did Kristen.

Katie exploded with a combination of outrage and embarrassment. "Lucilla! That is so rude!"

Dan watched as Kristen very calmly pulled back the plate and turned to walk back to the house. He was torn between supporting Katie with Lucilla and consoling Kristen on her retreat. Kristen won.

He hurried after her. "Are you okay?" he asked.

"Yeah, I am fine," she said. The intensely studied calm of her voice made Dan realize that she was not fine at all. They turned to see Katie launch one more verbal salvo at Lucilla and then turn to join them on the way to the house.

Kristen shook her head with disgust. Dan placed his hand lightly on her shoulder on the walk back inside.

When Katie joined them, she was on fire.

"I am so embarrassed and ashamed," she began. And for the next few minutes, she continued to apologize, all the time raging at Lucilla, while Dan and Kristen assured her that she didn't need to apologize for the actions of the old woman. It took a while.

By the time Katie had calmed down, Dan and Kristen had exchanged glances, and suggested that it might be time for them to go.

"Let me get upstairs and I'll set up this camera," Dan said. "And then we'll be out of your hair."

As he climbed the steps up to the attic, Dan remembered the chills he'd felt the last time. He reached the trap door and slowly opened it. A quick glance around showed him that the women had done some work up there. Some of the boxes were opened, and there were dresses hanging from a couple of the rafters.

He looked around to find a spot for the camera. The dresses were a problem, because they would block the view.

"Do you mind if I move a few things around up here?" he called down to Katie.

He heard the quiet conversation between the two women pause for a moment, and then Katie's reply. "Go right ahead."

He collected the dresses and moved them all to one side, leaving most of the attic now clear. He thought about moving some of the boxes as well, but then decided that he didn't want to work that hard.

There were a lot of boxes up there.

He set up the camera, aimed it at the center of the attic, and turned it on. "This should be good to go now," he called down to Katie.

There was sound of shuffling from down below, and Katie's head popped up through the door.

"Wow!" she said. "I didn't expect this!" She was pointing to the dresses.

"Well, the way you had them, they were in the way," Dan said. "They kind of blocked off the view."

Katie looked at him in consternation. "In the boxes?" she asked.

Now it was Dan's turn to be confused. "No," he said. "The dresses. They were hanging all over here, on these rafters." He pointed to where the dresses had been.

Katie stared at him. There was a long, ugly silence, and Dan fumbled for a way to continue.

"We didn't do that," Katie said. "The dresses were out here?"

Dan nodded.

"We definitely left everything in the boxes," Katie said. "Shauna said it was the only way to keep things clean up here."

Dan took a deep breath, then scratched his head. He gestured with his left hand. "And you didn't hang up these dresses?"

"Dan, we haven't been up here since the last time you were here," Katie said.

Behind her, Dan could hear Kristen moving about below. He was sure she wanted to see what they were talking about.

"No chance Shauna did this and didn't tell you about it?" he asked.

Katie shook her head slowly, almost lost in thought. She was still staring at the attic.

Dan began to get that bizarre feeling that something else, something alive, was in the attic. He slowly turned to look at the small window, where the dressing table had been set up. It was still there, but somehow it seemed different. He worked his way over to it. He didn't remember the mirror being there, but he couldn't be sure.

Behind him, he could hear a short conversation between the two women below. He heard Katie say: "This is so weird, so fucking, fucking weird."

He turned to see her head drop down below the floor of the attic, and a few moments later, Kristen's head appeared.

She looked around, and then continued to climb up into the attic. Dan caught her gaze and waved around at the attic. "All these boxes were stacked up the last time I was here," he said. Then, pointing to the dresses, "and all of these were in boxes, not hanging up."

Kristen stared for a while, then began to slowly walk around the attic, as if on patrol. She came over to join Dan at the small dresser.

"Look at this," she said.

"Yeah, it's like a little shrine," Dan said quietly.

Kristen picked up the hairbrush and studied it.

"You guys okay?" Katie's head had poked up above the floor again. "I think we should get out of here."

"Yeah, we're just leaving," Dan said. He pointed out the camera to Kristen, and the two of them walked over to the stairs and started down.

Back in the kitchen, Katie sat at the table, the edges of her body betraying her. Her voice trembled as she said "I don't know what's going on here." Her eyes flickered first to Dan, then to Kristen, then to the door of the attic, and back and forth.

Dan was about to respond when he heard Kristen say, "You

need to get out of here, Katie. Do you have another place to stay?"

Katie shook her head. "No. I mean, I can't leave. We bought this place." The look in her eyes was one of panic.

"Yeah, that's fine," Kristen said. Her voice seemed to channel a steady beam of calm towards Katie. "But right now, you need to find a place that feels safe. And that's not here, right now."

Dan watched as Kristen pulled out her keys and pulled off the key to her house. "You can stay at my place," she said. "I'm not using it much these days. And it's very safe."

It took a few minutes, but Kristen was able to convince her. "Go get a few things you'll need for tonight and tomorrow," Kristen told her. She gave Dan a quick glance and handed him the cookies. Then she turned and followed Katie to help her pack.

Dan put the cookies on a shelf in the kitchen and started towards his truck. Halfway there he stopped to look back at the house.

He glanced up to see Lucilla, still in the garden, hoeing away.

chapter 23

Kristen rode with Katie to give her directions, while Dan followed them down in his truck.

They didn't stop long at Kristen's house. By the time Dan had parked his truck a couple of houses down the street and walked up to the front door, Kristen was already saying her goodbyes. "Just call if you need anything or can't find anything."

Dan could hear Katie burbling with gratitude inside the house. Kristen stopped, went back inside to give Katie a hug, and then came back out to join Dan. He saw her take a deep breath, and then look him straight in the eye.

"We should go out to dinner tonight," she said. It wasn't a question.

"Anywhere you want," Dan said. He was still amazed that Kristen wasn't more upset.

She gave a big sigh. "Pizza," she said. Dan started the engine and put the truck in gear.

"I don't like crashers," Kristen said as they drove off.

Dan had no idea what she meant and let her know with a quick look and shrug.

"I do weddings, Dan," she explained. "I know what crashers look like."

Dan decided it was best to just let Kristen explain as much as she wanted, so he kept his mouth shut and drove. If Kristen wanted to talk about weddings, he would listen.

"There are two kinds," she said. "The quiet kind just sneak in the back door, and hope nobody notices. If they're smart, they stop at the display of gifts to make sure they have a couple of names right. And they assume that they'll blend in with the crowd—where everybody knows somebody, but nobody knows everybody."

She stopped and looked at Dan.

He shook his head to show that he was still completely lost.

"The other kind is always loud and obnoxious," Kristen continued. "They figure that nobody will want to take them on and make a big scene at a wedding and ruin it for the bride. So they overdo it, expecting that everyone else will look away and let them get away with it. A lot of times, everybody does."

Dan smiled. He imagined that Kristen, as the caterer, would not be the one to let them do that. It was a side to her that impressed him more than he could say.

"You know," Kristen said, "I knew her sister."

"Katie's?" Dan asked—and immediately knew he'd guessed wrong.

"Lucilla's," Kristen said. "She was a sweet old lady. And a good cook. She liked to share her recipes with me. Shaking her hand, it was so soft and light. Like a little pillow."

At least Dan was now sure of the topic they were discussing. He turned left and pulled out onto the highway.

"Not quite like Lucilla, huh?" he replied.

Kristen shook her head. "Not a bit. Not one bit." She looked at him. "She's a crasher."

"What do you mean?" Dan asked.

"She's an obnoxious crasher," Kristen said, her voice deep with disapproval.

"What do you mean?" Dan asked, shaking his head. "I don't get it. What's she crashing?"

"I don't know," Kristen admitted. "No idea. But she obviously doesn't want you to find out. Or me. I don't trust her. I think that was a bluff, to make sure we didn't get too curious."

Dan thought this over. He exited the highway and took a right turn towards the restaurant. A guy behind him was tailgating, and Dan was disappointed to see him take the same turn.

A thought suddenly struck him.

"I love that you are officially coming to stay, letting Katie stay at your place—that you feel like you can move in with me," he said, glancing over cautiously. "And yes, I would love you to do that."

Kristen gave a slight smile. "I was hoping you wouldn't mind, at least for a while. Maybe only a while."

"No, that's fine." Dan said, shaking his head. "For as long as you want."

He pulled the truck into a parking space in front of the restaurant and stopped. "Really," he said, looking at her. "For as long as you want."

Kristen gave another small smile and shook her head. "We'll see."

And then, as she climbed out of the truck she said, "You know how you suggested we could fix up your kitchen a bit?"

"And I meant it," Dan said.

"Well, you might want to wait until you hear what I think we need to do with that kitchen."

Dan realized that this might be the most expensive pizza dinner ever.

chapter 24

Dan was smiling as he drove to the Summit Ranger Station the next morning. He and Kristen had spent dinner and most of the rest of the evening making plans—plans for what they might do in the kitchen, sure, but Dan knew that also meant plans for how they might spend the next few years of their lives.

And every time he thought about it, he smiled again. He even smiled a bit as he thought about how he might do some of the work himself, pulling out the sink to get Kristen one she thought would work better—and maybe some nice local granite for the countertop they would have to replace.

He was smiling enough that Doris finally suggested that he seemed to be in a pretty good mood, which was an obvious invitation to tell her about it. But Dan resisted that temptation. He didn't want to jinx anything.

He was still smiling when his boss, Steve Matson, walked in the door, but his smile was short-lived. Steve explained that he was just dropping in to say hello, and both Dan and Doris knew that he was lying. His office was forty-five minutes away, and there was no reason for him to come see them unless he had something on his mind. And that was rarely good news.

Dan calculated the odds and came up with roughly one in ten that Steve was there to talk to Doris. The other nine pointed right at Dan.

And sure enough, within a couple of minutes of chatting with them both, Steve asked Dan if he had a minute or two to talk. It was a *pro forma* question, of course, and Dan played along, thinking it over very briefly before agreeing that yes, he did have a few minutes.

Steve led the way into the back office, and Dan followed with a feeling, somewhere back in his mind, that he was on his way to the principal's office.

They both sat, Steve in one of the two spare chairs in the office, while motioning for Dan to sit in his usual spot at his desk. Dan settled in, and Steve began with the most banal of small talk: about the weather, about campground reservations, about how things were going with Kristen. Dan knew that these were just the preliminaries and offered up short answers to each one of them; answers designed to get the questions out of the way, rather than expand on the topic.

Then Steve moved on to Doris, and how she was doing. Dan proceeded here with caution. He deeply appreciated Doris for the years of experience and local knowledge she brought to the office. It was true that she didn't always do things by the book, and that had become an issue from time to time, but the benefits vastly outweighed that. And Dan sure as hell wasn't going to be the reason Doris got into trouble.

He gave her glowing marks.

Steve then directed the conversation to Dan. How did he see things going up here?

By this point, Dan's warning antennae were buzzing. He tried to sound both calm and happy, and kept his answers short and cooperative. He didn't know what game Steve was playing, but Dan was not about to give him any easy moves.

"I know this new development project has been getting a lot of attention," Steve said. "I wouldn't be surprised to hear that they'd contacted you about it."

The way Matson said this sentence made it perfectly clear to Dan that Steve knew for a fact that the developers had talked to him. How did he find out? Dan wasn't sure he wanted to know. But he wasn't giving in. He just smiled at Steve and waited for his boss to continue.

"I guess you know that we're working on it," Matson said. "We'll have a full analysis and recommendations in time to be included in the EIR and the county hearings."

Dan took this in without making a response.

"Do you have any particular concerns?" Matson asked.

Dan opened up his hands in front of his chest. "I have some concerns, but I haven't really thought about it much. You've made it very clear that it will be addressed by somebody way over my pay grade, so…" He wasn't going to give Matson a reason to second guess him.

"That doesn't mean that you can't offer us your insight, Dan," Steve said. "If there are issues you think we might be overlooking, or giving too little weight, I'd be happy to hear them."

Dan assured Steve that he would let him know about that.

"I'd rather hear them from you directly than to find out about them later," Steve said.

Dan took a deep breath and let it out slowly. "Am I being reprimanded here?" he asked. "Is there something I've done that you think is a problem?" It sounded more confrontational than Dan intended, but he was getting frustrated with Steve beating around the bush.

Steve shook his head quickly. "No. No, you are not….This is not a reprimand. Nothing like that." Dan had to give him credit. Steve sounded concerned, even worried.

"Then what the hell is this about, Steve?" Dan pushed him. "If there's a problem, I'd rather hear it...'directly from you.'" He felt good using exactly the same words as Steve had used. Maybe that would break through the crap.

After a long pause, long enough for Dan to wonder if he'd really done something stupid, Steve said, "I heard they might have offered you a job."

Dan listened. He decided not to respond, but he also didn't look at Steve directly. He wondered if he should ask Steve how he found out. He didn't like that part.

"I know they're offering a lot of local people jobs," Steve continued. "And I've heard that they're offering some pretty crazy salaries, too."

Okay, so maybe Steve was just putting together the pieces, and guessing. Dan still kept quiet.

"I guess I would just want you to know that I would really hate losing you, Dan," Steve said.

This got Dan's attention, and he met his boss' gaze. He couldn't help let a small tinge of a smile cross his lips. He knew how much such an admission had cost his boss.

"That's just about the nicest thing you've ever said to me, Steve." Dan said, allowing the grin to grow.

"I mean it," Steve's sincerity was obvious. "I would totally understand if you took it, but I would really hate to lose you."

Dan decided to let Steve off the hook and shook his head. "I thought about it," he said. "They offered Kristen a job, too. Lots of money."

"But?" Steve prompted him.

Dan shook his head again. "Not my idea of what I want to do," he said. "I mean, for a couple of years, fine. But then what? Where do I go from there?"

Steve smiled. "Disney?" he suggested, and then two of them shared a laugh,

"Yeah, exactly. Why would I want to do that, when I can work here?" Dan waved his arm around to show off the dreary setting of the ranger station.

Steve looked around. "Do you want some OSHA posters, to decorate?" he offered. "I have extras down at my office."

Dan laughed again. "No, thanks. Besides, I think I've learned most of those lessons by now," he said. And then, as they sat together, Dan decided to raise the topic again, given the new foundation. "So what is the official USFS policy on that development?"

"Too soon to say, for now," Steve said. "You know. Washington wants us to try and work out a local solution first."

"The locals mainly just want jobs," Dan said.

"Except for the ones who don't want any development," Steve added. "And we're not likely to get into the middle of that. They are both defensible positions, and both reflect the mission of the Forest Service."

"So we don't take any position at all?" Dan asked.

"Hopefully, we take a position that allows both sides to win," Steve said. "Everybody knows what they don't want. I wish we could get them to agree on a few things they do want. In the future, I mean."

Dan snorted. "Not with these guys. They both believe that if the other guy wins, then they lose."

Steve smiled. "That's one of the reasons I'd hate to lose you, Dan," he said. "You get it. We'll try to raise some of the concerns about protecting wildlife and ecosystem, but we're supposed to manage the resource, and that includes using it to generate income and jobs. We'll also try to give the developers a way to proceed while doing that."

"I'm glad I don't have your job, Steve," Dan said.

"Well, the good news is that I don't really have to do that part, either," Steve said. "Because sooner or later, one side or the other is going to kick this whole thing upstairs. They'll write their congressman or senator or something. And when they do that, I will be taking my orders from somebody way above my paygrade."

"Doesn't that piss you off?" Dan asked.

Steve shook his head. "Only a little. It used to bother me more. But I know the rules. I know how the game is played. It only pisses me off when some developer tries to steal my best people."

Dan chuckled. "Well, if you really do get pissed off, I know somebody who's hiring," he said. "And from what I've heard, the pay is really good."

Steve stared at him, then broke into a grin. "I'll keep that in mind, Dan," Steve said.

Steve looked around the office again. "We could probably get you some new paint in here," he said.

Dan shook his head. "Not worth it. It would be more trouble to move all this stuff. Of course, we could just leave everything in place, and only paint what shows…"

Steve chuckled. "You know that would never fly."

Dan was relaxed now. He shot Steve a direct glance. "Are we done in here?"

Steve nodded. "Yeah. Thanks. I mean it. Thanks."

"I'll just try to remember this conversation during my next review," Dan said.

Steve shook his head sadly. "What conversation, Dan?"

Dan laughed and walked over to open the door.

"Oh, I almost forgot," Steve said. "There is one more thing."

Dan paused, his hand on the doorknob.

"I got a call from the Sheriff's office. They were wondering if you could give them a little help with that Arquette case," Steve said. "Cal will talk to you about it, but I think they'd like you to talk to some of the climbers around here."

"Me?" Dan couldn't hide his surprise.

"Apparently, they think you speak the language," Steve said.

Dan laughed. "Oh, I can talk a bit of the talk, but don't expect me to walk the walk," he said.

Steve smiled. "Fair enough."

"When is this supposed to happen?" Dan asked.

"They'd like you to attend the funeral on Saturday. I told them that we'd work it out somehow," Steve explained.

"Yeah, fine," Dan agreed. It didn't sound like a very good use of his time, but he'd work that out with Cal.

"Just keep me posted on the hours, so I can schedule appropriately," Steve said.

"Okey doke," Dan replied.

And then he opened the door to see Doris at the counter, and a room full of people waiting to talk to her.

Steve patted him on the shoulder. "I'll let you get back to work," he said. "Looks like Doris could use the help."

chapter 25

Which was how Dan found himself dressed in his more formal clothes, and seated in the third row at a funeral home in Sonora. He would have thought they'd have held the funeral in Yosemite, or at least somewhere out in the woods, but apparently that's a lot harder to do these days. And the rangers there were paying a lot more attention to people who wanted to scatter the ashes of loved ones in the park. There was even a page on the website about it and a required permit. Dan could only imagine how that would have gone over with Rod Arquette.

The crowd was smaller than Dan expected. He saw Cheryl in the front row, dressed in black from head to toe. Andy MacRostie sat next to her. A few people from around town had shown up. Barry, who owned the outdoor store was there, and Dan met his eyes and gave a nod. Cal had asked him to talk to anyone from the climbing community who showed up, but it wasn't obvious to Dan who those people might be.

Hideo Saito was there. He greeted Dan, and sat down next to Jim McDougal. McDougal greeted Hideo too loudly, and the two of them sat together on the other side of the aisle. A woman about Cheryl's age came in and asked Dan if the seat next to him was available. He gave her a small smile and assured her it was.

After she had settled into her seat, Dan started to make small talk. He looked around the room and suggested that he expected that there would have been more people at the funeral.

The woman next to him shook her head. "Rod was famous, but that doesn't mean he was popular," she said.

Dan took this as a reproof and sat back in his seat.

The woman leaned over and held out her hand. "I'm Chandra Bustamonte," she said. And then, when Dan didn't react to the name, she added, "Rod's first wife."

Dan apologized and introduced himself.

"I've heard about you," Chandra said. "You're a ranger here."

Dan admitted that this was true.

She looked at him again, more carefully. Her eyes narrowed. "Are you part of the investigation? Were you at the workshop where he was killed?" she asked.

"I thought it was appropriate to pay my respects," Dan said. "I am sorry about Rod."

Chandra waved her hand dismissively. "Oh hell, it was bound to happen," she said. "Nobody ever expected Rod to go quietly. Nobody."

Dan gave her a concerned look.

"I don't mean that I expected him to get shot," she said. "Well, I didn't not expect it, with the way he carried on. But there was no way that Rod Arquette was going to die in bed. At least, not in his own bed."

The conversation was making Dan uncomfortable, but as he looked around, none of the other guests seemed to be paying much attention. He saw Cal walk in on the far side of the room and sit down.

"I'm sorry," Dan said. "For your loss."

"Yeah, thanks," Chandra answered. She didn't seem to take the comment seriously. "I think my loss happened a long time ago."

When she saw the confused look on Dan's face, she continued. "Look, when I married Rod I was a starry-eyed kid, and he was an up-and-coming rock star. I was so amazed that he would be interested in me." She paused here, and Dan glanced over at Cal. Cal nodded.

"But after a while, I realized that he was interested in me the way a dog humps your leg," she said.

Dan quickly looked back at her face. She was not kidding.

"All that attention and intensity is all very exciting, until you realize that it's not you," Chandra continued. "The dog feels that way about every leg it sees."

She didn't seem bitter to Dan, but he was still shocked that she would talk this way.

"It didn't make any difference that we were married, or that we had kids. There were still always legs around that needed humping." She stopped to look at Dan. "I don't hate the guy. He gave me two really wonderful kids. I'm just sorry that I wasted so many years thinking it would be different. And I love my kids. He was part of that. He is part of them. Hopefully, a good part of them."

Dan murmured something about how he thought he understood.

"Were there any young women at the workshop…that day?" she asked him.

Dan shook his head. "No, well, one, but I don't think she was his type."

"That would make her a rare female indeed," she said.

Chandra indicated Cheryl Arquette with her chin. "She was smart. She knew what she was getting into." she said. "No surprises. As long as he came back to her on the weekends, she didn't care where he played around." Here she shook her head. "I don't think I could do that."

Dan asked her if she knew anyone else in the room.

Chandra pointed out Andy MacRostie. "I know him from somewhere, but I can't say where."

Dan was about to explain who Andy was, but Chandra interrupted him.

"You know, I am not bitter," she said. "He couldn't help it. He couldn't help being who he was. And I wasn't smart enough to see that. I am now."

Dan was now quite sure that this wasn't a conversation that he wanted to have, but he didn't see any way out of it.

"I mean, he left me for a kid who was nineteen years old," Chandra continued. "Nineteen. And he'd been fucking her for two years before that."

The look on Dan's face caught her attention.

"Oh, yes. When she was seventeen," she said. "She attended one of his climbing classes, and the rest, as they say, was history. And it was an ugly history, too. She was way too young to see what was going on, and by the time she figured it out, he'd already moved on."

Dan's face was frozen. He didn't want to give her any indication that she should continue.

"Dropped her. Broke her heart," Chandra said. "I guess you know she killed herself."

Dan nodded, glumly.

"Yeah, well, it just about destroyed her whole family, not that he gave a shit," Chandra said.

A group of people had walked into the room, and two young people came over to sit with Chandra.

She greeted them, then introduced them to Dan. "My kids," she said. "Annie and Marcus."

Dan said hello, and murmured how sorry he was. Then he stood up and made room for them alongside their mother.

"Nice talking with you," Chandra said to him. "If you need anything, with the investigation I mean, I'm happy to help."

Dan thanked her. "I've just seen an old friend over there,' he said, pointing to Cal. "I think I'll go join him."

But the family was already ignoring Dan, talking among themselves.

Dan sat down heavily next to Cal, and gave a deep sigh.

"You making new friends here?" Cal asked.

"That was Chandra Bustamonte," Dan said. "Our boy Arquette's first wife."

"How did you meet her?" Cal asked. He seemed to be impressed.

"I didn't," Dan explained. "I sat down, and she sat down next to me. Those are her kids. His kids, too."

Cal looked over at them. "Okay. How is she doing?" he asked Dan.

Dan shrugged. "Do you want to know what she told me, or what I think?"

Cal looked back at Dan. "Both, I guess?"

"She told me she was over him. And she still seemed kind of angry with him." Dan said.

"Understandable," Cal replied. "Which is more than I can say about the rest of this thing."

"Are you getting anywhere?" Dan asked him.

Cal shook his head. "Not really. Still with lots of suspects and not a lot of motives. Or some people who might have motives,"— here Cal tilted his head toward Chandra Bustamonte—"but were nowhere near the scene. At least that we know about."

A man in a dark suit stood up at the podium and began to speak.

"Do you see anyone else here you know?" Cal whispered.

Dan shook his head. "Cheryl and Andy MacRostie," he suggested. "And you know Barry…"

Cal nodded. "Those two guys over there were at the class…"

"Hideo Saito and Jim McDougal," Dan whispered back.

Cal leaned closer. "I guess MacRostie is going to keep running the classes," he said.

"Is that a motive?" Dan asked.

Cal shook his head. "I doubt it. Without Arquette, that's going to be a lot less popular. And a lot less profitable."

Dan thought this over. The man up front was trying hard to talk about Rod Arquette without mentioning his various foibles.

"He could keep the name…" Dan suggested.

Cal winced. "I don't see it…not without Rod making an appearance now and then. It sure wouldn't be the same."

"And Cheryl?" Dan asked. "Nothing on her?"

Cal shook his head. "Not that I've seen. Still a viable suspect, but we have no motive and no evidence."

"Chandra said that Cheryl knew exactly what she was getting into," Dan said.

"Seems that way," Cal agreed.

The man at the podium was now reading a poem.

"And Cheryl's daughter?" Dan whispered.

Cal shook his head. "She left the night before, with her dad. She was on a plane to Peru the next morning."

A woman sitting in front of them turned around to glare at them.

Cal nudged Dan. "Shhh!" he hissed quietly, pretending to be offended.

Dan allowed a tiny grin to flit across his face as he sat back to watch the rest of the ceremony.

chapter 26

As the organ music swelled to end the funeral, Cal pointed out a couple of men to Dan. "I'm going to go over and talk to those guys," he said. "If you see anyone else you think might know something, why don't you say hello?"

Dan looked around the room. A group of about eight or ten people had clustered around Cheryl Arquette, and it looked like a few more were waiting in line. Dan joined the line and waited his turn to pay his respects.

As the group in front him thinned out, Dan was able to get a good look at Cheryl. She did not look well. He said a few polite words to her, gave a short nod to Andy MacRostie, who was standing nearby, and walked out of the building. He hadn't heard if there was to be any kind of reception afterwards, and Cheryl hadn't mentioned it to him, so he walked out to his truck.

Cal was leaning on it, waiting for him.

"Did you learn anything?" he asked Dan.

Dan shook his head. "Just said a few words to Cheryl."

"Most of these climbing guys are all over the world," Cal said. "I had three names I was hoping to talk to here, but no luck."

"They didn't show?" Dan asked.

"One's on Denali up in Alaska, at least, that's what these guys think," Cal said. "Another two are climbing together in Patagonia or something. I guess that's what they do. They just travel around the world and climb stuff that nobody else can climb."

"Better them than me," Dan said. "Did those guys have any ideas about Arquette?"

Cal shook his head sadly. "He was not a popular guy. A lot of people weren't very interested in climbing with him."

Jim McDougal came over to join them. "Sad day," he said bluntly. "But a decent ceremony. It would have been nice to have a few more of the climbers show up. You'd think they'd want to honor one of their own."

Cal and Dan mumbled a response.

"But maybe they just don't like to think about the fact that they could die just about any day, out there on the rocks," McDougal said. "I mean, if I were a climber, I wouldn't want to spend a lot of time thinking about funerals."

"It is climbing season," Dan suggested. "A lot of these guys are probably climbing in other parts of the world."

"Yeah, and not wanting to think about death there, either," McDougal continued. Then, turning to Cal Healey, he said, "Hey, Sheriff, you got any hot leads on the murder? Am I still a suspect?"

Cal shook his head. "I'm not exactly looking to share that information," Cal said. "The investigation is ongoing."

"Ha!" McDougal almost shouted. "Just like in the movies. Well, you know what they say. Ninety-five percent of all murder victims know their murderer."

Cal gave him a wan smile. "Is that what they say?"

"Isn't that true?" McDougal asked him. "That's what I've heard."

"I guess it depends on whose statistics you believe," Cal said.

"Yeah, well, I don't know what you're waiting for. That's where I would look," McDougal continued. Then, looking at Dan, he said,

"Not that he's looking for any advice, right?"

Dan looked away and was relieved to see Hideo Saito in the parking lot. He gave him a small wave, and Hideo waved back.

McDougal sensed the cold shoulder. "I guess I better get going," he said. "Good to see you guys."

Dan and Cal nodded to him without speaking. Across the way, they could see Cheryl Arquette getting into a car. A small group of people lingered behind on the steps, one of them was Andy MacRostie.

"Are you going to the reception?" Cal asked.

Dan shook his head. "Wasn't invited. No idea where it is."

"Me, either," Cal said. "I guess I'll go back to work. Let me know if you hear anything."

Dan assured him he would.

Since Kristen's catering kitchen was on his way back to the Ranger Station, Dan thought he might stop by. It was just about lunch time, and who knew if Kristen might have a little something he could cadge.

He knocked on the door and peered in through the glass. He saw Kristen wave, and then backed away, waiting for her to open the door. She greeted him in her whites, which were just stained enough to let him know she'd been busy.

"Can I interrupt your regularly scheduled programming to take you to lunch?" he asked.

She laughed. "Nope, I'm way too busy. But if you want it, I've got some leftover potato salad and some cold roast beef."

Dan grinned. "You drive a hard bargain."

"And there's horseradish for the roast beef," Kristen continued. "I was saving it for dinner tonight, but we might as well eat it now."

She led Dan back into the kitchen.

"You got a weird call this morning, after you left," Kristen said. "Somebody from a newspaper?" She pulled out her phone. "Matt Moroni from The Stockton Record? He said wanted to talk to you, then wanted to know all about you."

"I hope you left out the juicy stuff," Dan said.

"I didn't tell him much," Kristen said. "I didn't like the way it felt. I just told him he needed to talk to you."

"Okay, no problem." Dan said. "Did he leave a number?"

"I texted it to your phone," she said.

With a start, Dan pulled out his phone and saw that he had a few messages and the text from Kristen. He decided to deal with them after lunch.

"What do you hear from Katie?" Kristen asked. "Is Shauna back home by now?"

"I don't know," Dan answered. "I guess I should check. Is Katie still living at your place?"

"I think she's gone back to her own house now," Kristen said. "So Shauna is probably back."

She placed a slab of chocolate cake in front of Dan. "I saved this for you," she said.

Dan grinned. "Man, that is a chunk of chocolate!"

"If you don't want it…" Kristen suggested.

"Oh no, I want it." Dan assured her. "Is there some for you, too?"

Kristen smiled. "I had some on my break this morning," she said, pointed to a dark smear on her jacket. "It was good."

Dan was wolfing down his piece of cake. The frosting was so dense and rich that he had to lick it off the fork numerous times.

"Looks like you liked it," Kristen said.

Dan stuck the last bite into his mouth and let it sit there as he savored the flavor.

"There's another piece in the fridge," Kristen offered.

Dan laughed. "Can we hab it tonide?" he mumbled with his mouth full.

"Yes, but you'll have to share it with me," Kristen answered.

Dan caught her hand and pulled her over to give her a kiss. "Any time."

It wasn't until he got to the Ranger Station that Dan remembered those messages. He returned the call from the newspaper writer, but was confused to hear that the number was no longer in service. He called Kristen to check, and she assured him she had copied it correctly. "I even read it back to him to make sure," she said.

"I can always just call the paper," Dan said.

He looked up the number and called. After working through a phone tree maze, he finally managed to talk to a live person. But that didn't help much. Nobody at the paper recognized the name Matt Moroni. Dan thanked them and hung up. If the guy really wanted to talk to him, he'd call back.

He dialed Katie's number down at her office in Mi-Wuk. This time he got an answer. Yes, Shauna was back. Yes, Katie was back in her own house with Shauna. And Lucille didn't seem to be complaining about anything, at least today.

Dan was tempted to tell Katie about Kristen's suspicions, but he couldn't see any real benefit to doing so. Katie was already worried enough, and didn't need anything to add to her concerns.

But Katie did invite Dan and Kristen back to the house, this time to join them for a drink after work. Dan said he'd check with Kristen, but it sounded like a great idea.

chapter 27

On the drive up to Katie's house, Kristen and Dan were talking about Lucilla. "How do we know that Lucilla is really Lydia's sister?" Kristen asked him.

Dan shook his head. "Lydia seemed to think so," Dan said. "Isn't that good enough?"

"But you told me that Cal said something about Lucilla being left behind when Lydia was just a baby…"

Dan shrugged as he thought this over. "They must have talked about it," he said. "You know, about the family and their parents and everything."

Kristen stared hard out the side window of the truck. "I just think there's something off about that lady."

"She didn't want your cookies," Dan suggested.

"No," Katie said. "Not that. She's…it's like she doesn't want anybody to get close."

"How would you feel if your parents had left you behind?" Dan asked. "Seems like that might have some long-lasting effects." He was about to say something about emotional trauma, but then he remembered Kristen's own history, and clammed up.

"I still think there's something not right about the whole thing," Kristen said.

They pulled up on the gravel in front of Katie's house. Dan put the truck in park and turned off the engine. "We can ask them about it now," he suggested.

Kristen looked up at the house. For once, Lucilla was not in the garden. "I wonder where she is," Kristen said. It was clear to Dan that she was not going to let this go.

Katie was prepared for them this time. She had put out a tray of cheese and crackers, and offered them wine, beer or cocktails.

Dan looked at the array of drinks, and then at the three women. He decided a beer was probably safest.

But Kristen immediately accepted a glass of bubbly, and Shauna and Katie joined her. Shauna held up her glass. "Here's to… the sounds of silence," she said, with a laugh.

They all drank to the toast, and Dan asked about the noises.

Shauna shook her head. "Not much to complain about recently," she said. "But I think it's just a question of time before she starts in again."

Kristen delicately brought up the topic of her questions about Lucilla's identify.

Shauna met this with a guffaw. "Ha! You mean she's not who she says she is? That would be rich." There was a hint of tension in her voice.

"I don't see how that could be possible," Katie said dismissively. "Not after all that's happened here."

But Shauna was not deterred. And it seemed to Dan that maybe she'd had a drink or two before they arrived.

"Oh man, we should totally try to check this out," Shauna said. And then, looking at Dan, "So how do we go about it, Dan? You know how to do this stuff. You solve mysteries."

Dan held his hands up in front of himself to ward off the idea. "Not me," he said. "Not a chance."

Shauna considered this. "There's no way we could trick her," she said. "I mean, she knows more than we do about it. And she'd never talk to us long enough anyway…"

"We don't really know very much about her, do we?" Kristen said. "But I can't think of anyone who could help us."

"The Mormons," Shauna was now fully engaged in the idea. "They do all this genealogical research. We could call them."

Dan pointed out that even if the Mormon Church had information about the family, there was no real way to make sure that Lucilla was who she said she was. "You could find out more about the family, but I don't think that would answer your question."

"But maybe we could find out something that Lucilla doesn't know, and trick her with it." Shauna was like a dog with a bone.

Dan smiled. "If you could get her to talk. The last time we tried that, it wasn't very successful."

"Ah, but we have ways," Shauna said, wiggling her fingers together in front of her grinning face. "We have ways of making old ladies talk…"

"Shauna," Katie tried to rein her in, but was laughing along. "Really."

Dan cut himself a small piece of goat cheese and spread it on a cracker. He damn near dropped it when Shauna exploded.

"DNA!" Shauna shouted. "We need to get some of her DNA!"

Katie was mortified and tried to shush her. "For god's sake, Shauna, she'll hear you."

Shauna gave an exaggerated look of embarrassment. "Oops," she said quietly, still grinning. "So how do we get her to pee in a cup?"

This set all three women off into laughter, and Dan began to think he was the odd man out, literally.

"But wait, maybe she drinks straight from the bottle!" Shauna hooted. "All we have to do is raid her trash and swipe some saliva. Only I don't think she drinks, does she, Katie?"

"I've never seen her," Katie agreed. "I mean, she must, but never outside, where we could see her."

Shauna's eyes narrowed. "I think it's time we had a little midnight raid on the garbage can," she said. "We can always blame it on the raccoons."

That's when Kristen held up her hand. "Wait a minute," she said. For a moment Kristen was lost in thought.

"Can you get Lucilla to pee in a cup?" Shauna asked her, with a wicked grin.

"Remember her giving me back that plate?" Kristen asked. "Maybe it would have her DNA on it."

"Oh, my God," Katie said. "Where is it?"

Shauna gave a groan and leaned back in her chair. "I don't know. What happened to it? Did you put it in the dishwasher?"

Kristen immediately stood and came back seconds later, with the plate held high. "Dan put it on a shelf back there. I think you must have missed it."

"Oh, my God," Katie yelled. "I forgot all about it!"

Dan chuckled. "It's not that easy, you know," he said. "I don't think you can just ask a lab to run that for fun. And that plate might not have anything on it."

Katie held the plate up to the light and stared at it. "There are some smears," she said. "It looks like it. And there's the cookie. That was in her mouth!"

"We could send it to one of those DNA places, where they tell you about your family," Shauna said. "It only costs like a hundred bucks." She was excited, talking too loudly again.

Dan shook his head. "Guys, I'm pretty sure there are some legal issues here," he said. "Those companies are careful about that stuff." He found himself staring at the plate.

When he looked up, he saw all three women were staring at the plate.

"I worked in Silicon Valley for a while," Kristen said quietly. "I did some work for one of those companies."

"Do you think they'd help us?" Shauna asked eagerly. "That would be so cool."

Dan shook his head again. "There are laws about this stuff, you know."

"Oh, but we could ask them to do it on the side, like, unofficially," Shauna said.

Kristen was quiet, gently biting on a thumbnail. She stopped and looked up.

"They wouldn't have to tell us who she is, just if she's related to Lydia," Shauna insisted, her voice getting louder again. "That's all we want to know." She was pushing hard.

"I don't want to rain on the parade," Dan said, "but I don't see how you can hope anyone will do that. And even if they do, what are you going to do then? Confront her and throw her out? She's already in the will, no matter who she is."

"But maybe she got there under false pretenses!" Shauna insisted. "Wouldn't that make the will invalid?"

Dan chuckled and leaned back in his chair. "Sure, maybe. Five years and a fortune in legal costs later. This is crazy. Besides, to prove anything, you'd need some of Lydia's DNA as well."

Shauna face fell into deep concentration, and she leaned forward, putting her elbows on her knees and resting her face on her upturned hands. Katie offered Kristen some more bubbly.

Dan was relieved to see that he had sidetracked the discussion.

"Besides, he said, "Maybe we have some images on the camera up there." He pointed to the attic. "That might solve the whole problem."

As the women stirred in their chairs, it was like an electric current had connected them all. Shauna sat bolt upright and raised a finger in the air, and all three women shouted in unison.

"The hairbrush!"

Dan gave a sigh and shook his head. He had a feeling it was going to be a long night.

chapter 28

By the time Dan and Kristen decided it was time to leave, the conversation had gone from "maybe we could do this" to "we are totally going to do this." Dan pointed out to Kristen during the drive home that what they were considering was almost certainly unethical, and probably illegal.

As they talked about it, Kristen slowly backed away from her promises to Shauna and Katie. "I don't think any of us know exactly what the laws are about this stuff," she said, referring to the use of DNA, "but I'm very sure that my friends in Silicon Valley will know exactly what's legal and what's not."

"And ethical?" Dan asked.

Kristen was quiet for a time. When she finally spoke, it was in a more guarded tone. "I know what you're thinking Dan. And you're right."

"I just think that you guys are jumping a little too far ahead in all of this," he said. "I know the old lady is driving them crazy, and you want to help. But she has a right to a certain amount of privacy."

Kristen gave a long sigh. "Yeah, you're right," she said.

Dan chuckled. "Shauna sure is crazy, in a fun way," he said. "For a minute there, I thought you guys were going to run out and grab Lucilla and yank a few hairs off her head."

Kristen smiled. "Oh, it was just girls letting off some steam," she said. "Shauna and Katie have a lot on their plates. It felt good to help them unwind."

Dan raised his eyebrows. "Is that what that was?" he asked. "It was getting a little hairy for me."

Kristen reached over and patted his arm. "That's all right, Dan," she said. "It was just talk. It's what we do."

That night Dan spent the evening getting his pack ready for the trail. He was scheduled to do a couple of days of trail work out of Gianelli trailhead, knocking down cairns, cleaning up campfire rings, and picking up trash. It wasn't his favorite trail, or his favorite activity, but he loved the fact that he would be out in the mountains for two days, solid.

Once his pack was set, he turned to Kristen, who had been working on the computer.

"Find out anything interesting?" he asked.

"Mmmm," Kristen responded. "Sort of."

"What does that mean?" Dan asked.

"Well, we're not going to be able to test Lucilla's DNA without her consent,"

Kristen said. "Not legally."

"I thought so," Dan said. Then he smiled. "And I'm not sure that you're likely to get her consent."

Kristen shook her head. "No, and Lydia's another problem. To test her DNA, we need the permission of her next of kin."

"Which is Lucilla," Dan pointed out.

Kristen turned and looked at him. "Maybe," she said. "Maybe not, but there's no way to show that without Lucilla's permission."

Dan came up behind her and rubbed her shoulders. Kristen leaned back, letting her head fall against Dan's torso. "That feels nice," she said.

Dan kept rubbing. "Sorry to spoil the fun," he said.

"Ah well," Kristen said. "It was fun while it lasted. I'm afraid that Shauna is going to be disappointed."

"Don't tell her tonight," Dan suggested. "Let her enjoy the fantasy until tomorrow morning, at least."

Kristen reached out and turned the computer off. "Okay, but I still think there is something funny going on," she said.

Dan smiled. "With me out of the house for two days, you can spend your free time down as many rabbit holes as you like," he suggested. "Think of the fun you can have."

Kristen shook her head. "No, I think I'm going back to my place," she said.

Dan's stomach gave a lurch. "Really? You know you can stay here."

"Yeah, I should probably check in on things, and tidy up after Katie," she said.

"Well, I'll be back here Thursday, late afternoon," Dan said. "Can we have dinner that night?"

Kristen smiled. "I'm not leaving you, Dan, I'm just keeping an eye on my place," she said. "If you're inviting me for dinner, I accept."

Dan laughed with relief. "Done," he said. "If that's all it takes, done."

Which was one of the reasons he was smiling when he hit the trail the next morning. That, and the fact that he was going to be spending some time hiking up ridges, down canyons, across meadows, and along the creeks of the Emigrant Wilderness.

When Steve Matson had suggested this trip, Dan was suspicious that Steve was just getting him out of the office, and out of reach of the evil clutches of those who were offering him more money. But once on the trail, he didn't care. The sun was bright. It was going to be a warm day, and Dan would have to make sure he kept hydrated. But at 8,000 feet, the air was clear, and any time Dan stepped into the shade, it was comfortable, if not cool.

At his first stop, Powell Lake, he found three campsites that were far too close to the water. He removed the fire rings, carrying the blackened rocks far into the forest. He dug up the dirt to hide the remaining ashes. At the last site he moved three large logs that had been set up as benches in an arc around the now-disappeared fire ring. And when he was all done, he collected armfuls of pine needles and scattered them on the ground.

He took a step back and admired his work. The place looked like it had never been used as a campsite at all. He dug into his pack, pulled out a yellow "No Camping, Habitat Restoration" sign, and posted it on a nearby tree.

He didn't expect that the sign would convince everyone, but at least it would discourage those who had some sense of civic responsibility.

chapter 29

After only a couple of hours in the backcountry, Dan could not say that he had made a major impact on the wilderness. But he was happy to admit that the wilderness had made a major impact on him. His head was clear, his nerves were calm, and there was a smile on his face. He greeted every hiker he met, and stopped to spend a few minutes chatting with them about the conditions on the trail ahead and their plans. He did make an effort to mention, in every case, the work he was doing to restore habitat, remove cairns, and haul out trash that other hikers had left behind. God, it felt good to be back out there again.

He hoped that would encourage those he met to follow the Leave No Trace guidelines, if not perfectly, then at least more earnestly. By the end of the first day, he was six miles in, had a pack full of trash, had lopped a section of trail overgrown with huckleberry oak, cleaned up four campsites that were way too close to the water, and knocked over countless cairns as he hiked along. He also demolished an entire cairn village that someone had created along the shore of Powell Lake. The creator may have thought of it as art, but Dan preferred the work of the Creator, at least in the wilderness.

As the sun went down that night, he sat by his tent, tracking the shadows of the peaks behind him as they climbed the walls of the Sierra crest to the east. It was his favorite time of the day in the mountains—the golden hour—and this time the light was even deeper, almost rose-colored as it climbed the peaks. The mosquitoes were few and slow.

Dan took a leisurely stroll up to the top of a nearby granite knoll, where he could get a better view of the mountains. He sat down on the sun-warmed granite and enjoyed the show, far better than any movie, in his opinion. Colors changed and ebbed, shadows deepened, and breeze dropped off entirely. The silence, except for the first owl of the night, was total.

When it was fully dark, he climbed into his bag and drifted off to the kind of sleep he knew he could never feel anywhere else—the sleep of a man who had worked hard all day at elevation.

The next morning Dan began his hike back out again, this time focusing on the southern side of the trail. Instead of visiting Powell Lake, this time he worked his way down to Y Meadow Lake, again checking for the detritus and damage that years of hikers had brought to the wilderness.

The campsites at Y Meadow were high on granite ledges above the lake—harder to access, and thus harder to find than the ones at Powell. Maybe that was why Dan found that they had been less affected by years of backpackers. And the lake was farther from the trailhead. That always seemed to be a factor. The farther you had to hike, the more likely you were to share the Leave No Trace principles.

He did the same at Chewing Gum Lake, where he found a string of campsites right on the lake shore, including one with a young couple of backpackers in place. He explained what he was doing— that the campsites so close to the water were illegal.

That led to an uncomfortable silence.

"But we thought we should camp in an existing site, instead of making a new one," the young man explained. His tank top revealed arms covered in tattoos, and a tiny goatee adorned his face.

Dan agreed. "As long as the site is legal. But a lot of these sites were created a long time ago, before our current policies were in place. That's why I'm going around and cleaning them up. The new regulations are to camp at least a hundred feet from water." Here he paused, to look at the lake only fifteen feet away. "And then camp on a durable surface, so you don't mash down plants with your tent."

The young woman, whose piercings were more than Dan could count without making a fuss, asked if they needed to move their campsite.

"You could," Dan answered. "That would be great. But I'm not asking you to do that. Let me show you what I'm doing at these other sites." He explained how he was removing the rocks around the fire ring, hiding them from further use, and generally returning the site to a more natural condition. "If you would be willing to do that when you leave here, that would be great."

The two backpackers murmured something that sounded like agreement. "So, wipe it clean, like it never existed?" she asked.

Dan smiled. "Yeah. And maybe even toss a few pine needles and rocks around, to make it look even less like a heavily used campsite."

He could tell the young woman was intrigued. With luck, she'd take it on like a game, and have some fun with it. He thanked them for their cooperation, and moved on to the next site. Behind him, he could hear them discussing what he'd said, and planning how they'd fix the site.

The junction with the main trail was a mess, and Dan spent the better part of an hour cleaning up bits of micro-trash and a section behind two logs that was blooming with used toilet paper. By the time he was done with that, he had a full belly of resentment for the hikers who left that.

But as he hiked back up the ridge from the junction, he ran into a family of five, complete with their protective dog on a leash. He smiled and greeted the kids. He always loved to see kids out on the trail, and asked them if they were having fun.

The only boy, a ten-year-old in sneakers with a pack that was far too large for him, happily agreed. Dan asked about the fishing rod sticking up out of the pack, and the kid admitted that he was hoping to catch a few. The youngest girl was too shy to respond. He guessed she was six or seven. But when he looked at the oldest child, a girl about twelve, her guarded response let him know that at least one person wasn't so enthusiastic. He knew that no family of five could hike with everyone happy at the same time.

Dan chatted briefly with the parents, the mom all the while holding back the dog, who clearly didn't trust Dan a bit. He gave them his usual spiel about leaving no trace, and asked the kids to help make sure that everyone did their part. They assured him they would do just that.

All of which put a smile on Dan's face, and helped him forget the trash he was hauling up from below. The last climb, up to Burst Rock, seemed to fly by, and then he was meeting the day-hikers. A few conversations with them on the way down to the trailhead restored Dan's belief in human nature—two different groups had thanked him for his work—and he arrived at the truck just in time to call it a day.

He rolled the windows down and enjoyed taking the rough dirt road slowly. As long as he didn't meet anyone on the way, or catch up to anyone ahead of him, the dust would all be behind him, and he could enjoy the mountain air.

He slowed down even more to take the big bumps in the road at the pack station, glancing up to wave to one of the hands who was out in the corral. Once on the paved road, he allowed himself to speed up, but still took the corners slowly to avoid running over any of the marmots who lived in the granite along the top of the ridge.

Instead of going to the Summit Ranger Station, he stayed left and drove out onto the highway, heading for home. It was only when he passed Mia's Pizza that he remembered that he'd promised to take Kristen out to dinner tonight. That would have to wait until his phone had service.

Cold Springs, Long Barn, Sierra Village, Mi-Wuk Village, Sugar Pine…Dan loved the names along this stretch of highway, speaking as they did to history and a love of the outdoors. But when he got to Confidence, the traffic in front of him slowed, and as he came around the corner, it stopped entirely. And he could see emergency vehicles with flashing lights far ahead.

And that was when Dan noticed the smoke, drifting high up in the trees above him.

chapter 30

With a start, Dan remembered to turn on his radio, and quickly learned of a fire down in the canyon on the left side of the road. He called down to the office in Mi-Wuk for instructions and was told to "offer any assistance they might need up there."

With the cars stopped in front of him, Dan turned on his emergency lights and waited for the cars in front of him to pull off to the right. Then he eased his truck down to the CHP officer who had blocked the road.

The officer waved him forward. Dan asked where the incident command was, and the office pointed him down the Confidence Road to the left, toward the denser smoke.

He didn't have far to drive. Once he had parked and reported in, he was directed to work with a team of volunteer firefighters from Mi-Wuk/Sugar Pine. They were stationed along the road to identify any new fires created by spotting—embers falling from the sky ahead of the main fire. He pulled his fire gear out of the truck, slipped it on, grabbed his shovel, his McLeod, and a mask from his truck and started hiking.

In red flag conditions, these embers were capable of landing as much as a mile ahead of the main blaze, making the establishment of a containment perimeter almost impossible. But these were not red flag conditions. With luck, they might actually get this one under control.

The group commander showed him a quick map of the area where his team was stationed and sent Dan down the road to join them. The smoke was thicker here, and Dan slipped on his mask. It was going to be warm work.

He waved to the guys as he joined the group, and one of them pointed to an area that needed attention. Dan indicated he understood and walked out into a small meadow surrounded by an open forest. In the meadow, they would have a chance at stopping the fire. Once it lit the trees in the forest, there was no way to control it.

As Dan walked out into the meadow, he could see other members of the team spread out along the direction of the front of the fire. He turned around to look into the trees. There he could see cabins. Some, he knew, were vacation homes for tourists, but others were houses for the locals. All of them seemed too close to the trees, too covered with dry vegetation, to be safe from the fire.

A helicopter roared overhead, trailing a bucket that soon dumped water over the fire. As it wheeled and roared off, another one flew directly over Dan and did the same. They were targeting an area that could only have been a quarter mile from where Dan was standing.

Off to his right, Dan got the first glimpse of flames shooting into the air as a large tree caught fire. It was too close. Dan glanced around the meadow. Still no embers here, but it would only be a matter of time after the tree went up.

Another helicopter (or was it the first one?) came over and dumped its water directly on the burning tree, and a cloud of steam exploded up into the air. The chopper roared off for another trip. He remembered this about firefighting. A lot of it was standing around, waiting for something to happen, some emergency work that needed to be done.

As he watched the chopper, Dan heard yelling behind him. He turned to see a small patch of the meadow in flames, one man already attacking it. Dan ran over and joined in the effort, smashing the grass with his shovel, tossing dirt on the base of the flames, hacking a firebreak in the grass with his McLeod. He wasn't really thinking; he was just working as hard and fast as he could. Somebody began spraying water from a backpack on the hottest spot.

It was frantic work. Every time they put out one section, they saw another area catching fire. Two more men joined them, and they began to shut the fire down.

Dan took a moment to look up. The tall tree was still burning, but it wasn't the flaming torch of a crown fire that would light up the rest of the forest. He felt a slap on his shoulder, and turned his attention back to the blaze in the meadow.

The men were moving more slowly now, partly because they were exhausted by the initial, frenetic effort, but also because they could now see that they were going to win. The grass was charred, but the flames were almost gone; only smoke and dust remained.

Dan threw a few more shovels of dirt on what had been the hottest area. One of the men handed Dan a bottle of water. Only then did he realize how hot he was, and how much he was sweating. He peeled off the mask, choking on the smoke, and finished the water at one go.

He gave the man a thumbs up and slipped his mask back on.

Another chopper roared overhead and hit the area by the tree again. This time there was less steam. Did that mean the chopper had missed, or that the fire was slowing down? From his spot in the meadow, Dan couldn't see enough through the smoke to tell.

On the other side of the meadow, another group of men were fighting to put out some flames. Dan started to walk over to join them when the group commander waved him back. His job was to worry about his own section. They would call him in if they needed help.

To his right, Dan saw a tall pine slowly tilt and come crashing to the ground. And then, behind it, another one came down only a few seconds later. He realized that another crew was dropping the trees, creating a defensible break between the fire and the houses behind them,

Another chopper roared by, this time hitting the very trees the crews had just felled. No steam this time. That was a preventative strike.

Dan looked around the meadow. He could see another group between where he stood and the blazing pine. On the other side, the meadow was almost empty except for the three men fighting their own small fire. Those guys looked like they might be winning, or at least holding their own.

In the middle, Dan stood with his group, four men, watching the clouds of smoke billow up, seeing glimpses of flames through the trees. He could see a line of firefighters now, right on the front of the fire. They were slashing and digging. Two big Caterpillar tractors were crunching through the brush, flattening everything and leaving only bare dirt behind.

He suddenly realized that he was no longer noticing the helicopters. There had been so many that they were now a part of the hellish landscape, just one more element to combine with the smoke, the fire, and the noise.

An ember fell down, almost at his feet. He quickly stomped on it and then, when the grass still caught fire, he frantically threw dirt on it. The grass was so dry that it seemed to catch fire by itself, sometimes a foot or two from the initial flames.

Dan whacked and dug, head down, focusing every motion on the fire. As he worked, he sensed other bodies near him, and soon more shovels were hard at work.

This spot was smaller, and they were able to put it out in only a minute or two. Dan looked up and gave the other guys a fist bump. There was something about that last bump that got his attention.

He looked carefully at the person behind the respirator. A thumbs up came back at him, and the firefighter walked back to sit down just a few yards closer to the cabins. That's when Dan noticed it wasn't a guy, but a woman behind the mask, covered in gear. He wondered if it could have been Katie. No, she wasn't tall enough to be Katie.

The realization that Katie's house was near here gave him a shot of adrenaline. He quickly looked around to get his bearings. The meadow was below her house, wasn't it? Or was it another, similar meadow? He tried to remember. The smoke and ash in the air were making it hard for him to recognize any landmarks, even if he could see past the trees that ringed the dry grass.

A large and delicate piece of ash, an oak leaf, gently drifted down in front of Dan, its edges still glowing red, but the rest a pale gray. He watched it land and dumped a shovel of dirt on it, just in case.

He turned to look at the fire line. It was now a solid wall of flame, but between those flames and the meadow was a twenty-foot dirt strip, carved by the Cats. Off to the right, the men who had been felling trees were making real progress. Dan could see a channel through the forest where they had cut a path.

As he turned to look behind, the cabins were still intact, still unburned. One of the guys in the meadow saw him looking around and gave a wave. Dan returned it wearily. He checked out his section of the meadow. He didn't want to jump to any conclusions, but things seemed to be getting slightly better.

All they needed now was for the weather to cooperate. A gentle breeze would take all of this work and throw it in the fire, literally. And a gust or two of real wind would make it critical. They would have to evacuate in seconds, if not minutes.

And the choppers kept flying, mission after mission, overhead.

chapter 31

Dan had no idea what time it was when he got home. It was well after dark, maybe after midnight. His clothes were covered in ashes and reeked of smoke. When he looked in the mirror, he was surprised by the black stripes and splotches that showed him what the ventilator had left uncovered. He was too tired to eat. He took everything out of his pack, stripped out of his clothes in front of the washing machine and tossed them all in. He was about to hit the start button when he remembered that he was going to take a shower, and he didn't want to compete with the washing machine for hot water.

After a short but very hot shower, he pulled on an old flannel robe, slipped on a pair of sandals, and wandered out into the kitchen.

There was something odd, slightly empty and cold about the house. Kristen wasn't there. That's when Dan remembered that she had told him she was going to spend the last two days at her place. His gut worried about that, even when his brain told it not to.

There was almost nothing to eat in the fridge. He pulled out a package of ramen from the cupboard and set a pot to boil the water. He dumped a shot of vinegar and six or eight shots of Tapatio sauce into the bowl, hoping to wake up his taste buds.

He picked up his phone and noticed a message from Kristen. It said that she would be at his house at six, and they could decide then where to eat.

Well, that sure didn't happen. She hadn't sent a second message. That was bad. He sent her a text to apologize for missing dinner, and explained about the fire. He hoped she'd understand.

The ramen was ready, and he burned his mouth trying to eat it too quickly. He didn't care. It was just one more thing to burn today. He just kept eating, blowing on each spoonful, forcing it down. When the bowl was empty, he put it into the sink and walked into the bedroom. He thought about brushing his teeth.

He sat down on the bed to think about it, and then lay back and closed his eyes. Within a minute, he fell into a deep sleep.

The next morning, he woke early. Five-twenty, the clock said. He closed his eyes and tried to rest. His body was sore from the workout of the day before. The glow of dawn gave a dim light to the bedroom.

A short while later he opened his eyes again. It was now eight forty-five. He blinked his eyes, scratched his head, and jumped out of bed to get himself ready for work.

He called Steve Matson to apologize, but Steve told him to relax. "Thanks for the work last night," he said. "Looks like things are in much better shape this morning. Why don't you take your time, maybe take the morning off, or the whole day, for that matter. With all the smoke, and the fire in the news, we're going to see a lot fewer people today."

Dan thought that this sounded like great advice.

The euphoria from the mountains had now completely evaporated out of his bones. He poured himself a bowl of granola and took it out to the picnic table in the backyard. A squirrel expressed her outrage at this, and Dan tossed a flake of granola in her direction. With his mouth full, he turned to his phone and started to check his emails.

The very latest, from just a few minutes ago, was from Kristen. She was happy to hear that he was okay, and she understood completely. What about dinner tonight? He quickly responded to that one. "Yes, anywhere you want. Just say the time and the place!"

He hoped she appreciated the enthusiasm. He was beyond worrying about sounding too desperate at this point.

Dan's eyes roamed down the list. There was a message from Cal Healey as well, asking Dan to call him. A few from Steve Matson that seemed routine, including one thanking him for helping out yesterday, and another one regarding new fire restrictions for all backcountry camping. Dan was expecting that one. If yesterday was any indication, fire season was now in full swing.

Dan checked through the list, deleting most of them, saving a few in his inbox for future action. He gave a quick look at his spam folder—326 messages—and deleted them all without even bothering to see what they were about. If it was really important, someone would probably send it again, or call.

He picked up his phone and called Cal but got the Sheriff's voicemail.

A noise on the side of his house got his attention.

"Are you here?" he heard his next door neighbor Ruth ask. "May we join you?"

He looked up to see Ruth and her husband Walt come around the corner of his house, Ruth's hands carrying a basket.

"I'll bet you were up at that fire last night, weren't you?" she said.

Dan smiled. "Yeah, I was," he admitted.

"Well, we brought you a little something to thank you," Ruth said, holding out the basket.

"Ruth's cinnamon rolls," Walt advised him. "Be very careful.

They are addictive."

Dan laughed. "Thanks, but you didn't have to do this."

"Of course not," Ruth agreed. "But it sure beats putting a sign up in the front yard. You can't eat that."

Dan peeled the cloth napkin open in the basket and took a deep breath. "Man, those smell good!"

"Just out of the oven," Ruth said. "Better eat one right now." She smiled with the easy grin of a drug dealer.

Dan agreed and took a hefty bite out of one of the rolls. He closed his eyes in pleasure and knew that Walt was grinning. "I told you," he heard Walt say.

Ruth waited for him to come back to earth, then asked about the fire. "They said on the news this morning that it's something like ninety percent contained."

Dan nodded, his mouth still full as he savored the cinnamon roll.

"Let's hope we don't get any more of those," Walt said. "It's still early in the summer."

Walt held out a copy of the day's New York Times. "We usually make you wait a few days for these," he said, "But I'm already done with this one."

Dan thanked him and set the paper on the table.

"The news said that only one house was burned," Ruth said. "Is that right?"

Dan shrugged. "Could be," he said. "I was off on one side, trying to make sure it didn't get any bigger. Not exactly the best place to get the big picture. But they sent me home. That means at least it wasn't getting any worse."

"Well, we just want you to know that we're grateful," Ruth said. "Truly grateful, Dan."

"Me too!" Dan said, pointing to the basket of rolls.

"Oh, don't be silly," Ruth said, "That's nothing. Not compared to what you do. Positively heroic."

Dan shrugged. "It's part of the job," he said. He hoped the adulation would end soon. It was making him uncomfortable.

Ruth obliged him by asking about Kristen. "Is she working today?"

"I think so," Dan said. "I got home so late last night, I'm not sure what's happening."

"Well, she was here earlier," Ruth said. "Around dinnertime. We told her we hadn't seen you."

"I sent her a text this morning," Dan said. "After I finally woke up. We're going out to dinner tonight."

"Oh, good," Ruth said. Dan detected movement from Walt, and so did Ruth. "Oh, don't worry, Walt. I'm not sticking my nose in. I'm just happy for them."

Walt met this with a skeptical look through his partially lowered eyelids.

"Well," Ruth said. "We should let you get on with your morning."

"No worries," Dan said. "I think the next twenty minutes will just be spent enjoying this roll. These are deadly!"

Ruth gave a short laugh, then her expression changed. "It was so sad to hear about that Arquette woman," she said, shaking her head slowly. "That poor thing."

Dan stared at her and stopped chewing. It was clear he didn't know what she was talking about.

"She must have been in so much pain," Ruth continued. "Right after her husband was murdered." Here she took Walt's hand and gave it a squeeze.

Dan swallowed and cleared his throat. "Really?" he asked. "What happened? Where was this?"

"Found her yesterday at her house in Tahoe," Walt explained. "Looks like suicide."

"It's in all the news," Ruth said. Then, looking at the Times on the table, "Well, I mean the local news. My Motherlode has it online."

Dan gave her a tired smile. "I'll have to check it out," he said.

"Did you know her?" Ruth asked. "Wasn't her husband a big-time climber?"

"Yeah," Dan agreed. "I knew them both, but only a little bit. We'd met a few times."

"I'm sorry," Ruth said. "I didn't know if you were close."

Dan shook his head. "Not close, just acquaintances. But I knew them."

Ruth looked down at her hands, then at Walt. "We should be going," she said.

Walt didn't answer. He simply stood up and gave a quick nod to Dan. "Thanks again for the firefighting," he said.

Dan smiled. "You're welcome. It really is just part of the job. But thank you for the goodies," he said, pointing at the basket.

chapter 32

After they'd left, Dan sat back in his Adirondack chair and allowed the noises from his neighborhood to waft in. It was still early enough that the sun was streaming in at a low angle through the trees. A chainsaw moaned in the distance, probably taking down a few dead trees and finally getting around to making the home more defensible against a fire.

Fires in the news had a way of getting people moving in the right direction.

And that damn rooster from three cabins over was still letting the world know that he ruled the roost, at least until a fox, raccoon, or mountain lion figured out how to get into the coop. Up here, that usually didn't take a full summer.

Overhead, a gray squirrel expressed its displeasure at Dan, surprised to find the ranger still at home at this hour. Normally the squirrel would have the run of the place by now, and it was letting Dan know exactly how it felt. The little fountain in the backyard should be free of human presence by now, and the squirrel wanted in.

So did a blue jay, perched on the lower limb of a cedar near the fountain.

Dan watched them both for a few minutes, amused by their obvious sense of entitlement to his backyard. Then he chuckled, realizing that they were entitled to it—he was the interloper here.

Still, he waited for a few more minutes, watching to see how close the squirrel would come.

Dan's chair was only ten feet from the fountain. Would the squirrel chance it? It crept down the small oak tree that sheltered the fountain, tiny fingers scratching on the bark, carefully keeping to the far side of the trunk, and watching Dan every second.

It stopped only three feet from the ground and squawked at Dan, face to face.

Dan didn't move.

The squirrel came down lower, just to the edge of the fountain. Would it drink? It was still looking straight at Dan, ready to leap to safety in a split second.

And just as the squirrel leaned over, inch by inch, towards the fountain, Dan's phone rang.

The squirrel exploded back up the tree, screaming in outrage at Dan. The blue jay fluttered up to a pine tree twenty feet away and chided Dan for his rudeness.

Dan glanced at the phone. It was Kristen calling.

"Hi there!" he said.

"Hey," Kristen responded calmly. The tone of her voice was delicious. It was like sliding into a fresh, clean set of sheets at the end of the day. "Are you recovering?"

"Oh yeah," Dan answered. "Nothing like taking a morning off and sitting in the backyard listening to the squirrels to restore your soul."

"Sounds lovely," Kristen said. Dan could tell she was smiling. "I was wondering about tonight. How about if I just cook us dinner?" she asked.

Dan's eyebrows went up. "Really? I mean, I'm always happy to eat what you cook, but I thought you'd like to take a night off."

"Well, let's take a night off from other people," Kristen said. "I'd kind of like to have you to myself tonight."

"That sounds good," Dan said.

Kristen laughed, which made Dan grin along with her. "There's something I'd like to talk to you about," she said. "And it's probably easier not in a restaurant."

Dan's stomach gave a tiny flip. "I hope it's nothing too serious," he said.

"I hope so, too," Kristen answered. "Can I come by about four?"

"Sure," Dan agreed. "You want to cook here, and not at your place?"

"Yeah, I do," she said.

That gave Dan the rest of the day to think about what Kristen felt was so important, and why she wanted to cook at his place. Maybe so she could leave when she wanted? Which meant: maybe so she could end the conversation when she wanted?

He decided that sitting in the backyard wasn't the solution to the problem. He got up, again sending the squirrel and blue jay into paroxysms of rage, and remembered that he could tidy up his yard, too. He dragged out a rake, and spent the rest of the morning cleaning up the pine needles and oak leaves, raking them into piles, then carrying them over to the compost pit, where he soaked them well and then turned them over into the compost.

By then it was lunchtime, and after a quick bite, he realized that he was tired enough to take a nap. He picked up his current book, a history of mule packing in the Sierra, and soon drifted off to sleep.

Forty-five minutes later his phone woke him up. Katie Pederson had texted him.

He opened it up to read that Katie was very worried about the fact that Lucilla had seemingly disappeared. She asked Dan to call her.

Dan gave a sigh. Katie, or rather Lucilla, was beginning to take up more of his time and attention than he wanted. Better get it over with now. He dialed Katie.

"Hi, Dan!" she answered after only one ring. "Thanks for calling. We thought you'd want to know. It looks like Lucilla's disappeared."

Dan gave a short laugh and said, "And how are you, Katie? And more importantly, how's your house?"

Katie absorbed the implied reprimand and apologized. "Sorry, Dan. We're fine. The firefighters did a great job, and things look a lot better this morning. Were you out here on the lines?"

"Yeah," Dan said. He asked if she had been out on the fire line as well.

"Of course!" Katie answered. "But they gave me a medical day off, and sent me home to keep me out of the smoke. Well, not home, because we were still officially evacuated. But we spent the night at the Baptist Church, and I'm back at the house now. It's fine. The fire never got up this far."

Dan told about his own afternoon in the smoke, and she thanked him effusively—enough that he finally had to cut her off to ask her about Lucilla.

"Dan, this whole thing is so crazy. I mean, it's really weird," she said. "She's just gone."

Dan asked her to explain.

"She not here, Dan," Katie said. "No word, no nothing. She's just not here anymore. And as near as we can tell, she didn't take anything with her. I can't imagine where she could be."

"My guess is that she got evacuated last night," Dan said. "Have you checked the evacuation centers?"

"She refused to leave yesterday," Katie said. "Just absolutely refused. I had to leave to go to work, and she was still here, holding the garden hose. I've checked the centers. They closed those down all but one of them down this morning, and we've checked everywhere."

Dan asked if she'd reported this to the Sheriff's office.

"Oh I don't want to bother them," Katie explained. "They have enough on their plate."

"Katie, this is exactly the kind of stuff they do have on their plate, and you need to tell them about it," Dan said. "This is what they do."

He heard Katie give a long sigh.

"Seriously," he continued. "You want them to know about this. They're the ones that have all the information, and they can send out an Amber Alert, or whatever they call it when it's an old person. And they have people all over who can keep an eye out."

He waited.

"Yeah, okay," Katie finally admitted. "Do I just call 911?"

"I'm not sure it's a life-or-death emergency," Dan said. "Just call their normal business number and ask them what to do."

Katie promised she would do exactly that and thanked him.

Dan ended the call and gave his head a little shake, as if to clear out the dust and pine needles. At least it would be a story he could tell to entertain Kristen tonight.

chapter 33

She arrived at four o'clock, on the dot, arms full of shopping bags bursting with food.

Dan helped her carry the bags into his kitchen and unpack them. "Are you planning for guests?" Dan asked her. It seemed like enough food for eight or ten people.

Kristen just smiled and continued to organize the food in the kitchen, putting some in the fridge, some on the counter, and depositing a couple of bags in the sink.

She had cooked dinner for them here before, and at her place as well, but something about this time seemed different. Dan was still slightly on edge. He moved to her and embraced her from behind, as she rinsed the asparagus in the sink.

"I missed you," he said.

She leaned back into him briefly and said "Yeah, me too." Then she leaned back over the sink and continued to work.

Dan took the hint and asked if there was something he could do to help.

Kristen turned around and surveyed the food, the fridge, the stove, and the counters. "You could set the table," she said.

Dan quickly moved to his silverware drawer. "You know," he said, "The place seems kind of empty without you." He moved on to get some glasses out of the cupboard.

"That's sweet, Dan," Kristen said. And then, as she began to chop mushrooms on the cutting board, she chuckled and said, "Is it a bit too quiet for you?"

"No, not exactly. Just empty," Dan said. He put the napkins in place and stood back to inspect the table.

Kristen glanced over. "Don't forget the wine glasses," she said. "And the wine," pointing with her chin at the bottle on the counter. "You should probably open it up now."

Dan looked at the bottle, a Pinot noir from Oregon. The price tag on it gave him a start. "Wow. This should be good."

Kristen didn't respond. As he watched her, Dan was reminded of the first time he'd watched someone play a real organ. He had taken a few years of piano lessons, struggling to make his fingers on each hand do what they were supposed to do. And then one day he'd visited a church with an organist, fingers flying from one keyboard to the next, feet dancing on the pedals, hands occasionally flying up to pull out a stop, or push three in.

That's what Kristen looked like when she was cooking.

She threw a quick glance over her shoulder and said, "You could snap the asparagus."

He moved to the sink. The asparagus sat in tight clump. He wasn't sure exactly what she meant.

Kristen stopped what she was doing at the stove and quickly picked up a spear. "Like this," she said, snapping the bottom inch and a half off the spear.

And then she was back at the stove.

Dan worked his way through the asparagus, not sure if he was doing it right, and absolutely sure he was doing it much too slowly.

"And you could slice the bread," Kristen added.

Dan knew he had a bread knife somewhere in the drawer. He finally found it and settled the loaf on the counter ready to cut.

"Not too thin," Kristen said.

Dan showed her where he thought he would cut the bread. She wrinkled her nose. "Thicker than that."

He moved the knife again and she nodded. "Good."

Dan finished slicing the bread and turned to watch Kristen cook, her white apron wrapped snugly around her waist, and her blond hair tied back in a ponytail.

With one hand Kristen was shaking one pan on the stove, rattling it and tossing the mushrooms around. Then she used a spatula on the potatoes that were turning golden brown in another pan. The noise of the steak sizzling in a third pan added to the symphony.

She turned and held out her hands for the bread, which she slipped into the oven. Then she pointed to the plates. "Give me those and I'll warm them up, too."

Dan handed her the plates. He was now very much an assistant in his own house. Kristen was in charge. It was impressive to watch her work, to see the energy and competence in action. And as she worked, he could see her slowly turn his kitchen into her workshop. He was a satellite, orbiting her whirling planet.

"You're amazing," he said.

She gave him a skeptical look while she flipped the mushrooms again.

"I mean it," he continued. "I don't think these pots and pans have ever been given such a workout."

"You could use a few more," she said. "Like a really good skillet. Next time, I'll have to remember to bring mine."

"I'm happy to get one, if you'll tell me what to buy." Dan said.

She turned the steak with a fork. "I could just bring mine."

"Anything else I need?" Dan asked, looking around the kitchen with a smile.

Kristen shot him a look. "We should talk about that," she said

But it wasn't until after dinner that they did.

Kristen started the conversation. "You know, Dan, I love being here with you," she said. "And I can even make this kitchen work."

Dan grunted his agreement. "I'll say, this was really, really delicious."

She smiled. "Thanks. I love to cook for an appreciative audience."

"Color me appreciative," Dan said.

"But." Kristen paused here.

"But what?" Dan asked. Was this the topic they had to discuss?

"I don't really have a place here, Dan," Kristen said. "This is your house, and I don't think that there's really room for me here."

The doors and windows in Dan's brain were suddenly blown open. He realized they were talking about her moving in with him, and he was dead certain he wanted it to happen. He went into panic mode. "That's not a problem," he blurted out. "We can make a place for you. The second bedroom would work…"

"That's your office, Dan," Kristen reminded him.

"I can move my office out here," he said, pointing to the living room. "You could have that room for anything you want."

Kristen was silent, thinking this over.

"What about your place?" Dan asked. He could not believe that he was saying this. "Would you rather that we try to make that work?"

Kristen shook her head. "The lease is up in about six weeks," she said. "That's what got me thinking. Do we still need it?"

"Well, I don't," Dan said with a smile. He loved that she had spoken of them as "we" as if they were a team, a couple. "And if you moved in here, you wouldn't either."

"I'd probably want to keep it for a while, just in case," Kristen said.

"Just in case?" Dan asked.

She laughed. "Yeah. Just in case."

"I'll be on my best behavior," Dan said. "I promise. At least for the next couple of months."

They both laughed at that, in part because they were relieved that they could joke about it.

"So may I invite you officially to move in?" Dan asked.

Kristen smiled. "Yeah, I am thinking about it."

"And if I buy a skillet?" Dan asked.

That got a laugh from her. "That would be a good idea."

"Of course, if you are going to move in, maybe we can just use yours?" Dan asked.

"Maybe," she said. Then she wrinkled her nose. "Dan, why does it smell like ashes and smoke in here?"

That's when Dan remembered his clothes sitting in the washing machine. He laughed. "I think I can take care of that," he said.

chapter 34

Which was when Cal called. Dan's phone beeped and glowed over on the coffee table.

Kristen told him to go ahead and answer it. "I think we're kind of done," she said, which Dan interpreted as a good sign. At least he hoped it was.

When Dan answered, Cal sounded stressed, and got straight to the point.

"I don't know if you've heard, but we've got a missing person here," he said. "Lucilla Manzella."

Dan told him that he had heard about it from Katie.

"So you're talking to her? You probably heard about this before we did. And what did she have to say?" Cal asked.

Dan summarized the conversation for Cal, including the fact that Dan had suggested she call the Sheriff's office, and then asked what Cal was thinking.

"I can't tell you," Cal said. "It's an ongoing investigation, and I can't comment on it."

That didn't sound like Cal to Dan. "Okay." Dan backed off. Then, just to make sure, "are you serious?" he asked.

"What do you know that you're not telling me?" Cal said.

Dan thought this over. "I can't think of anything," he said slowly. His mind was working through the details. Cal was obviously angry about something, and Dan didn't want to make it worse.

Cal waited for a moment. "Do you want to tell me about the wildlife camera in the attic?" he asked Dan.

Dan chuckled. "Oh yeah, well, we were trying to find out if there was anything to the noises that Lucilla was hearing up there."

Cal met this with stony silence.

"You still there?" Dan asked.

"And?" Cal asked pointedly.

"I don't know," Dan admitted. "I haven't had a chance to go back and check. I've been kinda busy, you know. I was out on the trail for a couple of days, and then I was up on the fire yesterday."

"Yeah," Cal said. He was still clearly angry.

Dan tried to smooth over the waters. "So you found the camera? Was there anything on it?" Dan asked quietly.

"Animals?" Cal asked. "No. Not a squirrel or a rat or a possum. But there were some pictures of an old lady shuffling around the attic."

"Are you serious?" Dan asked. His back was suddenly racing with chills.

"Yeah," Cal said. "She's right in there, moving around with the dresses and the boxes."

"Wait," Dan said. "You mean it was Lucilla?"

"Who the hell else would it be?" Cal asked.

"How did she get up there?" Dan asked. He told Cal about the staircase in Katie's house. "I thought that was the only way up there."

"Yeah, well, there was one on her side, too," Cal said. "The old man liked to be creative with his carpentry that way."

"So why would she complain about the noises up there, if she could get up there herself and see?" Dan asked.

"Maybe she wanted to find out for herself," Cal said. "She

might have been a bit on the odd side. We sent a guy up there to check it out. Unbelievable. Her place was full of all kinds of weird shit. About six baby Jesus dolls, each one with its own crib, and baby bottle, and diaper. Crucifixes on every wall. Lots of saints and little altars everywhere."

"Wow," Dan said. "I had no idea. Huh. Who would have guessed?"

"I'm glad to hear you say that," Cal said. "Because if you'd told me you knew about all that stuff, I was going to blow a gasket."

"Nope," Dan said. "I had no idea. Save your gasket for something else."

"That's good," Cal sounded calmer now. "At least there's one thing I knew about before you."

Dan let this comment slide.

"You know, Dan, there are times when it seems that you just stick your nose into things, even when it doesn't belong," Cal said.

Dan considered this. "Hey, Cal, I don't ever ask for this stuff," he said. "It just comes to me. People just seem to tell me stuff."

"I know that," Cal said. "It just comes to you. A lot of stuff just comes to you. A lot of people tell you stuff." Dan could tell he was still angry. "And sometimes I can't help wondering why."

Dan wasn't happy to hear this from his friend. "Maybe people think that telling me is easier than getting the official authorities involved," he suggested.

"And yet," Cal said. Dan could imagine him holding up a finger, wagging in the air. "And yet, it never turns out to be easier, does it, Dan? It always just turns out more complicated."

Dan looked for a way to calm things down. "You know, Cal, you don't have to do anything with this stuff from me. I mean, consider the source."

"Oh, I do consider the source," Cal assured him. "But I still have to listen to it."

"You can ignore anything I tell you, "Dan said. "Ignore like it came from some crazy old lady..."

"I could," Cal agreed, "but first of all, that would be an insult to all the crazy old ladies I know."

They sat in silence. Dan couldn't think of anything to say. He was just about to apologize, although he wasn't sure why, when Cal spoke again.

"And I can't ignore it. I can't ignore the source, because dammit if you don't somehow manage to find out something that's important.

"Do you think this is important?" Dan asked.

"How the hell do I know?" Cal said. "But the crazy old lady that told me about it seems to be right a lot of the time."

"Cal, I am not trying to get involved in these things," Dan said. "I really don't look for this stuff."

"Yeah, that may be true," Cal said. "But it sure as hell finds you."

There was another long pause. Dan was about to suggest that they talk again later when Cal started again.

"What do you know about those two women?" he asked.

"Katie and Shauna?" Dan asked. "Good kids. I don't know Shauna really well, but Katie is great."

"Any chance they might have run the old lady off?" Cal asked.

"No, I don't think so. Not a chance. Katie's a sweetheart. Wouldn't hurt anyone. And I don't think she'd let Shauna do anything, either," Dan said. He remembered the conversation about DNA in their kitchen, and wondered how he could bring it up to Cal. "How much do you know about Lucilla?' he asked.

He heard Cal sigh. "Is there something you think I should know about her, too?" he asked peevishly.

"No, I was just wondering if anyone other than Lydia knew who she was."

"I think maybe her sister would be enough, don't you Dan?" Cal asked.

"Yeah, maybe." Dan wasn't willing to give in completely. "But what if she isn't Lydia's sister?"

Cal waited a moment, digesting this thought. "And her supposed sister would lie about this?" he asked.

"I don't know," Dan said. "It's just a suspicion." He didn't want to suggest to Cal that it was Kristen's idea.

"We have a missing person alert out on Nixle," Cal said. "If she's around here, somebody will probably see her. Maybe she's just wandering around."

"You did hear that Lucilla refused to be evacuated, right?" Dan said.

"Yes, that's something I did hear," Cal said. "And I bet I heard before you did. But we're checking that, too."

"Do you really think that Katie and Shauna had anything to do with Lucilla disappearing?" Dan asked.

"Do I think that?" Cal answered. "No, I don't. But they are the last people to see her, and they are the only ones with any kind of motive. So…"

"Yeah, okay," Dan said. "Let me know if I can help."

"No, no, no, no," Cal said. "No help, Dan. We've sent out a Silver Alert, just in case somebody has seen her somewhere. And we'll go up there tomorrow and search the property more thoroughly if she doesn't show up."

"At her age, maybe she did wander off and got lost," Dan

suggested.

"Or worse," Cal added.

"I can't think anybody would have much of a motive to hurt her," Dan said.

"Except maybe your gal friends," Cal responded. "They were the last people to see her alive. That's the definition of a suspect."

"Okay, but not really," Dan said. "I really can't see it. And there is no evidence of foul play. She's only been gone since the fire. What's that, a day?"

"Exactly," Cal said.

"And do you think there is foul play?" Dan asked.

"That's what we don't know," Cal answered. "And that's why we're not making any more public comments. But there aren't a lot of places she could go, Dan. And we've checked them."

"There's a lot of ground to cover up there, if she's lost," Dan said.

"We're looking," Cal said. "Tomorrow, we may go back with a couple of tracking dogs if she doesn't show up."

Dan tried to put in a few good words for Katie. "I know this kid, Cal. She'd never do anything like this."

"Well," Cal said. "There's two of them. And we're just keeping an open mind."

Kristen, overhearing the conversation, told Dan that there was no way Katie or Shauna were involved.

"Sounds like you have company," Cal said.

"Kristen's here," Dan said. He wanted to say that she'd come home but wasn't sure how she would take that.

"Then I'll let you go," Cal said. "You've got more important stuff to worry about."

Dan laughed. "Thanks, Cal. I guess I do."

"Oh, one last thing," Cal said. "I guess you may have heard already, but Cheryl Arquette committed suicide last night."

"Yeah, Ruth and Walt told me this morning," Dan said.

"Yeah, well, there's more to that story," Cal said.

"What do you mean? Was it suicide? Are they sure?" Dan asked.

"Yeah," Cal said. "Sleeping pills in the bathtub, apparently."

"Jesus," Dan said. "And you believe it?"

"Yeah, they are pretty sure about it," Cal said. "Anyway, say 'Hi' to Kristen for me." He clearly wanted to get off the phone. Dan let him.

When the Sheriff hung up, Dan turned to Kristen.

"What?" she asked, "What's wrong?"

Dan started to tell her. Then he stopped. He walked over to her and kissed her. And when she kissed back, he kissed her again, longer this time.

When they finally came up for air, Dan said, "Welcome home. I missed you."

She smiled. "Me too," she said. "It feels good to be back."

Dan grinned and told her about the squirrel that morning. "He missed you, too."

"I doubt that," Kristen said. "But it's nice of you to say."

chapter 35

Dan reported to the Summit Ranger Station the next day, on time, feeling as if he had had a real vacation. And Doris noticed the smile on his face.

"You look pretty pleased with yourself for someone who has been fighting fires," she said.

Dan grinned. "I did get out on the trail for two days, you know," he said. "And I took yesterday off."

Doris gave him a look. "That must have gone well," she said.

Dan laughed and admitted that it had.

It wasn't much later that Katie Pederson called. "The Sheriff is here again, Dan. And this time they have a dog sniffing around."

"They're trying to track Lucilla," Dan explained. "They're hoping the dog can pick up a scent. Did you talk to them about it?"

"They won't talk to us," Katie complained. "They just asked us to stay out of the way."

"Well, there's not much you can do to help." Dan said. "And you've told them what you know, right?"

"That's another story," Katie said. "It's like they think we did something to her, like we're suspects. They kept asking us all sorts of questions about how we got along with her, and didn't we have some problems…"

"That's probably just standard procedure," Dan assured her. "Cal said he wanted to see if they could track her when I talked to him last night. I wouldn't worry about it too much."

"Dan, they came up here yesterday and asked for permission to look around. I mean, of course we gave them permission, and now they're back. And they already looked all over, in her place and in ours!"

This surprised Dan, and he told her so. "You know Katie, it might be a good idea to talk to an attorney before you let them climb all over your place."

"Oh, there's nothing here," Katie reassured him. "We don't have anything to worry about."

"That's because you don't know what they're looking for," Dan said. "I'd be a little cautious about that," he said. "I mean, you didn't do anything to scare Lucilla, did you?"

"Dan! Of course not!" Katie was vehement in her response. "But it's not like she had a car or anything. She didn't drive, at least I think she didn't. I mean, where did she go? And how did she get there?"

"Got me," Dan said. "Did the Sheriff find anything?"

Katie snorted. "Not that they'd tell us," she said. "But I can't imagine what they could find. It's not like we did anything to her." Her voice was now rising to near panic levels.

"Okay," Dan said, "It sounds like they are just following all the standard procedures. I'm telling you, I wouldn't worry about it. They'll find her in Reno at a casino or something."

"God, I hope you're right," Katie said. "I don't have a good feeling about this."

"What does Shauna say?" Dan asked.

"Oh, not much," Katie replied. "She's as confused as I am. Maybe a little more angry, but just as confused."

In the background, he could hear Shauna talking to someone.

"Dan, they want to dig up the rose garden!" Katie said. "They're asking us if they can do it. The dog is really sniffing around there."

"Katie, you really need to talk to an attorney," Dan said. "But of course, Lucilla spent a lot of time in that rose garden. The dog must be smelling that."

The voices in the background were getting louder. "I have to go now, Dan," Katie said. "Thanks. I'll call somebody. I have to go now."

And she hung up.

Dan looked up to see Doris staring at him. "What was that all about?" she asked.

Dan explained it to her.

"They're looking for Lucilla, who seems to have disappeared," he said. "They brought a dog in to try to track her, and the dog is going crazy in the rose garden, where Lucilla spent hours every day."

"Oh dear," Doris said. "You don't think…"

"No, I don't," Dan said. "But I'm sure the dog is right—it must smell her there. And she was always digging around in there, so the soil is disturbed."

"Well," Doris said. "If this were a movie…"

"It's not," Dan said. "They'll find out soon enough."

He sent a text to Katie, asking her to keep in touch, and assuring her that things would all work out. And he hoped that was true.

It was well after lunch (a Caesar salad with chicken that Kristen had packed up for him in the morning) that Dan heard from Katie again. And it wasn't good news.

First of all, she sounded very quiet, almost as if she were whispering.

"Dan, they are still digging in the rose garden," she said. "But I think they found something."

"What do you mean?" Dan asked.

"Well, the dog was sniffing and digging, and then they started digging, and now they've stopped," Katie said. "But they are talking on their radios, and everyone is standing around and looking down into the hole."

"Did you call a lawyer?" Dan asked.

"Yeah," Katie said. "Well, I left a message for one."

Dan started to remonstrate with her when she interrupted him.

"Sorry, Dan, I've got to go."

And she hung up.

Doris was talking to three backpackers who were trying to talk her into allowing them to have a fire in the backcountry. Dan walked over and lent the power of his height and uniform to the discussion, which ended it quickly.

After they'd left, Doris asked him about the call.

Dan shook his head. "I don't know, but Katie says that she thinks the Sheriff found something when they were digging in her garden."

"Oh, God," Doris said.

Dan shrugged and shook his head. "I don't know," he said. "I don't know what's going on."

Another group came in the doors, and Doris turned to help them.

Dan walked back into the rear office and checked his computer. There were some emails that he should really answer, but his heart wasn't in it. He deleted as many as he could, telling himself that he was making progress, but knowing that he was really just wasting time.

Steve Matson wanted data on the number of permits last month. Dan's friend Chris Martin wanted to schedule a day of trail work down in the Mokelumne Canyon. There were four memos from HR about new procedures that needed to be followed. Dan was tempted to delete them all, but worried that doing so might prevent him from getting paid or getting Doris paid. But he certainly couldn't read the dense language and comprehend it right now.

Out in the main office, he heard more voices. It was time for him to go out and see if Doris needed help. Besides, maybe that would distract him.

When the last visitor left, it closing time. Dan looked at the clock, and then at Doris.

"A busy day," she said. "But I still can't help thinking about Katie. Have you heard any more from her?"

Dan checked his phone one more time. "Nope," he said. "Nothing." He suggested that Doris could leave, and Dan would lock up.

Doris wished him a good evening, and asked him to give her regards to Kristen.

What Dan wanted to do was to call Katie and ask for news. But there was little point in that. If she needed help, she would call. If she needed more serious help, she would call somebody else, like that attorney. At least, he hoped she would.

He turned off the computer, turned on the voicemail system, took a last look around the office to make sure that it would be ready for the next day, and started to walk out.

That's when his phone rang. It was Cal Healey.

"Hey," Dan said. "How are you doing?" He thought about mentioning Katie and her garden, and then decided that Cal might not take that well.

"What do you know about this whole thing?" Cal asked. It was clear to Dan that Cal knew about Katie's phone calls to him.

"Not much," Dan said. "I think I told you everything last night."

"Yeah, well, think some more," Cal said. "We found a body out here today. It's not Lucilla. Forensics says it's a younger woman, and it's been here for years."

"Sorry," Dan said. "I can't help you with that one. You mean it's older?"

"Fifty to a hundred years," Cal said. "Very rough estimate."

"That's before my time, Cal," Dan said. "I only got here about five years ago."

Dan heard a noise from the phone. He guessed it was Cal, sucking on a tooth.

"So it's not Lucilla?" Dan asked.

"Definitely not," Cal said. "Body is too young, and it's been there too long."

"Lucilla spent a lot of time in that garden," Dan said. "Way more than anywhere else. Do you think she knew?"

"Maybe," Cal said. "That sure is something I'd like to ask her, if I could find her. But right now, she is nowhere to be found."

"I wish I could help," Dan said. "But I don't know anything."

"That is sadly true, Courtwright," Cal said. "You really don't know anything. I don't know how you manage it."

Dan smiled. This was the Cal he knew. "I try to keep it that way, Cal. Saves on worries."

"I wish I could say the same," Cal said. "Let me know if you do manage to learn anything, would you, Dan?"

"Yep, but I am going to try really hard not to," Dan said. "Learn anything, I mean."

chapter 36

That evening, Dan was hoping to tell Kristen about the day's developments, but she was working, catering a reception for someone down in Jamestown. Which was probably just as well, because he was having a hard time believing it all. He kept rubbing his eyes and twisting his head around, trying, somehow, to get his mind and body to loosen up, to relax.

There was something eating at him. He knew he should call Katie and check in with her, but he also knew that Cal would not appreciate that. So he sat at home, trying to read a book about the Galapagos, and watching his mind wander all over the world. By the time Kristen got home, he was nodding off, somewhere between San Cristobal and Isabela.

Kristen, once she had heard the whole story, was adamant that he reach out to Katie.

Dan explained his concerns, but Kristen wasn't having any of it.

"You need to let her know," she said. "You need to offer to help her."

"Help with what?" Dan asked. "I can't get involved in that."

"She trusts you, Dan," Kristen said. "And sometimes, just hearing from someone you trust can really help."

"Yeah, well I don't think I helped her much today," Dan said.

"Yes, you did," she said. "It's just that other stuff happened as well."

Kristen fixed Dan with one of her looks—the one that said she knew what she was talking about. The one that said he'd better not argue. "Just send her a text message and leave it at that."

So that was exactly what Dan did. "Hope you and Shauna are doing okay," he wrote. He thought about adding more, then decided that it would just be asking for trouble.

"Did you tell Cal about the dish I have with Lucilla's DNA on it?" Kristen asked.

Dan could feel the bottom of his stomach slowly sink away into the abyss. He shook his head.

"He'd probably want to know about it, wouldn't he?" she asked.

Shit.

Dan nodded. "Yeah, I guess he would," he admitted. He picked up his phone and clicked on Cal's number.

It was late. Maybe Cal wouldn't answer.

Dan was in luck. He left a short message and got up off the sofa, leaving his book behind. The Galapagos could wait until tomorrow, at the earliest.

Kristen finished putting away the food she had brought home and walked over to give him a kiss. Before she got to him, his phone rang.

Kristen glanced at it and handed it to him. "It's Cal."

When Dan answered, Cal cut straight to the chase. "Hey, I saw you called. What's up?" Cal's voice sounded tired.

Dan explained the long conversation with Katie, Shauna, and Kristen, and how Kristen had ended up with a plate that had Lucilla's DNA on it.

Cal gave a sad chuckle. "Man, you just never stop, do you?"

"In all fairness, Cal, I don't think you can pin much of this on me," Dan said. "I was just a bystander."

Cal chuckled again. "Like always, Dan. You tend to stand by in some of the most interesting places."

"So anyway, do you want the plate?" Dan asked.

Cal sighed. "Yeah, I should probably get that," he said.

"And the hairbrush?" Dan added. "We think that might be mainly Lydia's."

"And the hairbrush," Cal agreed. "You got any blood or semen samples?"

Dan laughed. "Nope, fresh out of those."

"Well, that is a relief," Cal said.

"Hey, does this mean that I am no longer a suspect in Arquette's murder?" he asked.

"Yeah, I think you can take your name off that list, at least for now," Cal said. "But don't leave town."

"Damn," Dan said. "I was planning to head to Paraguay tomorrow."

"Probably a good idea," Cal said. "I don't think we have an extradition treaty with them."

"That was my thought," Dan said.

"You know, we found the gun," Cal said.

"Did Cheryl have it?" Dan asked.

"Buried in a squirrel burrow up where she shot him," Cal said.

Dan paused. "You think the squirrels were in on it?" he asked.

Cal laughed out loud. "If they were, then you would be back on the suspect list," he said. "But I think she just jammed it in there, and we didn't do a good job of looking for it. It was way in there, under a big granite boulder, so the metal detectors didn't pick it up."

"So how did you find it?" Dan asked.

"What did old Sherlock say? When you've eliminated everything else…"

"I think it's something like, 'When you have eliminated the impossible, whatever's left must be true,'" Dan said.

"Yeah, well, when we figured it couldn't be anywhere else, we went back and looked again. There weren't many options."

"Good idea," Dan said. "Smart, even."

"Yeah, I thought so," Cal said.

"So you have means and opportunity," Dan said. "But you had that before. And what, exactly, was her motive?"

"We're still working on that one," Cal said.

"Did you manage to talk to Sam and her father?" Dan asked.

"They'll be back in a day or two," Cal said. "And we're still tracking down some of his old climbing buddies."

"And Cheryl is supposed to have done all that hacking and email stuff?" Dan asked. "What was the point of all that?"

Cal replied with a grunt. "She sure had access to their computers. But no, I have no idea why she did that. Or how."

"Crazy," Dan said. "Remember what his first wife told me, how Cheryl was fine with all his past history."

"That's what she said," Cal agreed.

"Did she leave a note?" Dan asked. "Cheryl, I mean."

"Yep, and it was short and to the point," Cal said. "Just apologized to Sam and her ex-husband, and said she had to do it, that she couldn't allow it to continue."

"It being what?" Dan asked.

"We're working on that," Cal said. "That's where those climbers might help. But those guys are like trying to catch a live trout with chopsticks. They're all over the place, and they're never in one place for long."

"Dirt bags," Dan said.

"Well, I don't know…"

"No, that's what they call themselves," Dan explained. "Dirt bags. They live out of a van or car, and live for climbing rocks. No permanent address."

"Well, that part's true," Cal said. "One guy is halfway up a wall in Yosemite. Another one is somewhere in the Hindu Kush, wherever the hell that is."

"Pakistan, Afghanistan," Dan said. "Big mountains."

"Great," Cal said. "You want to go track them down?"

"Not there," Dan said. "Thanks, anyway."

"This is a pretty good wild goose chase," Cal said.

"Well, you got who shot him," Dan said. "That's the main thing."

"Yeah, I guess," Cal said. "Now I get to track down disappearing old ladies."

"And other bodies that appear," Dan reminded him.

"Yeah, well, the first old lady may have just run for the hills," Cal said.

"Who? Lucilla?" Dan asked.

"According to our local banker, who can't divulge anything officially, she pulled out whatever money she had on the day of the fire. No word of where she went, but we're hoping somebody gave her a ride, and will tell us about it."

"And you're sure it was her?" Dan asked.

"Unlike people," Cal said, "security cameras don't lie."

chapter 37

It had seemed like a great idea at the time. A few days later, Steve Matson had asked Dan to take a drive up towards St. Mary's Pass to check out reports of a large group of people camping right at the trailhead. That was a violation. You could disperse camp along the road in that area, but not in the parking lot of the trailhead. It wouldn't have been a top priority, except that there was a group from the Sierra Club headed up that way to do some trail restoration, and it wouldn't look good at all if they discovered that the local rangers were asleep on the job.

And while he was at it, he could stop in and check on Andy MacRostie. The Arquette Climbing School had adopted a nice section of granite only a few miles west of the trailhead, and they were trying to do some business with tourists and the like. Dan could stop in and make sure that Andy was abiding by the conditions of his permit.

Dan was happy to get out of the office, even though he felt a tiny pang of guilt leaving Doris there on her own. She would get some help later in the day, though, when a couple of the local volunteers showed up to handle some of the visitor traffic.

Meanwhile, Dan was cruising up the highway, past Kennedy Meadows. He pulled out at the first viewpoint and did a quick survey of the snow levels on Granite Dome. It was a dry year, and the rest of the summer was going to be a nail-biter, fingers crossed that no major fires broke out.

Back in his truck, Dan drove up through Deadman Creek Canyon, admiring the steep towers of black volcanic rock on the south side of the highway, and the sheets of clean white granite on the north side. He continued up into the steep switchbacks that eventually would top out at more than 9,000 feet. Underneath the volcanic rock of the pass, there were walls of lovely, clean granite.

That's where he would find Andy MacRostie. Climbing on volcanic rock is like scraping your skin with a cheese grater. And that's only if you don't fall. Granite, on the other hand, is a whole different story, polished in places until it literally glistens in the sunlight. A fall could certainly still kill you, but at least with granite, it wouldn't be a death of a thousand cuts.

Dan found and quickly identified Andy's van, complete with the Arquette Climbing School logo on the side, parked across the highway from a nice granite wall.

Before he could park his truck, though, the radio crackled on.

"Dispatch to Courtwright. What's your location?"

Dan picked up the radio and called in to Sarah.

"We have a report of an injured climber up by Blue Canyon Lake," Sarah said. "How close are you to that?"

"Ten minutes from the trailhead," Dan said. "I'll go check it out."

"The report is that a climber has fallen up on the cliffs above the lake," Sarah said. "We'll send up a team, but it would help if you could get there and let us know what we need."

Dan stared at the van in front of him. It took only a second for him to decide. He got out and walked up the trail toward the granite, quickly locating Andy in a pile of equipment.

MacRostie greeted him with a wave, and then introduced him to the two climbers—what looked like a father and awkward teenage daughter. "Dan Courtwright, folks. A proud graduate of our Search and Rescue workshop."

Dan told him about the fallen climber and asked if he could help. Andy turned to his two customers. The young girl looked disappointed, but the father immediately reacted.

"Don't worry about us," he said. "Go help."

Andy looked at Dan. "They might learn something," he said, suggesting that the climbers come along.

"In your van, not my truck," Dan responded.

Andy turned and gave the keys to his van to the father. "I'll make it up to you," he said. "A free class whenever you want."

The man agreed. Andy grabbed two climbing ropes, two helmets, and a pack full of gear and walked toward Dan. "Is it okay if I ride in your truck?" he asked. "In case they need to bug out early?"

"Hop in!" Dan said, and didn't bother to wait for Andy to fasten his seat belt before racing out onto the highway.

"Do you know the area?" Dan asked. "Blue Canyon Lake?"

Andy gave a shrug. "Nasty rock. Sharp, steep, and crumbly," he said. "Not a place I'd pick to climb."

There is no parking area for the Blue Canyon Lake trail. There's a wide spot in the road, and people have parked wherever they could fit a vehicle over the years. There were four cars on the near side of the road, and two more in the wide spot on the far side. Someone had lit off a few flares on the highway, and a man was directing traffic. He quickly waved Dan over to park behind a black pickup perched on the side of the canyon.

"Glad you're here," he yelled. "There's a kid up there, she's fallen. Up on the cliff." He pointed up the trail. "I can manage this down here."

Dan looked at Andy. "You ready for some exercise?" he asked. The trail up to the lake was less than a mile, but desperately steep.

Andy smiled and handed Dan one of the ropes. "Think you can carry this?" he asked.

Dan radioed in that they were now at the trailhead and would be leaving immediately for the lake. And he stressed that they needed some traffic control on the highway, ASAP. He hoisted the rope over one shoulder and pointed to the primitive trail. "Let's go."

Dan was used to hiking in these mountains, and he normally kept a pace that few other people could match. But he never pushed it. As he liked to say, "If you're hiking so fast that you can't get your breath to have a conversation, you're going too fast."

But this was different. A life might be hanging in the balance. He paced off up the trail at a speed that soon had his thighs burning. He knew that it would only be a minute or two more before his lungs couldn't keep up, and he would be gasping. Behind him, he heard Andy MacRostie struggling to keep up. Struggling, but not falling behind.

Dan wasn't sure how long he could keep up the pace. He knew that the trail wound up the canyon, with three very steep patches, and a couple of easier slopes in between. Just when he thought he would have to slow down, he hit one of those flatter sections. He kept the cadence of his strides the same, but the flatter terrain allowed him to get a bit of his breath back.

And then the next steep section loomed. This time he shortened his strides, still keeping the same pace, but biting off a smaller piece of the climb with each step. They were close to 10,000 feet now, and even Dan was gasping as he drove forward.

Up ahead, a lone hiker was working her way back down the

trail. When she saw them, she stopped and stepped out of the way.

"It's right up there," she said, pointing to where Dan knew the lake sat, in a narrow bowl in the cliffs. "There's a bunch of people up there, but they can't get to her."

Dan nodded. He wasn't going to use up any breath for unnecessary conversation. Behind him, he could hear Andy panting loudly, blowing his breath out hard with every step.

Up above them, Dan heard someone yelling, and looked up. A man was waving to him, encouraging him to keep hiking.

Dan shook his head. No worries there.

The last, steep, final stretch was in front of them. Dan and Andy forced themselves upward, pushing their bodies hard. It was a small sense of satisfaction for Dan to note that in the last fifty yards, he had pulled a few feet ahead of Andy.

And then the people started shouting, all at once.

"She's up there in those rocks!" one woman was yelling and pointing. Dan followed her arm to see the very steepest section of the rock. "Can you see her?"

Dan stared. It was a massive slope of black stone. Andy came up beside him, gasping. Together they stared at the mountain.

At the edge of the talus field near the base of it, there were two more people—a young boy and an older man.

"Go over there," the woman pointed to them. "They can show you better."

Andy touched Dan's shoulder and then pointed to a tiny white speck in the middle of the slope. "Might be her there," he said. "Maybe a shoe or something? A hat?"

Dan studied the rock. It was nasty stuff, loose and jagged, with a couple of avalanche chutes running through it. Above it there was a massive field of volcanic talus—chunks of rock perched at the angle of repose, where a single rock moving might set off a slide over half the cliff.

"We sure aren't going to be able to hike the ridge and come down," Andy said. "Chances are, we'd bury her under that talus."

Dan knew he was right. They were now halfway to the two people at the very base of the slope. It was clear that the young boy was deeply upset, his face bright red and contorted with pain.

When he saw Dan, he shoved the older man away and came to meet Dan. "You've got to help her," he said. "She's up there and she fell. Right up there." He was pointing.

Dan thought he could see a ledge, or at least a couple of larger boulders. Maybe someone was in the rocks that had piled up there. He looked at Andy.

Andy started laying out the ropes. "You folks need to get back now," he said. "We'll go up there and take care of her, but this rock is crazy unstable, and if you're standing down here you could be killed."

The older man pulled the kid back. He made eye contact with Dan. "We just found them up here," he said. "I'm just trying to help. She was hiking up on the ridge when she slipped or tripped, and fell down there. This guy was going to climb over there by himself, but I told him it would be too dangerous."

Dan nodded. "Good job. The last thing we need is two people hurt up there. Let's get everybody well back now."

Andy had put on his climbing shoes, and he gave Dan's hiking boots a disapproving look.

Dan lifted one of his feet. "They're all I've got."

Andy handed Dan a helmet from the backpack. "I'm assuming I'm going to lead?" he suggested.

Dan was sure we wanted Andy to lead. "Lead on," he said. "Just tell me what to do, and what you need."

"Well, the first thing we need to do is get over this talus," Andy said. A steep field of rough boulders lay between them and the crags where the girl was supposed to be.

"My favorite thing," Dan said. "A talus field on the side of a mountain."

"Won't it be fun?" Andy said. "Just follow me."

Dan looked up at the jumbled rocks. "You know how all that talus got there, right?" he asked Andy. He pointed to the cliffs higher above them. "It all started up there and fell down."

Andy laughed. "Over how many centuries, millennia?" he asked. "We'll just be on it for a few minutes. Fingers crossed."

Dan took a deep breath and followed Andy onto the talus.

"Just stay behind me, not below me," Andy reminded him. "Clear of anything I might kick free."

"Got it," Dan said. "Besides, that way I have a better view when you get hurt."

Andy was picking his way along carefully through the rocks, teetering on one, then leaping off another to climb higher.

Dan was struggling to keep up. "Remind me to do more aerobics," he said. "This is killing my thighs."

Just then a rock shifted under Dan's weight, and he slid down into a narrow slot between two boulders. Andy heard his grunt, and the percussion of the rock movement, and turned around.

"You okay?" he asked Dan.

"I think so," Dan answered. He pointed to a rock next to him. "That one is not to be trusted."

"Don't break an ankle out here," Andy said. "This is supposed to be the easy part."

"Nobody told that rock," Dan replied. He wedged himself up

out of the hole. He was reasonably sure he had cut his shin, but hoped it wasn't bad enough to bleed through his pant leg. He didn't want to stop and look.

After another few minutes, Dan looked up to see Andy contemplating the rocks above them.

"Are you thinking this is where we start up?" Dan asked.

Andy continued to stare at the rock.

Dan looked up at the rock. He could see some larger chunks, maybe the bedrock of the mountain, peeking through the talus. "Looks like fun," he said.

Andy took one long look at the chaotic rock wall in front of him. "I guess we should rope up," he said. "It's really more of a scramble than a climb." He was still staring at the rock. "Pretty standard stuff. Not very technical, but plenty of torture talus with suicide scree."

"If she's hurt, bleeding, we need to get up there now," Dan said. "I don't think we should wait for an entire team."

Andy nodded. "Yeah." He was still staring at the rock, not at Dan. "We need to stay out from under each other," he said. "This shit looks like it could go at any minute. If I kick something loose, I don't want you below me."

"Take it at an angle," Dan agreed. "That way, when I belay you, I'll be off to the side."

Andy grunted agreement. "If I can find anywhere to put in some protection," he said, more to himself than to Dan. He was still looking up at the rock. "Shit."

Dan looked at him.

"This is gonna be a bitch," Andy said.

chapter 38

Andy inched his way out into the loose vertical jumble of rocks. Dan heard Andy say, "What the hell was she doing out here on this stuff, anyway?"

Dan didn't reply. He was too focused on paying out the line to Andy.

He watched as Andy tested each rock, leaning upwards into the slope while he slowly followed a crooked route up the slope. Dan heard Andy swear again, and saw a rock go tumbling down the slope.

Andy was trying hard to work his way from one large rock to the next. Somehow, they seemed more stable than the smaller stuff. He reached one boulder, tested it, and launched himself onto it with a grunt and a gasp. He rested there for a minute, turning back to look at Dan.

"You're a lot better at this than I am," Dan called out to Andy.

He heard Andy grunt. "Too many climbs start with this shit at the bottom. By the time you get to real rock, it's a relief."

Just then the rock under Andy shifted slightly, and he leaped off, landing on all fours on the slope. It seemed as if the whole mountain were slowly moving.

"You okay up there?" Dan called to him.

"Just testing my reflexes," Andy said. Dan could see small stones still rolling down the hill from where he was. Some were picking up speed. Andy clung to the rocks and waited until things had stopped moving.

Which limb would he move first? Andy lifted his left hand off the slope and began to slide again. Ahead was a large rock that might be more stable. With a lurch he pushed off with both feet, Dan could see the mountain slide out from under him as he did so.

His right leg slid out from under him, but he reached out with his hands and grabbed the rock. Slowly he pulled himself up onto the top of it.

"I think it gets better up here," Andy said. And then, almost as quickly, Andy was sliding fifteen feet down the mountain, brought up short by the chock he'd put in the rock, and the rope in Dan's hands.

Dan watched as Andy rode out the slide, keeping his hands and feet on the slope, and his head uphill. The rockslide slowly came to a stop.

"This is insane," he said to Dan.

"I've got you," Dan reassured him. "Take your time."

Andy shook his head. "This is nuts. I've got nothing to anchor to out here," he said.

Andy started moving again, slowly easing himself across one of the avalanche chutes. There was less rock here, the mountain had been swept clean, and he started to gain confidence.

Andy was moving, slowly edging up to the base of the rocks where they thought the girl had fallen.

"You okay doing that?" Dan asked him.

"Beats that fucking talus," Andy said. "This big stuff is pretty stable."

Dan eased the rope out for Andy. The climber was now only ten or twelve feet below the girl, and on solid rock. He quickly clambered up it and gave Dan a wave. "Good!" he yelled.

Dan waited for Andy to set the belay. He could hear Andy talking to the girl. That was a good sign. He saw Andy lean back, testing an anchor, and then turn to Dan. "Gotcha!" he said. "Go ahead and tie in."

Dan carefully tied into the end of the rope, checking the knot twice. He waved to Andy, who pulled up the slack and told him to start climbing.

Dan stepped up onto the first chunk of rock and was relieved to have it stay put. He'd watched Andy methodically move up the rocks, each arm and leg seeming to know exactly what to do next.

That wasn't how Dan climbed. He pushed to a ledge here, a hold there, and then stopped, trying to plan out his next move, never wanting to be in between safe havens. And he was sweating. He knew where he had to go, because he could follow the chocks and slings that Andy had placed. But he still had to work out how to get there.

Andy saw him pause. "Go up to the right," he said to Dan. "See that rib of rock above you? That will go."

Dan moved slowly, one foot on one rock, and a pause to check. Test the new rock with some weight. Pray that it didn't give way. And then the next foot. Soon he could grip the rib of rock with his fingers, and he could climb this section more easily.

"Doing great," Andy said.

And Dan was doing great. It helped that he had seen Andy climb this, and even though he hadn't memorized the moves, he did see how Andy handled some of the sections. He was confident enough to relax a bit, which was just enough for him to have one foot slip and send a coconut sized rock careening down the mountain.

Andy's belay was tight, and Dan only fell about eighteen inches.

"You okay?" Andy called down to him. "I've got you. Take your time."

Now Dan was sweating and shaking at the same time. Now each move seemed to be more difficult—the holds harder to reach, the ledges more slippery for his feet.

He struggled up the slope, finally getting to the last section where Andy had set off the small slide.

He looked up at Andy as if to say, "Now what?"

Andy pointed to a spot below him. "Don't come any higher," he said. "Hang there. Take five. Don't try to climb it, just swing across. The rock on the other side is solid."

Dan looked across the narrow chute. He'd never done this kind of thing before. "Are you sure?" he asked Andy.

"Yeah. It beats trying to climb up an avalanche," Andy said. "Just get out on the edge, and then kick up and out with your feet. Keep your feet high, so that you can bounce along."

Dan walked his feet up the rock a step, putting all his weight on the rope.

"That's good, like that," Andy said. "Now tiptoe across."

Dan shook his head. "I don't think I can tiptoe," he said. "Maybe more like scurry in a panic."

"That will work," Andy said with a chuckle.

And then Dan shoved off, shuffling his feet along as he swung across the chute. A few stones clattered down, and then he was swinging into the crag on the other side, his feet not quite keeping up with his body. He slammed into the rock with an "Oof," and grabbed on.

"Nice," Andy said. "You've got it."

Dan knew he did not have it. His feet were swinging free, and his hands were doing all they could just to keep him on the rock.

Only the rope held him above the abyss.

"I've got you," Andy said. "Trust the rope."

Dan relaxed his hands a bit, and somehow found a landing spot for his left foot.

And then it was easy. His right foot fell into place, and soon he was moving up the rock towards Andy.

Andy stuck out a hand and pulled him up onto the pile of huge boulders.

"Thanks," Dan said.

Andy nodded toward the top of the rocky crag. "Let's get to work."

As they came over the top of the crag, they saw the girl. She was lying at an odd angle among the rocks, her face pale. And she wasn't moving. Dan eased down next to her and was relieved to see her open her eyes.

"Hey," he said quietly. "How are you doing?"

He felt Andy crouch down next to him and saw him reach out to touch the girl's leg.

In a tiny whisper, she said "I'm hurt. Bad." The fear in her face was obvious.

Dan gently patted her leg. "That's okay, we're going to get you out of here."

Andy began to check the basics, rattling them off to Dan as he did so. "I don't see massive bleeding," he said to Dan, then, to the girl, "That's good. That's a good thing. Can you breathe?" he asked. Dan recognized the steps to basic diagnosis, the acronym MARCH—massive bleeding, airway, respiration, circulation, and head.

The girl gave a very slight nod of her head. "It hurts a lot," she said.

Andy was pulling off his pack, digging into it for the first aid kit. "Okay, we are going to take care of you," he said to her. He was taking her pulse on her neck. "Can you tell me where it hurts?"

She looked at him. It looked as if her eyes were having trouble focusing. "Everywhere," she said.

Dan pulled out his radio. "I'm calling for a chopper," he said to Andy. "Are you okay taking care of her while I get on to Dispatch?"

"Stay with me, honey," he heard Andy say. The girl had closed her eyes again. "Stay with me here. You need to stay with me."

Dan got Dispatch and explained the urgent need for a chopper. It would be at least forty-five minutes away, he knew. And they would need a spine board. There was no way they could move her without one. How would they manage that, up here on this slope?

"Right here, honey," Dan heard Andy saying. "Can you drink something?"

Dan reached into his pack and pulled out his windbreaker. He rolled it into shape and handed it to Andy. "See if you can get this to support her head," he said. "Like a neck brace."

Andy carefully held her head and tried to gently ease the bundle into place. "Is that better?" he asked.

The girl didn't respond.

"Hey," Andy said more insistently. "You need to stay with me here. I'd like you to drink something, and I can give you something for the pain."

The girl opened her eyes again. Andy carefully held the tube of his hydration pack to her lips. "Just little sips," he said.

Dan's radio crackled. The chopper was on its way. He checked his GPS and repeated the coordinates to dispatch. It shouldn't be hard for the chopper to find them, but you never knew. He glanced down at the people below. He could see at least one orange jacket, a SAR team member.

He ended the call and turned back to Andy and the girl. Andy was talking to her urgently. "You've got to hang on," he said. "The chopper will be here soon, so just hang on, okay? That kid down there needs you!"

The girl opened her eyes.

"He needs you," Andy repeated. "You're his big sister, and you have to make sure he's okay, because he really loves you. He wanted to climb up here all by himself to save you."

The girl gave the faintest of smiles, then closed her eyes again.

"Don't leave me," Andy's voice had a note of panic. "You can't leave that kid. He needs his big sister. He needs you to help him grow up."

Dan moved behind Andy and opened an emergency blanket. He held it over the girl's face, giving her some shade. They were crouched down among the boulders, and the heat radiating off the rocks was baking them. He could only imagine the effect it was having on the girl. She'd been there for what, two hours at least?

His radio came to life again, this time with Angela Thomson, at the Search and Rescue Command Center. She had apparently arrived down below at the highway.

"What's going on, Dan?"

Dan brought her up to speed on where they were and what they were doing.

"What the hell were you thinking, heading up that stuff on your own?" Angela asked.

"We were thinking that the girl needed help, and more people on this slope is not going to make it any safer," Dan said. "Just the opposite."

"That's not the way we do it," Angela replied. She then started in on what Dan guessed would be a long rant.

He turned down the volume on the radio. And looked back at the girl.

Andy was now keeping up a steady stream of encouragement to her. "You're going to be fine," he was saying. "Little Jimmy down there is praying something fierce for you. The chopper is going to be here soon, just hang on, and don't let that kid down."

Dan wet a bandanna and wiped the girl's forehead with it. He looked out beyond the boulders. He could see the peak rising above them, and the intense blue sky beyond it. Down below, he could just make out a tiny corner of Blue Canyon Lake, the water so clear that he could easily see the rocks on the bottom. Some of them were enormous. In the distance, he could barely hear Angela's voice, now calling out his name, trying to get his attention.

A puff of breeze came through and fluttered the mylar blanket. Dan tried to rearrange it so that it gave her more shade.

Dan picked up the radio again and told Angela that he was too busy to talk right now. They didn't need more help, but they needed to focus on what was happening up on the mountain. He didn't wait for an answer.

Next to him, Andy was still muttering, chanting, pleading with the girl.

To Dan, it seemed as if her color was worse now, even paler than when they arrived. But maybe that was just the effect of the shade of the blanket.

It fluttered again, and then Dan heard the chopper. He tapped Andy on the shoulder to let him know.

Andy nodded to show that he understood, then returned to his pleading, now with even more urgency. "The chopper is here," he was saying. "You did it. You're going to be okay. Jimmy's waving at the chopper, he's telling it where to go."

This last was pure fabrication. Andy couldn't see much beyond the rocks and the blanket.

Dan stood up and waved the chopper in. It circled around once, hovered for a few minutes, and then began to lower a medic down on a cable. The blast was blowing rocks and dirt everywhere. Dan hoped liked hell it didn't break something loose. And then Dan was afraid the medic was going to land on the loose talus above them, and might either slip down the mountain or cause an avalanche of rocks to hit them, but the chopper rose up again, and made another pass.

This time the approach was spot on. The medic landed on the biggest boulder above them, and quickly unhooked from the chopper. He nodded to Dan and Andy. "Dave," he said as a way of introduction. Behind him, Dan could hear the trickle of small rocks rolling down the mountainside.

Dave didn't waste any time, and once he arrived, there was no question of who was in charge. He quickly interrogated Andy about her condition, all the while unfolding the spine board. He told Dan to move off to the side and settled himself next to the girl.

Dan couldn't tell if she was responding. If she was, her answers were too quiet for him to hear.

The medic told Andy to hold her head, and then wrapped another cushion around her neck. He told Dan to help him settle the spine board into position. He told Andy to hold her arms in close to her body while he adjusted her legs.

It happened faster than Dan could keep track. One minute Dave had landed with them, and then it was just a blur of movements: here, do this, hold this, move over there. Meanwhile, Dave was keeping up a steady stream of communication with the helicopter,

Andy, Dan, and the girl.

Suddenly, Dave stood up and waved. The chopper came back. There was the suspense of trying to reconnect the cable, but with only a gentle breeze, even that went fast. With a cloud of dust blasting them, Dan and Andy watched the chopper take off, hoisting both Dave and the girl into the air. A few rocks trickled by, tiny ones. The blast of air disappeared.

And then they were alone.

chapter 39

The thump of the helicopter faded away into the distance.

It was quiet, almost silent. Dan could hear the gentle wash of air over the peak above them, but nothing more. That, and one more rock dribbled down the slope.

After a couple of hours of frantic activity, Dan looked around. The peak above them was still there, reaching up towards the deep blue sky. Blue Canyon Lake was still there, far below. He leaned against one of the boulders and tried to edge into the shade it provided. The sun had moved west, making for even less shade.

Andy was still sitting on the ground, near where the girl had lain. He hadn't moved.

Dan pulled out a bottle of water and offered some to Andy. Andy pointed to his hydration tube, then took a drink from it. That's when Dan noticed the tears streaming down Andy's face.

He decided to give the man a minute or two to compose himself, and climbed out to the top of the jumble of boulders. Now he had a clearer view of the lake and the area below. There was a small crowd there—more hikers than Dan remembered, and more than a few orange shirts or vests; the SAR team had assembled.

"Looks like we've drawn a crowd," Dan said.

Andy didn't respond. Dan took a quick glance, to see Andy trying to wipe the tears from his face.

"You okay?" he asked.

Andy nodded, silently. He clearly wasn't okay.

"You did good work here," Dan said, trying to offer the man some comfort. "More than anyone could expect."

Andy wiped his nose on his arm and was nodding his head up and down. "Yeah," he choked out.

Dan looked back down at the route they would have to follow to get back to the trail. From this direction it looked just as ugly. "This isn't going to be any easier on the way down," he said. "Do you want to request a chopper to get us out of here?"

Andy shrugged, still not making eye contact with Dan. Then he shook his head. He gave a huge sigh. "We can do it. It's not that hard or dangerous. At least we won't have to worry about the chopper knocking more shit loose. On a rappel, you might slide some, but it won't be fatal."

Dan gave a dry chuckle. "Well, that's comforting," he said.

"We just have to take it slow and easy," Andy said. "And keep your feet spread out."

Dan looked back down the mountain. His stomach was tight. The fact that Andy didn't seem to be in the right frame of mind worried him. And he wondered why Andy was so upset. What had happened during the rescue? Why was he so concerned about the young girl? It's normal to want the rescue to be successful, that is always part of the process. And to Dan's eyes, she had a good chance of pulling through, now that she was on the way to the hospital. Her vital signs were fair, and she was still conscious when the chopper lifted her off.

His radio crackled, letting him know that the SAR team below was ready to go, if he wanted their assistance. He looked back down the mountain. He could see the orange shirts, clustered together. And over to the side, a small group around the young boy, the girl's brother.

Dan looked back at Andy. Something was puzzling him.

"Jimmy?" he asked.

Andy didn't look up, but Dan could tell there had been a reaction. Dan waited.

Andy shook his head, then turned away and started to get up.

"You called her brother 'Jimmy'" Dan said.

"What?" Andy said. "No, I didn't." He was making a great show of collecting his gear, getting ready for their descent.

"He didn't tell us what his name was," Dan said. "Nobody did."

Andy shook his head and turned away.

Something told Dan not to let it go. "Why did you call him Jimmy?"

A thought shot into his head, clobbered his stomach, and finally knocked the strength out of his knees. Jimmy was the name of Janice Scott's brother. Janice, the young woman who killed herself because of Rod Arquette.

He stared hard at Andy MacRostie. Andy still wouldn't look back at him. The sunlight slowly broke through the clouds in his brain.

"Jimmy Scott," Dan said. The breeze up in the rocks suddenly felt very cold. It was a long way back down to safety.

Andy tried to push past Dan, to start the climb back down the mountain. But there wasn't really room on the rocks.

As they collided, Dan grabbed him from behind and stopped him.

"What the fuck is going on?" he asked.

Andy tried to pull away, to push past him. For moment, the two struggled, leaning over the steep talus below. Andy was younger, stronger, but Dan's height and size gave him an advantage. While

Andy was trying to get free, all Dan had to do was hang on. Both of them were trying not to plummet down the mountain.

They struggled for a few seconds, then Dan sat down, pulling Andy down on his lap in a bear hug. They collapsed in a pile on the edge of the boulders, the steep slope a chasm below them. Dan could see the open air when he looked past Andy's head.

Dan held on tightly until Andy stopped struggling. "We're not going anywhere until you tell me what the hell is going on," he said.

And then he waited. He couldn't see Andy's face; it was turned away. But Dan held him tightly, arms wrapped around his torso.

He waited at least fifteen seconds, maybe more.

"He was my best friend," Andy said. "Two peas in a pod."

"Jimmy Scott?"

Andy nodded. "Down in LA," he said. "We were brothers on the street."

"So what happened?" Dan asked.

"I watched him die," Andy said. "It could have been me." He turned to look at Dan. "It could have been me, but it was him."

Dan waited. He knew there was more.

"Just died right in front of me," Andy continued.

"When was this?" Dan asked.

"Five years ago, maybe six," Andy said, "And that was a message, man. A message loud and clear."

"What did you do?" Dan asked.

Andy snorted. "I got clean," he said. "I got clean and I got the hell out of there."

Dan took this in. He knew how many addicts failed when they tried to quit. "That was hard work."

Andy stopped and stared at him. "You have no idea," he said bitterly.

Dan had to agree with that. "So how did you do it?" he asked. "Did you get some help?"

Andy shook his head. "Not like that. No twelve steps or anything."

"That's even harder," Dan said.

"Not when you have something to focus on," Andy said. "And I did. That fucker Arquette destroyed an entire family, the son of a bitch. That got me through some very tough times."

Dan took this in. "Is that why you killed him?" Dan asked.

Andy started. "I didn't kill him!"

Now Dan was confused.

Andy was shaking his head. "You don't understand. I never wanted to kill him," he said. "Never. That was not the plan. I wanted to make him so fucking desperate that he wanted to kill himself. I wanted to expose him to the world for the asshole he was. And then I wanted him to kill himself."

Dan took this in. "You wanted him to die like Janice Scott did," he suggested.

Andy nodded.

"Didn't happen," Dan said.

Andy shook his head. "It was never going to work," Andy said. "The son of a bitch didn't care that much about anyone except himself. He was such a dick."

Dan held on tight. He wasn't going to let go until he had some answers.

"And so you shot him?" Dan asked again.

Andy jerked. "Hell no!" he said. "I told you, I wanted him to kill himself."

"Okay," Dan asked. "So who did kill him?"

"The cops already know," Andy said. "Cheryl did."

It still didn't make any sense to Dan. "Why? What was the deal? They seemed pretty darn happy to me."

Andy gave a short, hard laugh. "They were, until she found out that Arquette was fucking her daughter."

chapter 40

The slope below seemed to waver in front of Dan. He was no longer completely sure what was down, and what was up. At least Andy had stopped struggling.

"Can I go now?" Andy asked him. His voice sounded calm, almost tired.

Delicately, moving as if he were climbing a friction slab, Dan slowly moved one hand, not stopping until he found a place to brace it against solid rock. Andy waited.

Then the other hand, allowing Dan to ease himself into a more comfortable position, still perched near the edge of the boulders.

Andy waited patiently. Finally he asked. "Can I move now?"

Dan sighed and gave a quick nod. "Slowly," he said. "I still want to get down this thing in one piece."

Andy took a deep breath. "Me, too," he said.

Dan was still looking down the slope. "Do you think we could try a rappel straight down from here?" Dan asked. "I mean, instead of the way we came up?"

Andy looked over the slope. "Yeah," he said. "It sure as hell looks at least as good as how we got up here. I'm looking for a spot to land."

Dan leaned over to look down the slope. "Those rocks over there to the right?"

Andy grunted. "If they're solid," he said. "If they're not, we're stuck in no man's land."

"That's kind of where we are, anyway, isn't it?" Dan asked.

Andy conceded the point. The two continued to scan the mountainside.

"The guy on top will have to be really careful," Andy said. "No moving around, nothing. Because if he kicks a rock free, it will be very definitely less than optimal."

Dan considered this, wondering if he should go first or second. Second, he decided.

"And when the second guy comes down, whoever goes first better find a place to hide," Andy said. "Tuck in behind the rocks and pray nothing big breaks loose."

Dan took a deep breath. "Maybe you should go first," he said. "You'll probably do a better job of leaving the rocks where they are."

Andy shrugged. "I'm not making any promises on this thing," he said.

Dan turned and looked at him. "Are you up for this?" he asked. "Because if you're not, we can get the chopper back here."

"Simplest and safest," Andy replied. "Hanging that chopper in the air over here is no picnic either. That just involves more people. There's no telling what will break free. This is a lot simpler."

Dan watched as Andy began to set up the anchor. Although Andy was clearly the expert here, two sets of eyes are always better than one. They ran a large loop of webbing around a good-looking knob the size of a basketball. Andy found a good crack that would hold a chock and tied into that as well, testing it three times to make sure it would hold. Then he quickly clipped in the hardware and set up the rappel off the loops.

"That should work," Andy said.

Dan inspected it one more time. He knew he could not do any better. "Looks good to me," he said. "Want me to check your knots?"

Andy held the rig out away from his body, and Dan ran his hands along the rope, tracing the line and counting the loops. "Looks like you're all set," he said.

Andy backed up and positioned himself on the edge of the rocks. He inched back, until his feet were on the last possible lip. He looked up at Dan. "I'll try to kick all the loose stuff free," he said with a grin.

"Yeah, that would be great," Dan said.

"I'm not doing it for you," Andy said. "The more I kick loose, the less there is to fall on me when you come down."

And with that, he stepped backwards over the edge and slipped out of sight down the mountain.

Dan was careful to move slowly over to the edge. He wanted to watch Andy's descent, to see where there might be problems, but he made damn sure he didn't do anything to start a rock down the slope.

He could see Andy carefully picking his way backwards. This was not a place to kick free of the wall and descend in big, easy bounces. That would only increase the chances of some of the loose rock breaking free. And if that happened, who knew when it would stop. Or where. Or what it would take down with it.

Dan watched as Andy tested a foot placement here, eased to one side over there, aimed for a larger and more stable rock when he could, and delicately danced over the sketchiest parts of the slope.

Then, suddenly, the slope underneath Andy crumbled, and Dan watched as a cloud of rock and dust flew down the mountain. Andy kicked free, bouncing off to the side, and was able to find a spot to wait out the cascade of rocks.

After a few moments, he looked up at Dan. "That's one to watch out for," he said with a grin.

Dan knew that there was no guarantee that the remaining rock wouldn't crumble when Andy continued. Or when Dan descended.

Andy stayed left now, not aiming at the chunk of rock they had identified as their next belay point. Instead, he worked his way off the line, staying out of the sketchiest rock slope. When he was even with their belay target, he carefully worked his way back to the right. He gave one final, slow, bounce, and landed on the massive crag of black rock.

He bounced on it once or twice, testing to make sure it was solid. It was so large that Dan was confident it would be stable, but he was relieved that Andy had checked anyway.

Andy stood solidly on top of the rock and then eased himself down the face, coming to a stop on a ledge well below the top. Andy looked up at Dan. "Give me a minute to tie into something down here," he yelled up to Dan. And then he disappeared behind the crag.

Dan watched as the bottom of the rope danced and then Andy flaked it off to the side.

A minute later, Dan heard Andy yell, "You're good to go!" and saw his arm waving from behind the rock.

Dan inspected the anchor set up one more time. It still looked as strong as when they began. His breathing was faster now, and he knew his heart rate was higher than it should be. He clipped into the rope and tested everything again. A hundred feet, straight down. And below that, just more vertical exposure. Not the time or place for anything to go wrong. He knew he was in control of his descent, but it seemed that things were happening faster than he would like.

Dan took a deep breath and stood up, feet spread apart, and leaned back. Everything held. He bounced a couple of times, testing the rope and the anchor. Everything held. He turned around, looked at Andy and waited until they had made eye-contact. Then he waved. Andy waved back.

"Here goes," he said. And he stepped off backwards over the lip of rock, onto the vertical slope of the mountain.

chapter 41

In the first couple of steps backward, Dan knew that Andy was a lot better at this than he was. Andy had artfully judged just exactly how much rope to let through the brake to get him to the next solid-looking rock.

The first time Dan tried it, he stopped short and kicked a baseball-sized rock down the slope.

"Rock!" he yelled.

He could hear it rocketing/pocketing down the slope. He waited to hear if more rocks joined the chorus, but he was lucky. The sounds ended in a trickle of noise far below. He didn't dare look down to check.

The next time, he overshot the mark, and found himself just below the big rock he had targeted. His feet struck the smaller rocks below it. To his relief, they held, and didn't move. He decided he needed a new technique. He lowered himself by inches until he could put his right foot on a good boulder. He tested it. It held.

Then he looked for the next one. It was three feet further down, on the right. He switched feet first, putting his weight on his left foot, then slowly let the rope out, inch by inch, while he reached down with his right foot again.

Got it.

It would be slow going like this. He wondered what Andy MacRostie was thinking down below. As long as no rocks went plummeting his way, Andy was probably fine.

The next rock was over to the left just a bit, and Dan eased himself down to it, still keeping his weight on the rock above as long as he could.

And now he began to feel a rhythm. Choose the next rock. Keep one foot planted. Ease the rope out. Test the new rock. Stand on it. Choose the next rock.

He could do this. He got that feeling, the feeling that he had this under control. One rock, then another, test, stand, another rock.

He was halfway down now. One part of his mind working away on the rocks on the slope, the other part wandering through the revelations from Andy. Wheels were spinning, or at least, slowly turning.

He heard Andy say something below and stopped.

He turned and looked at Andy, surprised to see him off to the side of his path.

"You'll need to work over this way more," Andy said.

"Easy for you to say," Dan answered.

He searched the slope off to the left and picked out his next rock. He pushed off with his right foot and felt something move. Suddenly, there was a roar, and a cloud of rocks and dust went crashing down the slope, leaving Dan coughing. His feet slipped out from under him, and he was now face first on the rocks, his right arm banging hard into the talus.

He held on, praying that nothing above him would break free in the chaos.

He lay there, hanging from the rappel line, his face just inches from a jagged corner of a rock.

"You okay?" he heard Andy yell.

"Yeah," Dan said. "Are you?"

"Fine," Andy assured him. "You missed me by a mile. Are you good to go?"

"Yeah" Dan answered. At least, he thought his was. His right forearm hurt like hell, where it had cracked into the rocks. He looked at it to see a nasty gash that went through his shirt and was already bleeding into the cloth. He touched in gingerly with his left hand. It was right along the bony edge of his forearm. Dan hoped it hadn't gone all the way to the bone.

He moved his right hand and fingers. It all hurt, but he could move it. He decided that his arm wasn't broken.

"Are you okay?" Andy asked again.

This time Dan realized that he was high above Andy, who couldn't see him. "Yeah," he called down. "I'm great."

He tried to settle himself, then find a place to put one of his feet. It didn't look good. The first rock just kicked free and ricocheted down the slope. His heart was flying around, not even looking for a place to land.

"Don't try to put any weight on anything," Andy called over to him. "Just try to slide yourself over to some more stable rock."

Dan stared at the rock. This was definitely not fun.

He pushed the toe of his right foot against the slope, and gave a gentle nudge. Like moving on eggshells, he tried to take all of his weight on the rope, only delicately sliding over, using both his hands and feet, not taking too much weight on any of them.

A tiny tree, only a foot tall, had rooted in the rocks over to his left. Dan guessed it would be at least ten years old, already gnarled and twisted. He grabbed it with his left hand and pulled himself over.

"Nice," Andy congratulated him.

Dan held onto the tree and took a deep breath. And another

one. He settled his feet on a couple of rocks below. All sense of rhythm and flow was now gone. He took another breath. His heart was beginning to reenter the stratosphere.

He glanced at Andy, only twenty feet away now. Dan did not look down.

Andy grinned and gave him a quick nod. "You got this."

Dan gave a sigh and looked down at his feet. That rock over there to the left looked good. He tested it, stepped on it.

"That's it," Andy said.

Dan shifted his weight and now both feet were on the rock. Just above him, he could see a rib of rock underneath the talus, part of the crag that Andy had landed on.

He reached up and grabbed it.

"Good," Andy said. "It's probably easier of you climb up that, and then down over to me."

Dan realized that there would be slack in the rappel line then. If he slipped he could fall. But the rock looked solid, and easy. He pulled himself up and followed the rock sideways as it led him over to a spot just above Andy.

Andy talked him down the last few feet. "Just down a bit with your left foot, there's a ledge," he said. "That's it. Good. Now find that same ledge with your right foot. Good. And now just six inches down with the left…"

Suddenly Dan felt a hand on his left heel. Andy was guiding his foot into position.

Three more moves, and he was standing next to Andy.

"Nice work," Andy said.

Dan didn't reply, partly because he didn't want Andy to know how scared he'd been. And partly because his mind was still working through all that Andy had told him.

chapter 42

Andy helped Dan tie into the anchor and unclip from the rope. He was in climbing instructor mode now.

"Hang on here," Andy said. "I'll bring the rope down and get us set up for the next one."

Dan was glad to sit down. When he did, he was surprised to see his knees shaking up and down like the proverbial sewing machine. How much more of this could he do?

Andy gave a shout as the rope came tumbling down to them. Dan leaned back into the rock and let it cascade past him. He watched as Andy tied into a new anchor, set the rappel rope, and tested it.

"From here on down, it should be easy," Andy said. "By the time we get halfway down the rope, we should be able to just scramble over that talus and down to the lake."

He handed Dan the rope. "You want to go first this time?" he asked.

"Let me think about it," Dan said. He had decided he wanted to clear something up before they got off the mountain.

"You know what I keep asking myself?" he said to Andy. "Didn't Andy MacRostie have enough of his own shit to deal with?"

"What do you mean?" Andy asked. He didn't look at Dan.

"Why pick up Jimmy Scott's burden?" Dan asked. "Why take that on? Didn't Andy have enough of his own problems? Why not tackle those? Why the focus on Janice Scott?"

Andy looked away, not meeting Dan's eyes. "I told you, man. We were like brothers."

Dan looked at him. "I think you were a lot closer than Jimmy's brother," Dan said.

Andy just shook his head. He still wouldn't look at Dan.

Dan took a gamble. "I'm sorry about your sister," he said to Andy.

Andy jerked and looked up to meet his gaze.

Dan could tell that Andy was thinking, considering how to respond. Would he lie again?

Dan kept his eyes locked on Andy's. Finally, Andy looked away.

Andy still didn't answer, but his head gave a slight nod, and his shoulders shrugged just a fraction of an inch. "Yeah, thanks," he said.

They sat together in silence, both staring down at the rocks below, and the crowd of people thirty or more people waiting below that.

"There are a lot of people down there," Dan said.

Andy flaked the rope down again, making sure there were no loops in it, clearing the way for their rappel. As he gave the rope a final shake, he asked Dan, "Are you going to tell the sheriff?"

Dan had been thinking about this. "Only if you don't," he said.

"I didn't kill him," Andy said. "Hell, what I did…it didn't even make him that miserable. And it sure didn't get him shot. The fucker did that all on his own."

Dan looked at him. "Yeah," he agreed. "But you did kind of screw things up there for some of us." He could think of at least three criminal charges that could be brought against the guy.

"Not as much as Arquette did," Andy replied.

Dan gave a wan smile. "That's a pretty low bar," he said.

Andy nodded, then gave a huge sigh. He was still looking down at the people below. "I guess the whole thing's over now," he said.

"I'm not sure," Dan asked. "Is it over for you? Do you want it to be over?"

Andy considered this. "Yeah." He looked up at Dan. "Yeah, I do."

"So," Dan asked, waving his hand in the general direction of the crowd below. "Do I keep calling you Andy, or Jimmy? Jim? Got another name?"

"Whatever," the other man replied.

"Those people down there," Dan said, gesturing again. "They are going to want to know. They're going to tell people about us. There are reports to fill out. What name do you want to tell them?"

The other man thought for a minute, then turned to look at Dan. He looked him straight in the eyes. "Jim," he said. "No, James. I'm James Scott."

Dan gave him a quick nod. "Okay, James Scott. Are you ready for me to head down this mountain?"

"Yeah," James said. "I guess so."

Dan began to clip into the rope. He watched while James Scott checked out the knots, and then he tested the anchor. "Don't fuck it up too badly," James said. "I have to come down, too."

"Looks good," Dan said. His stomach was still giving a flutter or two, even though he'd done this many times. But not on rock like this.

"You'll be fine," James assured him. "We've done the hard part."

"More climbing accidents occur on the way down," Dan reminded him.

James smiled at him. "Spoken like a climbing instructor. Take it slow," he said. "You'll be fine."

Dan gave a glance over his shoulder down the mountain. "I don't think I'll wait for you down at the bottom," he said. "It's probably safer if I get the hell out of the way of anything that might get loose."

"You mean all those people?" James asked.

"No," Dan said. "I'll just try to avoid any rockslides you start."

"Good idea," James agreed. "Besides, I always enjoy the challenge of trying to hit a moving target."

chapter 43

For the second time, Dan stepped off backwards into the yawning open space beneath him, hanging only by the rope sliding through his rappel brake. The first few feet were easy, on solid rock that allowed him to walk back down the mountain.

Below that, the rocks were less stable, but he was slightly comforted by the fact that at least very little could fall down on him from above in this section.

But each backwards step took him into sketchier territory. A small rock tumbled free and fell, finally stopping only twenty feet farther down. He would have to make sure to miss it down there. And then a large boulder slightly shifted under his right foot. The deep, echoing sound of the movement sent vibrations to his left foot, and palpitations to his heart.

It shifted, rocked in place, and then stayed put.

It occurred to Dan that he was the only person who was sure of James' identity. If James wanted to keep that secret, an accident right here would do the job. He glanced up.

"How's it going?" James called down from above.

"So far, so good," Dan replied. "I think the rocks are getting bigger."

"The bigger they come…" James suggested.

"Yeah, the harder they fall," Dan agreed. "But they also tend to stay in place a little better. At least they weigh as much as I do."

He was gaining confidence now. He noticed with relief that there was now the odd tuft of grass in the talus, a clear sign that it had been stable for long enough for a little soil to accumulate.

He bounced over one large boulder, and found himself now in a steep field of large rock—some the size of a suitcase, some as big as a refrigerator. And over there, there were some large rocks the size of cars.

"I'm down!" he called up to James.

He found a flat boulder and eased off the rappel. He looked up and waved at James, then unhooked from the rope and called up. "It's all yours!"

He could see James, far above, peering down at him. James waved his arm twice toward the crowd and the lake.

"I'll wait until you get clear," James said.

Dan waved back.

Crossing a talus field was his least favorite part of off-trail hiking. There was no pattern or logic to the rocks, and picking a path was always a challenge. He searched for ways to stay on top of most of the rocks, looking for the path of least resistance. But each rock was a potential landmine, capable of tilting, sliding or moving. And they were all large enough to do real damage to his ankle or leg.

It was slow going.

Thirty feet into the journey, Dan had to stop and rethink his path. A huge rock stood in his way, and he didn't want to climb up it, for fear there would be no easy way down on the other side. And going uphill would take him off the most direct route to the bottom.

"Welcome to talus torture," Dan told himself.

He backtracked two or three rocks, then stretched to reach across a deep hole and clamber up the far side. He was breathing harder now.

Suddenly, behind and above him, he heard the crack of a falling rock.

He froze and pushed himself uphill to shelter against a boulder. A clattering of rocks shattered into the talus. Then it was quiet.

"What was that?" Dan yelled up to James.

"What?" he heard James reply.

Dan peered out from behind the boulder. James' head looked out high above him.

"You okay?" James asked.

"Yeah," Dan said. "A couple of rocks fell down here."

"I'm waiting for you to get clear," James said.

"Keep that thought," Dan called up.

He waited. Silence.

Dan stepped out and checked the slope behind him. It was quiet.

He moved forward, stepping onto the next block of talus, aiming for the one after that. A big step down onto a large, flat boulder, and then a series of easy steps through what almost looked like a trail— five flat surfaces in a row, like steppingstones.

The last one rocked under his weight, but only a half a inch, just enough to send a jolt to his nerves.

Dan took a big step up and climbed up onto the next boulder, then stopped to look ahead. It was still a good seventy yards to get out of this stuff.

He took a deep breath and moved on. At one point he had to climb up on a large rock and then ease himself down the other side on the seat of his pants. It wasn't elegant, but he wasn't worried about what the people watching thought. He just wanted to get done with this. If it tore open his pants, he would just have to live with it.

Behind him, he heard James call out that he was coming down.

Dan turned and waved at him, but James had already started

his rappel.

Ahead, Dan could see a couple of the SAR team members working their way out a few yards into the talus. They weren't coming to help, he knew. They just wanted to greet him.

He saw that Katie was leading them and gave her a wave.

She waved back, then stopped where she was. Smart girl, not wanting to get any farther into this mess of rock.

But Dan was on the home stretch now. The rocks were more stable, there were tufts of grass everywhere, and he could even see where there might be a deer trail here. He followed it, taking advantage of the local knowledge of the wildlife.

A few minutes later he was surprised to look up and see Katie in front of him.

"Hey," he said. "Fancy meeting you here."

She smiled. "Nice job up there," she said. "You're quite the rock climber."

Dan looked at her and laughed. And he was delighted to see that she was laughing too.

"Ain't I, though?" he grinned. "It wasn't really hard, just nasty."

"Yeah, I could tell," Katie said. She joined him as they clambered through the last ten yards of talus to the grass.

"At least you had expert help," she said, referring to James.

Dan grinned. "Yeah, no shit."

A few more steps and they were on flat, solid ground. "God, that feels good," Dan said.

He stopped and looked back for James. He couldn't see him. Dan reached out for Katie's arm. "Where is he?" he asked.

They were both looking now, searching the slope for the young climber.

And then, far below where Dan had expected, he saw a

movement.

"There," he said. "He shot down farther than I did."

Now they could see James, coil of rope over his shoulder, working his way over the blocks of talus. He was moving well, far faster than Dan had done.

Katie chuckled beside him. "You are in deep doo-doo with Angela," she said.

"Oh, good," Dan said. "I'll prepare myself for a lecture."

Katie reached out and touched his arm. "Here," she said, holding out a pair ear plugs. "You might be able to use these."

chapter 44

It wasn't that simple.

There were eight SAR team members up by the lake, and it was Blake who noticed Dan's leg was bleeding.

"Hey," he said. "We need to take a look at that."

Dan looked down to see that his pant leg was covered in blood. "Let's do it down at the road," he said.

But Blake was insistent. "Nope," he said. "I didn't carry this gear all the way up here just to use it back down on the road." He pointed to a nearby rock and told Dan to take a seat.

The rock was hard and sharp. Dan slipped the coil of rope over his head and threw it on the rock. It wasn't soft, but it would be easier to sit on than the rock.

That was when Katie noticed his arm.

"Geez, Dan, you're a mess," she said. "Let me see that arm."

Dan surrendered. While Blake gently rolled up his pant leg, Dan held out his arm to Katie, and she did the same with his sleeve.

Blake quickly opened up one of the packs, and Dan was soon getting swabbed and patted with a range of wipes and pads.

"This is kinda nasty," Blake was saying. "You might need a few stitches to put this right."

Dan looked down at his leg. Blake had cleaned most of the blood off, and Dan could see a deep gash in his shin. Even though Blake had wiped it clean, it was soon filling again with deep red blood.

Katie leaned over to see. "Ooh, that doesn't look great, Dan," she said. Then, turning her attention to his arm, she added. "I think we can just patch this up and you'll be good here."

Blake put a large pad on the leg and then began to pull off long strips of tape.

"I should have shaved my legs," Dan said.

Blake laughed. "I'll give this a wrap with some non-adhesive first," he said. "That should help."

Dan heard radios around him echoing the voice of Angela, asking for a report.

Someone behind him answered. "They're down, they're safe," Dan heard. "Just getting organized here and we'll all head back down to you."

Katie looked away for a minute, and then said "Hi, Andy! We're just patching up your partner here a little bit."

Dan saw James Scott walking past them. James looked over and made eye contact with Dan.

Dan could see that James was conflicted. Should he stop and help? Or at least wait for Dan? But that would require him to interact more with the others—something Dan suspected he didn't want to do. Dan wondered where the climbing students were.

Another SAR team member offered Scott a bottle of water. He hesitated, and then took it. "Thanks," he said.

"You guys did great," Katie said. She was just about done with Dan's arm.

Dan looked at James Scott. "Some of us did better than others," he said.

Blake was wrapping his leg tightly now. "How does that feel?" he asked Dan.

"Good," Dan admitted. "Good enough to get me down the mountain." He nodded to James, who took that as a signal to start hiking.

The rest of the group quickly joined them on the trail.

Dan looked around but didn't see the girl's brother. "Where's the kid?" he asked. "Her brother?"

"Already on the way down," someone answered from behind Dan. "We've got someone taking him straight to his sister at the hospital."

They were now at the first steep section of the trail. Dan paused for a moment to look back up at the mountain behind him.

"Are you okay?" Katie asked him. "Want me to help you a bit?"

Dan shook his head. "No, I'm fine. Just taking it easy." He began down the slope, far slower than he had climbed up it. Ahead of him, James Scott was leading them all, seeming to race down the trail.

Blake, hiking in front of Dan, stopped to watch him get past a particularly steep section of the trail, offering his hand to Dan. Dan waved him off. "I got it," he said. He was embarrassed that everyone was being so solicitous. "Guys, I'm fine."

Blake acknowledged this and turned to continue hiking down the trail.

That was exactly when Dan's foot slipped and he fell down hard on his ass.

He quickly leaped back up, swearing under his breath, as he heard voices calling out to him, asking him if he was hurt, encouraging him to take it slower, others explaining that Dan had slipped and fallen.

Dan stopped and turned around to face most of the group. "Hey, guys, I'm fine," he said with a little laugh. "I appreciate the concern, but I just slipped. No biggie. Let's just get down to the road, okay?"

Murmurs of agreement were mixed in with suggestions to be careful and take it slow.

Behind him, Dan heard Katie mutter in a voice just loud enough for him, alone, to hear. "Jesus, Dan. Try not to kill yourself, okay."

Dan waved his hand at her over his shoulder. "I'll do my best."

Down at the highway, cars were parked in every direction. Dan noticed at least six with their lights flashing, and a couple of CHP officers directing traffic. They had closed the road and were waving cars through one direction at a time.

The last hundred feet of the trail wound around in a tight series of turns and switchbacks, which was why he didn't see Angela Thompson until she was almost of top on him.

Her hands were on her hips, and she didn't look pleased.

Behind her, Dan could see a couple of Sheriff deputies talking to James Scott. He wondered who started that conversation. The van was still there, so his climbing clients must have been around as well. Dan didn't see them, though.

Angela began by asking him what he thought he was doing up there. It was as if she wanted the rest of the SAR team to hear the whole conversation. Maybe she was thinking of this as a teachable moment for the whole group.

But she didn't wait for his answer. She immediately launched into a list of all the things that he should have done, and didn't, as well as a list of those things he did, but shouldn't have done.

Dan knew there was no response he could give that would satisfy her, so he kept his mouth shut and tried to appear as if he were listening.

Just when it seemed that Angela was reaching peak volume and intensity, one of the deputies interrupted her.

"Sorry," he said. "But we have orders to escort Mr. Courtwright down to Sonora immediately."

Angela stopped, almost stunned into silence. "For what?" she asked.

"Ongoing investigation," the deputy replied. "That's all I know. He's wanted immediately down the hill."

Angela gaped at him, then at Dan. She gathered herself together and told Dan to expect a follow-up meeting to discuss all of this in full detail, and make no mistake about it.

Dan agreed, and then followed the deputy down the road. "Are you going to drive me?" he asked. "Or can I take my own car?"

The deputy turned around. He checked behind Dan to see how far they were from Angela. Satisfied with what he saw, he turned to Dan. "Cal just said to get you out of there," he admitted. "He didn't say how."

It took a moment for the answer to sink in. Dan gave a short laugh and said, "Well, then, thanks, you did great."

"There's a time and place for everything," the deputy said. "And that wasn't it."

Dan wondered about James Scott. "What about…Andy MacRostie?" he asked.

"Already in a squad car on his way down the hill."

Dan climbed into his truck and pulled out on the highway. As soon as he had phone service, he would call Cal about that. Meanwhile, the CHP officer directing traffic at the lower end of the line looked at him carefully, then stiffened and gave him a smiling salute as he drove by.

Dan was embarrassed to admit it to himself, but that felt good.

chapter 45

Dan put it off for as long as he could. He made it all the way down to the turnoff to Twain Harte before he had to admit that he could no longer claim that he didn't have cell phone service. And that meant that he probably needed to call Cal Healey.

He pulled off the highway and turned on his phone. As he waited for it to boot up, he watched cars roaring by in both directions. It seemed a long way from being high in the silence of the mountains with James Scott.

His phone pinged and let Dan know that he had both emails and voicemail messages. He took a deep, slow breath, and leaned back in his seat. He might as well check them first.

The emails were easy to dismiss. The usual bureaucratic memos, some spam, a note from Kristen that she would make dinner tonight, and the most recent one from Cal, asking Dan to call him.

There was only one voicemail, and it, too, was from Cal.

That seemed conclusive.

Dan called Cal's cell phone. It rang through and connected to Cal's voicemail, so Dan left a message.

He thought about calling Kristen, but then decided it would be more fun just to head home and see her in person. After his adventures, his workday was over, anyway. He smiled, just thinking about seeing her.

He had just slipped his phone into his shirt pocket when it rang again.

The screen said "Cal Healey."

"Hi, Cal," Dan answered.

"Did I get you out in time?" Cal asked. "Or did Angie chew you a new one?"

Dan laughed. "Your timing was perfect. She's had to postpone the operation until later."

"Good," Cal said. "Hey, listen, do you have a minute?"

Dan assured him that he did.

"While you were up dancing around in the mountains, we've been doing some work," Cal said. "I think things are close to being wrapped up on this whole Rod Arquette thing."

Dan grunted an acknowledgment. "Good for you." He didn't want to spoil Cal's day.

"We finally tracked down Cheryl's husband and daughter," Cal said. "At least, they finally got back in this country. So I think we've got a pretty clear idea of motive."

"Yeah," Dan said. "I guess I know what that is."

"What do you mean?" Cal asked.

"Arquette was screwing the daughter, right?" Dan said.

Cal's exasperation was audible. "Courtwright? What the hell? Does this stuff just suddenly come to you in a dream? Or you do have some kind of direct link to…I don't know what? When did you figure that out?"

"Relax, Cal," Dan said. "We just had a little conversation up on that mountain, and I learned a few things."

Dan waited as Cal went silent.

"You still there?" Dan asked.

"You mean with Andy?" Cal asked. "Because I'm not sure I'd completely trust anything that he told me."

Dan smiled. "Yeah, I know what you mean. But I believe him about that."

"Yeah? Well, just for your information, we've also talked to the police and coroner down in Southern California. Who do you suppose identified the body for the coroner in Santa Monica when Jimmy Scott died?" he asked Dan.

"I'm guessing you're going to tell me that it was Andy," Dan said.

"That's right," Cal said, still sounding upset. "Turns out they were bosom buddies. I guess that would explain all the emails and stuff about Arquette and Janice Scott."

"Do you have him down there?" Dan asked.

"Sitting in a cell right now, cooling his jets," Cal assured him. "We'll have a nice long chat later today."

"You might want to talk to him about Jimmy Scott," Dan suggested.

"Oh, that's exactly what we're going to do," Cal agreed.

Dan debated with himself about telling Cal who Andy really was. He decided that he'd given James enough time to tell someone. He took a deep breath, let it out slowly, and said, "He's, uh, maybe not who you think he is."

"Who?" Cal asked. "MacRostie?"

"Yeah," Dan said. "That's not who he is. He's actually James Scott. Jimmy Scott. Janice's brother."

There was another long silence from Cal.

"So when, exactly, did you hear about this, Dan?" Cal asked, his voice steeply controlled.

"Up on the mountain," Dan said. "That's why I called you as soon as I had service. He kept calling the little kid up there 'Jimmy.' Only we didn't know his name," Dan said. "Still don't."

Cal still didn't respond.

"All this in the middle of a pretty sketchy rescue," Dan continued. Somehow, he wanted to keep talking, to explain it all to Cal. Maybe that would make things better. "He was just yammering away, and I realized that some of it didn't make sense. And then I realized that he must be thinking about this girl we were rescuing, and her little brother. And he was calling the brother Jimmy. That didn't make sense to me. Until it did."

Cal voice, when Dan heard it, was quiet. "Yeah, it does," he said. "It makes perfect sense."

"So anyway..." Dan continued.

"Got it," Cal said. "So let me ask you this again. Is there anything else you found out that I should know about?"

"I don't think so," Dan said. "He didn't kill Arquette. He wanted to drive him crazy. He wanted Arquette to kill himself. Just like Arquette did to his sister."

"Yeah, well, that wasn't going to work," Cal said. "Not from what I saw of Arquette."

"Right," Dan agreed. "That's what he found out, too. And then Cheryl found out about Arquette and Sam."

"Yeah," Cal said. "We got that part,"

"I think you'll find James pretty helpful," Dan said.

"Yeah, I bet," Cal answered dryly. "Hey, thanks for this. I gotta go."

And he hung up on Dan.

chapter 46

Dan got home with only two thoughts on his mind. The first one was about Kristen. Ever since he had learned that she had been assaulted as a young woman, he was unsure about how and when to talk to her about certain things. And the story of Rod Arquette had now become one of those things.

It wasn't that he wanted to hide it from her, but he also didn't want the story to bring up ugly memories—to send her into a dark place that he had already seen a few times. It was not any fun at all. And he couldn't stand to see her in pain.

He promised himself he would proceed with all due caution on that one.

The other one was to get out of these clothes and get cleaned up. That could be done right away. He walked into the kitchen, poured himself a full glass of water, and drank it down without stopping. Then he turned to the bedroom.

As he walked by the dining table, he was surprised to see it covered with paper—drawings and plans for something that Kristen had been working on. At first he thought it was the layout of one of the events she was going to cater, with sinks and cooktops and refrigeration.

And then he looked more closely at one of the drawings. He held it up in front of himself, and then turned towards the kitchen. There was the window. At least that stayed. And the sink, although that now looked larger, as did the stove. And there was what looked like an island in the middle of the room.

His first reaction came in his stomach, a sort of queasy, nervous sensation.

Dan had lived in his house for more than five years now, and he had always been happy with it.

Now, it looked like that wasn't going to be good enough, and he wasn't quite sure how he felt about that. Actually, he was sure. His stomach was telling exactly him how he felt.

He glanced up to see his elderly neighbors Walt and Ruth walking up to his front door. He grinned. They would certainly take his mind off the kitchen.

He opened the door and invited them in. As usual, Ruth apologized for bothering him, but then happily entered his house. "You know, we just heard on the radio about that big rescue up by Sonora Pass," Ruth said. "And we were wondering if you knew anything about it."

Her husband Walt, towering over Ruth, handed Dan the last couple of days of the New York Times. Dan knew that he'd find the sudoku completed, but the crossword was always waiting for him.

As Dan smiled and took the papers from Walt, Ruth noticed his leg.

"Oh my God, Dan! What have you done?" Her tiny frame leaned over to get an even closer look at the damage. "Do you need to go to the doctor? Walt can drive you if you need him to…"

Dan laughed. "No, I'm fine. All that is from a while ago. It may look nasty, but underneath, there's a very tidy bandage," he assured her.

"And your arm!" Ruth shouted. "Dan, what have you done?"

Dan was still smiling. "I just slipped on a rock," he said.

"Nothing major."

Ruth stared hard at him. "That's a lot of blood for nothing major," she said.

Dan looked to Walt for help.

"Well, if it's all taken care of now," Walt suggested.

"It is," Dan confirmed. "No need to worry."

Walt looked at him. "Did you do that up there?" he asked, referring to the rescue.

Dan shrugged and nodded at the same time. "Yeah, I was up there."

"And is the girl going to be all right?" Ruth asked. "The radio didn't say. It just said that she was badly hurt."

Dan shook his head. "No idea. We got her on a chopper and that's all I know."

"Well, how did you hurt yourself?" Ruth asked. "Did you fall?"

"He already told us," Walt noted. "He slipped on a rock."

"Well that's fine," Ruth said. "But if the rock is up on a cliff, it could be really dangerous." She looked at Dan, waiting for him to answer. "Was it?"

"It was just part of the job," Dan said. "I stepped on a rock that was loose and slipped down and bashed my leg. No big deal."

"I wonder if Kristen would agree with that," Ruth said, rather severely.

Dan gave a laugh. "Well, we'll have to wait and see about that," he said.

While Ruth continued to fuss, Walt had wandered over to the table and was looking at the papers. He turned his head one way, then the other, then stopped to look over at the kitchen. Then he turned and looked at Dan, raising his eyebrows.

Dan shook his head and gave an awkward grin at Walt. "Just

ideas, I think."

Walt gave him a look that let him know that Walt didn't believe that for a second.

"What's that?" Ruth asked.

Walt quickly stepped away from the table, shaking his head. "Nothing," he said.

But Ruth saw through him immediately and went over to pick up the plans. She stared at them for a moment, not understanding what she was seeing. She looked back at Dan, shaking her head expectantly.

Dan took a deep breath. "We're looking at doing some things here with the kitchen," he said.

It took a minute for the message to sink in. Then it hit Ruth. "Oh, Dan, that's wonderful," she said. "I am so happy for you."

Walt gave her a bemused look. "Because he's thinking about a new kitchen?" he asked.

"Walt, don't be ridiculous," Ruth scolded him. "It means they're serious!" Her exasperation was visible.

It was at this point that Dan saw Kristen's car pull up. Ruth noticed it as well.

"We'd better be going," she said. "I'm sure that he and Kristen have a lot to talk about."

As they moved toward the door, Dan thanked Walt for the newspapers.

Out on the front porch, Dan could hear Ruth talking to Kristen. "I am so happy for you, Kristen," She was saying. "And for Dan. Especially for Dan."

Dan could see Kristen looking a bit confused as she heard this.

"But oh, dear, you will have your hands full," Ruth continued, glancing back meaningfully at Dan. She gave a sigh and shook her head as she trundled off toward her house, Walt following patiently behind.

Kristen walked in and looked at Dan. "What was that all about?" she asked.

Dan smiled sheepishly and said, "I think it was welcome to the neighborhood."

Kristen stopped and stared at Dan's leg. "What happened to you?" she asked.

"I slipped on a rock," Dan said. "Dumb mistake."

"Looks awful," Kristen said. She was clearly concerned.

"It's fine," Dan assured her. "I'll go change my clothes."

Kristen gave him a quick peck and let him head off to the bedroom.

Dan went in and sat on the bed. He untied his boots and pulled them off, leaving his socks on. He unbuttoned his shirt and pulled it off. The bandage on his arm was still leaking just a tiny bit. He decided it was fine, and stood up to get a clean one out of the closet.

That's when Kristen walked in. She stopped and looked at him, clearly staring at his arm.

Dan shrugged, then turned to pull out a shirt and pull it on.

"I guess you saw those drawings," Kristen said quietly.

Dan nodded, buttoning up his shirt.

"I meant to tell you about it before you saw them," she said.

"It's okay," Dan said. He was still unsure how to react. He walked over to his dresser and took out a pair of jeans. "You already told me about it anyway, remember?"

"I mean, they're just ideas," Kristen said. "And you did say you were willing to make some changes."

Dan sat down on the bed and slipped off his pants. This time there was no hiding it. The bandage on his leg was impressive.

Kristen gave him a skeptical look. "Did you go to the doctor for that?" she asked.

Dan shook his head. "Better than that," he answered with a grin. "I had Katie Pederson do it."

Kristen sat down next to him on the bed. Her right hand came up and brushed against his cheek, then moved around to caress the back of his head.

Dan smiled. He could feel his body relax, as if he were slipping into a hot tub. His shoulders sagged slightly, and he leaned into her. God, it felt good.

"I'm sorry," Kristen said.

Dan shook his head. "No need to be sorry." His mind was still working through what it all meant, and how real it was going to be. Deep inside something dangerous moved. He could feel it. "I guess I'm just a little bit scared about all of this."

He could feel Kristen beside him, tiny trembles shaking her body.

He quickly looked at her in alarm. There were tears in her eyes, but they were smiling.

"I'm sorry," she repeated. "I'm the one who is supposed to be afraid, remember?"

Dan gave her a smile and pulled her close. He wanted her to feel him hold her. And he wanted to hide his own eyes, now clearly watering madly.

"Are you okay?" Kristen asked. "Is it okay? Are we okay?"

"Yeah," Dan said. "We're fine."

Now was as good a time as any, he thought.

"There's something more I need to tell you," he began. "About Rod Arquette. I'm not sure how to say this. I don't know if I should tell you." Of course, now he had to tell her. He was just trying avoid the inevitable.

Kristen waited patiently. She seemed calm.

"I'm not sure how to say this, but it's something I learned while I was up on the mountain." He knew he was dancing around the bush. Better to just come out and say it. "I guess the reason that Cheryl shot her husband was that he was sleeping with her daughter."

Dan waited. He thought about putting his fingers in his ears, to protect them from the explosion.

But Kristen didn't explode, at least, not at first. Dan could see her struggling to control her breath. Her face flushed and she grew very still.

She looked at him. "And why didn't you think you should tell me this?"

Dan paused awkwardly. "Well, I know that you…"

"You think that you can't tell me the truth?" she asked. "You think that you have to hide things from me?"

Yep. This was what Dan had hoped to avoid.

Kristen continued. "You think that because some asshole attacked me that I'm not capable of dealing with it? Is that what you think?"

Dan mumbled something that he hoped would communicate that he didn't think that.

"Because I am perfectly capable of dealing with it," Kristen plowed on. "In fact, I am better prepared than most people to deal with it."

Dan managed to look her in the eyes. She was incensed.

He shook his head and mumbled more apology. "I just didn't want to reopen an old wound," he said.

Kristen kept right on going. "I have a right to get angry," she said. "That wound won't ever go away. And I don't want it to. It's part of me. It's who I am."

Dan nodded in agreement. He took a deep breath. "I know that. I just didn't want you to…"

"I have a right to be angry," Kristen interrupted him again. "I'm not a crystal unicorn. I won't shatter. I don't need you to protect me. I'm strong. But part of being strong is that I will get angry. I will always get angry about things like this."

Dan was nodding again. "I know," he said. "I just don't like to see you unhappy."

Kristen looked at him. "You can't control that," Dan. "I have a right to feel what I feel."

Dan muttered a quiet "Okay."

"And I'm angry right now," she said. "Are you okay with that?"

Dan shrugged. "I guess I have to be." He said it hopefully.

"People like Rod make me furious," she said. "And you can't take that away from me."

"I know," Dan said. "I don't want to take it away from you. But I feel awful when I see you unhappy."

Kristen looked at him. The edge in her voice softened just a hair. "I'm not angry at you."

Dan gave her a tiny smile. "It's hard to tell sometimes," he admitted.

Kristen paused, then gave a little chuckle. "Trust me, Dan. When I'm angry at you, you'll know it."

Dan grinned. "That sounds scary."

Kristen nodded. "Good. It should scare you." But she was smiling now.

They continued to stare at each other, neither one knowing or wanting to know how to move on from this. Finally, it was Kristen who decided.

"Want some dinner?" she asked.

Dan thought this over. "I think so," he said cautiously.

"Good," Kristen smiled. "Then stay out of my kitchen so I can get to work."

Dan watched her move away.

Kristen stopped and looked over her shoulder. "Our kitchen." Dan followed her and watched as she set to work furiously peeling some potatoes.

After a few minutes she turned and walked over to him and embraced him, her hands still moist from the potatoes. "See how tough I am?" she said.

Dan smiled. "Yeah, I do." Her body felt like cashmere up against his.

Kristen pulled her head back to look him in the eyes. "Don't worry," she said. "When I do need your help, I'll ask you for it."

Dan gave her a grin. "Good. Thanks."

She pulled away and went back to the kitchen counter.

"If you want to help, you could set the table...." she suggested quietly.

Dan did as he was told.

chapter 47

A month later, the house was in free fall. The contractor had taken everything apart. The sink was disconnected, so they were washing their dishes in the bathroom. There was no stove, so they were living off takeout, dining out, and the microwave. With the floor torn up, they had learned to wear shoes at all times, to avoid both splinters and the occasional bent nail. And the fridge was out on the back porch, where Dan had built a locking mechanism to keep the local wildlife from helping themselves.

It had been this way for far longer than either of them had expected, with no real end in sight. There were promises about when it would be done, but they had learned to treat those with complete and utter disbelief.

Dan and Kristen had just finished eating out in the backyard—a delicious dinner of a roast chicken from the local grocery store, some macaroni salad, also from the grocery store, and a ready-made salad from that same grocery store. Dan stood up to clear the table and bring out a bowl of fruit and some cookies—from the same store.

With his hands full, he heard his phone ring inside. He propped the door open with his foot, put the dishes down on the dining table, and looked over at his phone.

Cal Healey was calling.

"Hi, Cal," Dan answered.

"Are you guys around?" Cal asked. "I'm right around the corner and thought I would stop in and see how the big project is going."

Dan glanced out at Kristen in the back yard, then at the demolished kitchen.

"Sure, come on by," he said. "Hope you don't mind visiting a war zone."

Cal chuckled. "That's one reason I thought I'd stop by. It will make me feel better about my front yard. See you in five."

Dan went out and let Kristen know that Cal was coming over.

"Did you let him know the place is a disaster?" she asked.

"He said that's what he wanted to see," Dan answered.

Kristen stood up and hurried into the house. "Well, I should at least make myself presentable." And she disappeared into the bathroom.

Dan collected another armful of dishes and headed back to the house. By the time he had unloaded them on the table, Cal was at the door.

Dan told him to come on in.

Cal took a look around the demolished kitchen. "Wow," he said. "I really like what you've done with the place."

"A work in progress," Dan said. "I warned you."

"No kidding," Cal said. "In fact, that's one of the reasons I wanted to come by. Maggie says that she can't imagine Kristen can cook in this mess, so she wanted to invite you to dinner sometime this week. How about Friday night?"

Dan smiled. "I'll check with Kristen, but…"

"We accept!" they heard Kristen call out from the bathroom. "That would be lovely!"

Dan grinned at Cal. "I guess we accept," he said.

"Great," Cal said. "Maggie thought you might enjoy it." He

looked around at the construction. "Well, I think I can see where you're making progress," he said.

"Waiting on the cabinets," Dan said. "Then we can get the sink in. The countertops are over there, in the hallway…"

"So what do you figure?" Cal asked. "Another month?"

Dan shook his head. "No idea. We've given up trying to predict the future. Whatever it is, it will be a while."

Cal glanced at Dan's arm. "That looks a lot better," he said.

Dan nodded. "Yeah, it's fine."

Cal laughed. "If I recall correctly, that's what you said when it happened. What about the leg?"

"Same," Dan said. "It's healing up just fine. Just needs time."

"Like the kitchen?" Cal asked.

"Maybe less time than that," Dan answered with a grin. "Hey, speaking of that, have you charged James Scott with anything?"

Cal gave a groan. "Like I told you, it's in the hands of the DA," he said. "She's trying to work out how to balance him obstructing a murder investigation against the credit the guy deserves for pulling that kid off the mountain. And he's fully cooperative now."

Dan nodded. "That's what I was wondering."

"The guy withheld information about a murder," Cal said. "And I don't really get why he did that."

"I thought about that," Dan said. "The only job he had was with Arquette's school, and maybe he was hoping he and Cheryl could keep it going. I hear that he's not doing so well on his own."

"Not exactly my problem," Cal said. "But even if the DA lets him off, I don't know where he goes from here. I can't imagine many climbers wanting to deal with him."

Dan thought of Eric Lenhardt and Willoughby Partners. "If the DA does let him off the hook, I think I might know someone who would be interested."

"Better you than me, buddy," Cal said.

"I saw what he could do when it really mattered," Dan said. "The guy was good. And he was totally focused on getting that girl out of there."

"That's one of the reasons the DA is hesitating," Cal said. "The kid's parents are suggesting that he deserves some leniency. They want to give him some kind of medal."

"Hey, how's she doing?" Dan asked. "Any news on that?"

"As far as I know, she's doing better," Cal said. "I heard she's out of the hospital and in rehab now. Hoping for a full recovery. That's why the parents are raving about what a great guy your buddy is." He shot Dan a look. "You, too, by the way. They think you're a regular superman."

Dan showed Cal the scab on his arm. "There must have been some kryptonite up there," he said.

"Either that, or they're dead wrong." Cal said.

"I guess I could call in and say hello, check in on her," Dan said.

"You should do that," Cal said. "Let them fawn all over you. Seriously, her dad did call to ask about the guys who rescued her. He was pretty damn grateful. I think she's making progress, but it's probably going to be a long slog." He stopped here to look around the kitchen again.

Dan caught the look and laughed. "Us, too," he said. "If you tell me where she is, I'll stop in and see her sometime."

Kristen came out to join them. Dan wasn't sure what she had done, but she was stunningly beautiful.

"Hi, Cal," she said. "You are the bearer of wonderful invitations."

Cal gave her a quick hug and waved his arm around at the construction. "Maggie seems to think you've suffered enough," he said.

"I promise we'll return the favor as soon as we're done with all of this," Kristen said.

"Don't worry," Cal said. Then after a pause to look around again, "I may not live that long anyway."

Dan looked at his friend carefully. "You do seem to be aging quickly," he said. "I'd be a little worried about that myself."

"You think I should pack it in?" Cal asked. "Hang up the badge and totter off into the sunset?"

"Well, at least do it before you drop dead in the saddle," Dan agreed. "I mean, you can't have that much time left, right?"

Cal chuckled. "Just remember, kiddo, I'm only a few years ahead of you."

"And I will never catch up," Dan said. "And I'm okay with that."

"Hey, Cal," Kristen wanted to change the subject. "Whatever happened with Lucilla? Did you ever find her?"

Cal took a deep breath. "Nope, we never found her." He paused here, as if considering how much he wanted to tell them.

Dan was prepared to wait him out. He knew his old friend. But Kristen wasn't so patient.

"But, I mean, you had that DNA and stuff, right?" she said. "What did you find out about all of that?"

Cal gave another sigh, then looked at Dan. Dan wasn't going to help him out and shrugged.

Cal looked back at Kristen. "We don't know what happened to her," he said. "She's pretty much dropped off the face of the earth."

Kristen took a moment to consider this.

"So, she's still a missing person?" she asked.

Cal gave a small grimace. "She's not exactly missing," he said.

"We're looking for her, believe me, we're looking for her. But don't know where she is. And neither does anyone else."

"But Katie and Shauna filed a report, didn't they?" Kristen asked. "So you're still looking for her?"

"Not because of them," Cal tried to explain. "They really don't have any connection to her. I mean, they said she had disappeared, but that's not why we're looking for her. She's run off."

Kristen was not about to give up. "What do you mean she's run off? That means she's still missing."

"She took all of her money out of the bank," Cal said, controlling his voice. "She left. She got someone to give her a ride to downtown Stockton, and she…simply disappeared."

"So you can't find her," Kristen said. It was a statement, not a question.

"And we are really looking," Cal said. "But I don't think she wants to be found."

"But she's an old woman!" Kristen said. "She may not able to take care of herself."

Cal gave a dry chuckle. "So far, she's done a pretty good job."

Kristen wasn't done. "Did you check that DNA?" she asked. "Did you run those tests?"

Cal nodded. "We did." He paused here again, then plowed ahead. "You know, there was no connection between Lucilla and Lydia," he said. "They weren't related."

It took a minute for Kristen to react. "I knew it!" she exulted. She looked at Dan. "Didn't I tell you?"

Cal held up his hand. "No connection to Lydia or her husband," Cal said. "But she was related to someone else up here. Remember the bones in the rose garden?" he asked.

Kristen and Dan were dead silent, waiting for Cal to continue.

Cal chewed on his lip for a moment. "Turns out, that was Lucilla's mother."

Outside, it seemed as if the sun were going down quickly, and shadows grew longer out in the backyard.

"Oh God," Kristen said. "That poor woman. And we chased her away."

Cal shook his head. "Not exactly."

"What do you mean?" Kristen asked. "We certainly did. If we hadn't poked out nose in her business…"

"Turns out Lucilla has a bit of a record," Cal said. "Including three outstanding warrants from back East."

Kristen was unconvinced. "She was just an old lady, living out the last years of her life. We should have left her in peace."

Cal shook his head. "I don't think so," he said. "One of the warrants is for trying to poison her husband. It's for attempted murder."

Dan and Kristen stood in stunned silence.

Before they could find a way to speak, Cal's radio squawked at him. He held up his hand to hold the conversation and spoke quietly into the microphone on his shoulder, turning away from Dan as he did so. After a moment, he turned back to face them.

"Gotta go," he said. "Some idiot just drove his car into somebody's house down in Sonora."

Dan and Kristen watched him hurry out the door and drive off in his vehicle.

"Wow," Kristen said quietly. "She poisoned her husband."

Dan walked over and put his arms around her. "Probably about remodeling their kitchen," he said with a grin. "Don't let it give you any ideas."

ALSO AVAILABLE:

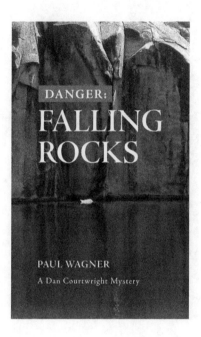

When a Wall Street tycoon insists that his family join him for an annual backpacking trip into the Sierra Nevada, some of his children are not enthusiastic about the idea.

And that's before people start turning up dead. Ranger Dan Courtwright is first on the scene. And with his friend Sheriff Cal Healey, he sticks with it to the terrifying finish, which is a real cliffhanger. Literally.

DANGER: FALLING ROCKS is available on Amazon.com.

ALSO AVAILABLE:

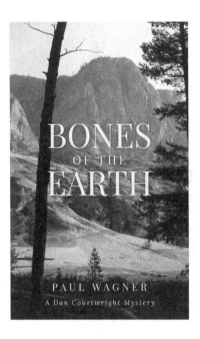

When a pair of hikers discover what they think are human remains, Ranger Dan Courtwright is skeptical. Then he sees the bones inside the hiking boot.

What follows leads Dan on a tangled path through the history of his section of the Stanislaus National Forest as he digs up the clues to a decades-old crime. And those lead him right into the terrifying face of evil.

BONES OF THE EARTH is available on Amazon.com.

ALSO AVAILABLE:

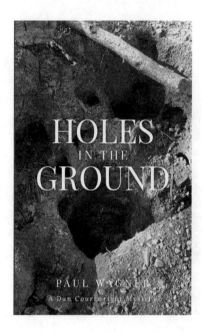

A hiker passing through the Emigrant Wilderness on the Pacific Crest Trail may or may not be who people think he is. With trail names, who can tell?

But when a body turns up in an abandoned mine shaft, Ranger Dan Courtwright finds himself in the middle of a much bigger story, and it is up to him and Sheriff Cal Healey to get to the bottom of it.

HOLES IN THE GROUND is available on Amazon.com.

ALSO AVAILABLE:

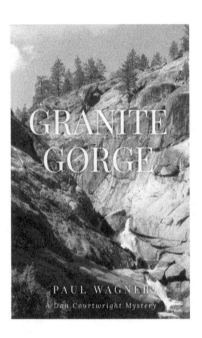

There are five trails that lead into the Granite Gorge of the Mokelumne River, but none of them connect to each other. It seems as if there are five ways in, and no way out.

But when Ranger Dan Courtwright offers to help restore some of those old trails, he discovers more than he expected. And is lucky to get out alive.

GRANITE GORGE is available on Amazon.com.

ALSO AVAILABLE:

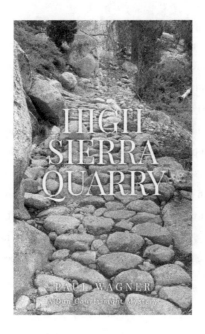

When a young woman hiker is reported missing, the Forest Service takes part in the search. But the more Ranger Dan Courtwright learns about the case, the less sense it makes to him. And the more dangerous things get for everyone involved, especially Dan.

All of which leads to confusion, consternation, and murder.

HIGH SIERRA QUARRY is available on Amazon.com.

Acknowledgments

My books are invented, whole cloth, from my memories of adventures in the mountains, both real and imagined. But they would not be possible without the help of some key players. My two daughters, Liz and Estelle, both read the first draft and make helpful and insightful comments. Robin Lewis is a prince and manages the design and production of these books with patience and style.

Karen Johnson adds her wonderful suggestions to the text. Finally, a note of thanks to my wife Margaret, who is kind enough to proof my work, and tries to keep me from making the most egregious errors. She is often successful.

Printed in the USA
CPSIA information can be obtained
at www.ICGtesting.com
LVHW011955221024
794499LV00013B/491

9 798985 605884